POSSESSION

CLUB X #3

K.M. SCOTT

Books by K.M. Scott

If I Dream (Corrupted Love #1)

Crash Into Me (Heart of Stone #1)
Fall Into Me (Heart of Stone #2)
Give In To Me (Heart of Stone #3)
Heart of Stone Volume One Box Set
Ever After (Heart of Stone #4)
A Heart of Stone Christmas (Heart of Stone #5)
Unforgettable (Heart of Stone #6)
Unbreakable (Heart of Stone #7)
Heart of Stone Volume Two Box Set

Temptation (Club X #1)
Surrender (Club X #2)
Possession (Club X #3)
Satisfaction (Club X #4)
Acceptance (Club X #5)
The Complete Club X Series Box Set

SILK Volume One
SILK Volume Two
SILK Volume Three
SILK Volume Four
The SILK Box Set

Books by K.M. Scott writing as Gabrielle Bisset

Blood Avenged (Sons of Navarus #1)
Blood Betrayed (Sons of Navarus #2)
Longing (A Sons of Navarus Short Story)
Blood Spirit (Sons of Navarus #3)
The Deepest Cut (A Sons of Navarus Short Story)
Blood Prophecy (Sons of Navarus #4)
Blood Craving (Sons of Navarus #5)
Blood Eclipse (Sons of Navarus #6)
The Sons of Navarus Box Set #1
The Sons of Navarus Box Set #2

Stolen Destiny (Destined Ones Duology #1)
Destiny Redeemed (Destined Ones Duology #2)

Love's Master
Masquerade
The Victorian Erotic Romance Trilogy

Kane Jackson, the ruler of the fantasy section of Club X, has always been different from his brothers. The bastard son of Cassian March III, he grew up without the money and privilege Cassian and Stefan enjoyed from the March name, instead only knowing his father as the man who abandoned him and seeing himself as unloved and unwanted. He let love in once and like everything else in his life, all that came from it was pain. His heart hidden behind the walls he's built since then, Kane is now just the dark figure who rules over the fantasies of others but has none himself.

Abbi Linde can't seem to get a break. Too many bad men and bad choices have left her bruised and broken, but the opportunity to dance at Club X could change everything. For the first time, she might be able to make a life for herself and find the happiness she longs for. After what feels like a lifetime of heartbreak, Abbi still believes one day her dreams will come true and she'll find the love that's eluded her.

Even the darkest heart craves the light, but will the darkness be too much for love to overcome with these two souls?

PROLOGUE

KANE

THE LIGHTNESS OF MY MOTHER'S hospital room pressed down on me as if it wanted to crush me or push me out. Dark and somber, I was an intruder in this place. Or at least that's how I felt every day I came to sit next to my mother as she withered away toward her death in her hospital bed.

A sad ending to a sad life. She'd always wanted more. More money. More of my father. More from me. The money never came. Neither did my father. And me? I don't know why I'd never been enough for her. Maybe it was because I looked so much like the man she'd wanted more from with my black hair and blue eyes that resembled his so strongly.

She didn't stay awake long, and most days she didn't even recognize me. The cancer had eaten away at her brain, so when she looked at me sometimes I knew she had no idea who I was sitting there. But then every so often I'd see a look of recognition in her eyes, and she'd reach for my hand and give me a tiny smile.

"Kane."

"Shhh, don't talk. I'm here."

"It's almost time. You need to get ready. Don't want to be late," she said as if I had somewhere to go. I had nowhere to go. Just there and the prison cell that waited for me in three days.

"It's okay, Mom. I won't be late."

"The school called, Kane. They say you miss a lot."

She slipped back into the past, but not too far this time. Just a few months, before I killed a man and got sentenced to prison. Before the cancer had come to take her away.

I watched as she looked up at me and waited for my answer to her unspoken question of why I missed so much school. Quietly, I answered, "I'm sorry, Mom. Holly likes to—"

My mother's eyes narrowed in anger. "A girl? You miss school for a girl?"

She never liked Holly. She never liked even the idea of me with anyone. Wanting to avoid the same argument we'd had every time I mentioned Holly's name, I simply nodded and smiled. "Okay. I won't anymore."

"Good. You don't know. It's not right."

I sat with my eyes closed as she rambled on incoherently, the words strung together making no sense. At least today I'd gotten a few minutes with her really there with me.

Taking my hand in hers, she squeezed it softly. "Your father is going to want to change you now, Kane. Don't let him."

My father and I becoming close had always been her biggest fear. She hated him as much as she loved him, and now that she saw the end coming, she worried he'd finally remember I existed for more than a visit or two every decade.

I looked down into her eyes and saw she was there with me now. "Nobody's going to change me, Mom."

She closed her eyes and sighed. When she opened them again, I wasn't sure she still knew who I was, but in a quiet voice, she whispered, "Good. You were meant to be who you are now, Kane."

Who I was now was a man convicted of murdering the man who'd taken everything I loved from me. How could she think anyone could be meant to be that?

I nodded and forced a smile, believing she must have slipped away again. "Okay, Mom."

"You were meant to hurt, Kane. From the minute I found out I was carrying you, I knew this. You were meant to hurt. Never forget that."

She closed her eyes and drifted off to sleep, somehow comforted like she'd always been by what she believed I truly was. Maybe she was right. Maybe that was my place in this world. With the exception of Holly, all I'd ever done was hurt from the day I was born.

As I watched my mother sleep, her words echoed in my ears.

You were meant to hurt, Kane. Never forget that.

Chapter One

Abbi

M Y VISION BLURRED AS THE final blow from Aaron's fist pounded into my cheekbone, knocking me back against the closet door. The pain radiated up into my eye as I lost my balance and fell in a heap on the floor. He bellowed something about it being my fault, but his words were drowned out by the sound of ringing in my ears. I closed my eyes to push away the pain and felt the toe of his boot jam hard into my left hip. Crying out in pain, I quickly stopped myself, knowing how much he hated when I complained.

Aaron leaned down close enough that I felt his hot breath on my aching cheek. "One more fucking word, Abbi, and I swear to fucking God I'll kill you! And don't fucking cry! One tear and I swear I'll hit you so hard."

I lifted my hands to shield myself from another blow, but that only angered him more and he slapped me hard across the face. My head bounced off the broken door, and for a moment I saw only black in front of my eyes.

"When I get back, you better have this mess cleaned up. Do you hear me?" he roared near my ear.

Unable to form even the simplest word, I nodded so he wouldn't hit me again. Terror raced through me as I felt his palm cup my cheek. Opening my eyes, I saw him crouching down next to me. His dark brown eyes flashed his rage, and he whispered in a voice laced with anger, "Baby, you know I hate it when you make me do stuff like this, don't you?"

I answered as I knew I must. "I'm sorry, Aaron. I didn't mean to make you angry."

Gently stroking my swelling cheek, he leaned in and kissed me on the forehead. "I'll be back in an hour. We'll go for a nice dinner and then come back here, okay? Give me one of those Abbi smiles I love."

As the corners of my mouth slowly hitched up, the pain in my cheekbone once again exploded into my eye, but I kept my smile pressed in place so he'd think his suggestion made me happy. Inside, I wanted to throw up at the thought of ever doing anything again with him.

"That's my girl. See you in an hour."

Barely able to speak, I whispered, "Okay, Aaron. I'll make everything right. I promise."

My eyes fluttered closed as I watched him walk out the front door to our apartment. The sound of a door closing had never sounded so comforting before in my life.

I couldn't do this anymore. One of these days he was going to kill me over something small like the toothpaste tube not being rolled up correctly or a dirty glass left in the sink.

I couldn't give him that chance. I may not ever have been truly strong, but I couldn't be weak anymore.

All I wanted to do was close my eyes and go to sleep so I wouldn't feel the pain, but if I did and he returned, he'd fly into another rage, so I gingerly pushed myself up onto my hands and knees. I tried to take a deep breath to prepare myself to stand, but a sharp pain stabbed through my chest and I nearly fell back onto the floor in agony. Panting, I straightened myself up and reached out to grab onto the doorframe, slowly standing on shaky legs.

"Oh, God," I moaned as I got the first glance of the wreck our place was after Aaron's rage. My grandmother's treasured blue glass vase lay shattered on the floor near the couch where he'd thrown it at my head after I hesitated with my answer to some question I couldn't remember now. I'd had that vase since she gave it to me right before she died, and now it was gone, smashed into a hundred splintered pieces.

I picked up the bits of blue glass from the carpet, cutting my fingers as I collected the shards of the most important possession I owned, my mind numb. How had things gotten to this point? In just ten months, Aaron had turned into a monster. Sweet and caring when we met, he'd changed overnight when we moved in together. After dating three months, he went from the man I loved who doted on me to the man I feared would kill me one day.

Scanning the room for my phone, I saw it lying face down near the coffee table. I bent down and picked it up, turning it on as I prayed to God it still worked after Aaron bounced it off the wall. A crack ran diagonally across the screen, but miraculously, the home screen appeared after a few moments.

Gemma's number was on speed dial, so I just pressed 2 and hoped the call went through. Her phone rang, and a feeling of relief washed over me. Gemma would help. She always did.

"Hey, Abbi, what's up?" she asked in her usual sweet voice.

"I was wondering if I could take you up on your offer to stay with you for a little bit. I think I need to leave here."

"Oh, honey, what happened? Are you okay? Did he hit you again?"

"He's coming back in a few minutes, Gemma. Can you come get me?"

She instantly kicked into protective mode. "I'm coming right now, Abbi. I want you to stay on the phone with me until I get there, okay? If he comes in, hang up and call 9-1-1. I'll call too so the cops know to come quick."

"Okay."

"I'm getting in my car now, so I'm just a few miles away. While you're waiting, gather up some clothes, honey. We'll take whatever we can and find someone to help us get the rest of your stuff later."

I made my way around the glass that lay all over the floor to the bedroom to get some clothes. My head throbbed with every step as I struggled to find what I needed.

"My eye hurts, Gemma. It's hard to see through my left eye."

"I'm driving as fast as I can, Abbi. It won't be long now. If I'm not there when he gets back, I need you to promise me you'll call 9-1-1. You can't let him hit you anymore."

As I tried to find something to wear, I remembered Aaron had thrown out nearly all my clothes that morning because he'd sworn I'd cheated on him. All that was left in the drawers and the closet was a bridesmaid gown and two sweaters with holes in them. The sight of a closet full of all those empty hangers was too much, and tears began to flow down my cheeks.

He'd taken everything away from me.

"Abbi, what's wrong? Why are you crying? Is he there? Hang up and call the cops now!"

I slumped against the side of the bed and let the tears come. "No, he's not here. It's just that I don't have anything left. He took all my clothes and threw them out. I have nothing to wear except the jeans and sweatshirt I've got on now."

"Oh, sweetie, don't worry. We'll get you something to wear. You can borrow my clothes until then. We're about the same size, so don't cry. I'm turning onto your street now, so grab what you need and I'll get you out of there."

A few minutes later, I heard a car pull up in front of the apartment, and fear tore through me at the thought that Aaron had come back so soon. Struggling to stand, I got back up on my feet and prepared to call the police. The sound of the door opening made me freeze where I stood, but in seconds I saw Gemma's sweet face appear in the doorway.

Her smile quickly faded as she got her first look at the aftermath of his rage on my face. As she came toward me, I saw in her eyes how bad I must look.

"Oh, honey, are you okay? Does it hurt enough to go to the emergency room?" she asked as she examined my broken and bruised face.

I hung my head, ashamed of what I'd let him do to me yet again. "Please let's go, Gemma. I need to leave here. I didn't get anything packed, though."

She sprang into action, clearing off my dresser into her purse and grabbing whatever underwear and bras she could lay her hands on. "I've got some things here. Whatever you need, I'll get it for you. We need to go now, honey."

Nodding, I quietly said, "Okay."

Looking around, I knew this might be the last time I saw this place I'd called home for the last six months. I'd loved this apartment when we first moved in with its new carpet and freshly painted walls. Aaron had promised we'd make a life together in this place.

Gently, she guided me out to her car, and as I watched my home fade into the distance, she drove me away to hers where for at least that night I could be safe.

I WOKE UP HOURS LATER on her living room couch, every muscle and bone in my body aching so much I wanted to cry, but I feared that would hurt even more. Gemma sat in a chair nearby ready to offer a glass of water and some painkillers she had left over from when she had a tooth taken out months before.

She placed two large white pills in my hand and smiled. "If I remember correctly, Vicodin killed most of my pain then. Hopefully, they're still good."

Popping them into my mouth, I took a gulp of water and washed them down, hoping they'd work quickly to ease the pain that seemed to be everywhere in my body. Sighing, I lay back down against the pillow, loving the coolness against my battered cheek. "Thanks. If they knock me out, know that I'm not trying to be a rude guest."

Her dark green eyes lit up, and she flashed me one of her terrific smiles. "Never. You rest and when you wake up later you can have something to eat. I'll make you those rice balls you like."

I looked over at her as she tried to remember what they were called. "Arancini. That's what the rice balls are called. Aren't you Italian? Shouldn't you know that?"

She made a face and flipped her jet black hair off her shoulder. "Yes, I'm a proud Italian woman, but that doesn't mean I know those rice ball things are called Arancini. I'll make my world famous sauce too. Remember how much you loved it that one time I made it for you?"

I closed my eyes and smiled at the memory of Gemma's Italian dinner party months before. Aaron and I had just begun dating then, and her dinner had been one of his first times meeting my friends. Everyone loved him, except Gemma. Even from that first night, she'd sensed something about him she didn't like.

If only I'd listened to her gut feeling then.

"Sounds great. I'm sure I'll be hungry later."

"Honey, I want you to know you can stay here as long as you need to. I know you're still looking for a job, but that doesn't matter. You can stay as long as you want."

I looked over at the back of the chair where my purse hung. "All the money I have is in my wallet, but you can have it. It's not much, but it's all I have now until I find a job."

"I'm not going to take the last of your money, sweetie. About the job, though, what about where I work? I like it there, and I was thinking you would too."

Gemma danced at Club X, and even though she'd raved about it dozens of times, I wasn't sure it was the right job for me. "I've never danced like that. Why would they hire me?"

"Because I can tell them you're a great person who they should hire. Kane will listen to me."

"Don't they require experience?"

"You were a Storm cheerleader, Abbi. That's more experience than most dancers have when they begin. You'd do fine."

I hung my head at her mention of my time as a cheerleader for the Tampa Bay Storm, the local arena football team. I'd worked so hard to get a spot on the squad, but after showing up with a black eye twice and not being able to do the routines because of a beating Aaron had given me, they'd kicked me off.

"That's not the same kind of dancing, Gemma."

She reached over and squeezed my forearm.

"Honey, it's a good job and you'd be able to work with me. Think about it."

Sighing, I nodded. "Okay, I'll think about it. What's it like?"

"It's not a bad job, Abbi. The hardest part for me is making sure I can fit into the outfits. You know how I love sweets. Other than that, it's just dancing."

I stared at her knowing there was more to the job than that. "And? I've heard about Club X. Isn't it more like stripping?"

She nodded and shrugged. "For some. I don't do the nude stuff. Maybe someday. You wouldn't have to either, unless you wanted to. You certainly have the body for it, though."

At that moment, all I knew about my body was it hurt all over. The Vicodin hadn't kicked in yet, and my cheekbone felt like it could explode out of my face at any moment. Dancing, nude or otherwise, was the last thing on my mind.

"I don't know. I could go back to waitressing. I always made decent money doing that."

"You could, but dancing pays a lot better."

More money piqued my interest. "How much better? More than you used to make at the diner?"

"Let's just say that it's not out of the question for me to make seven hundred to a thousand on a really good week, depending on where Kane puts me. If it's with people who tip well, I can do pretty good. Way better than I used to make waitressing."

"And that's without going nude?"

"Yeah, but that's working all five nights at eight hours each. Some girls don't work the whole eight like I do, but I guess if they're stripping they make more money in less time."

"So what kind of dancing is this if you don't take off your clothes?" I asked, suddenly curious about this job of hers. If the money was that good, it wouldn't take me long to make enough to get the hell out of Tampa and begin a new life where nobody knew me. I'd miss Gemma, but she'd understand. We'd both seen our share of bad because of men, and even though hers never beat her, she was no stranger to heartbreak.

"The top three floors of the club have fantasy rooms, and each room has a place for dancers. It's sort of like a room next to a room. A window in one wall of the fantasy room separates me from the people in the room. So all I have to do is dance for them. Not everyone who reserves a room wants a dancer, but when they do, that's how it happens."

"Do they see you?"

Gemma seemed to think about my question and nodded again. "Yeah, but it's not really like they're there, at least not for me. I listen to the music and just dance."

The way she described it didn't sound so bad. I could probably do that. The dancing nude sounded terrifying, but if it meant a lot more money, maybe I could get over how scary it all sounded.

"Do the ones who strip also dance behind the window?"

"Some do. Others do the usual kind of erotic dancing in the room with the members. I couldn't do that. I know a few girls who do, but it's not for me. Then there are others who act out the fantasies people want."

"Just so I'm getting this straight, they don't make you do anything you don't want to, like dance nude, right?"

Gemma smiled and shook her head. "They don't. Trust me, you're going to love the guys who run the club. The one owner never comes out of his office, it seems. He and his fiancée take care of all the club business together. Cassian and Olivia are really sweet. Then there's Stefan. He used to be a huge horndog, but since he met his girlfriend, he's a changed man. And the one who's in charge of the dancers and the whole fantasy thing is named Kane. You're going to love him. Trust me."

A childhood of twice a week Bible study marched through my brain at the mention of his name. "As in the son of Adam and Eve who killed his brother?"

"Not Cain, with a C. His name is Kane, K-A-N-E. Like candy."

"That's with a C too," I said with a chuckle that

sent a stabbing pain shooting through my ribs. "What's this Kane like?"

Gemma leaned forward in her seat like she had something important to say. "All the girls love him. As long as you do your work, you'll love him too. I've seen him rough up a few of the members when they got out of line with a couple of the dancers. He doesn't take any shit when it comes to us. Owners aren't always like that, but he is."

The idea of a man protecting women instead of beating up on them sounded good. She'd almost convinced me to apply for the dancer job.

Almost.

"I'm going to call him and see when he can give you an interview," she said as she jumped off the chair to get her phone.

"No..." Leaning off the couch, I reached out to stop her but my hand only caught air. She was off like a shot toward the other room so full of enthusiasm for us working together, but I wasn't so sure I could do it. Even though I'd be fully clothed, dancing for people in fantasy rooms scared me. It seemed so—exposed, even with clothes on. What if I couldn't do it?

I rolled back onto the couch to ease the pain of my aching ribs. Closing my eyes, I tried to push away the memory of Aaron's fists hitting my side and the pain shooting through my bones as he punched me over and over. He was probably back at the house by now, furious that I hadn't cleaned up the mess he'd made and left without telling him where I was going.

A spike of fear pressed into my mind. What if he figured out where I was and came looking for me? If he found me here, Gemma could get hurt, along with her beautiful apartment. Pushing myself up, I slowly swung my legs off the couch to stand. I needed to get out of there before anyone else found themselves on the receiving end of Aaron's anger or his fists.

"Hey, I got you an interview for Thursday night. What are you doing?"

I looked up and saw Gemma staring down at me. "I have to go. I don't want Aaron to find me here and hurt you too."

She placed her hand on my shoulder and stilled my movement. "Abbi, sit down. I'm not going to get hurt, honey. Don't worry. If he comes here, I'll get the cops and they'll take care of him."

I lowered myself to the couch and hung my head. "I just don't want to see you get hurt too. He'll be furious if he figures out where I am."

"Then he'll have to deal with me. I'm pretty fucking sick of his bullshit, so he doesn't want to mess with me today. For now, you can stay on that couch until you feel better. I don't have work tonight, so I'll be right here the whole time. I won't give him the chance to hurt you again."

Looking up at her, I saw in those beautiful green

eyes of hers she meant business. "Okay. I think the Vicodin are kicking in anyway, so I'll just stay here and hope I feel better."

"Good. And when you wake up, I'll make the Arancini. Then tomorrow you can start a brand new life and in a few days you can start a new job."

I closed my eyes as she chirped away about all the great things I truly wished would come true. A brand new life and a new job sounded exactly like what I needed.

CHAPTER TWO

ABBI

SIX O'CLOCK THURSDAY CAME FAST, but the closer my interview came, the more unsure of myself I felt. My ribs still killed, and the bruise on my cheek had turned a deep reddish-purple color. As I stared into Gemma's bathroom mirror, at least I could be thankful that my face no longer looked like a Botox appointment gone horribly wrong.

Blowing my bangs off my face, I shook my head in disbelief that Gemma would ever find a way to make me look presentable. I looked mangy. That's what I felt like too. Like a stray dog who'd been kicked too many times and just couldn't believe life would ever be any better than it was right at that moment, bruises and all.

I heard her buzzing around in her room getting ready for her shift at Club X and couldn't help but be infected by her enthusiasm. Gemma was like that. When she felt happy, she made everyone around her happy. I loved her for that, especially since it was her strength that had made leaving Aaron possible. Her singing, no matter how off key, made me smile, and looking in the mirror again, I saw something of that person I'd been before everything happened with Aaron.

God, how had I let myself get so torn apart?

"Hey, chickie, what do you think, black pants or blue? I like the black. Blondes always look great in black."

I turned around to see her holding two pairs of dress pants up in front of me. Gemma leaned her head toward the black pair and rolled her eyes toward them. "I guess the black then since you're doing the mind trick thing to get me to pick them. But wouldn't a skirt be better?"

Her gaze traveled to my legs, and I looked down to see a huge black and blue mark on the inside of my left knee. I hadn't realized Aaron had caught me there. Sheepishly, I looked away, too embarrassed to face her.

"Easily explainable, if you want to wear a skirt, Abbi. I mean, people trip over things every day. No biggie. I doubt anyone will even notice it."

"No, you were right with the pants," I said quietly as I took them from her hand. "What do you think I should wear on top?"

She began fussing with the back of my hair as she explained what she'd picked out for me to wear as a shirt. "On top, I think you need to let Kane see the blessings the good Lord has given you. I have an adorable little top that you'll look great in. You get the pants on and I'll be right back."

I did as she said and stripped off the T-shirt she'd given me. Standing there in front of the mirror in just my bra, I looked down at the blessings the good Lord had given me, thankful they weren't bruised too. I examined my arms to make sure Aaron hadn't caught me anywhere with a wild punch, but somehow I'd been pretty much spared from the neck down, except for my ribs, my left hip that still ached, and that bruise on my leg.

Gemma came up behind me and held out the shirt for me to see. "Check it out! I admit I'm partial to green, but even I don't look as great as you will in this pale green number. I love the bows on the shoulders too. So cute! You're going to look fantastic in this."

Slipping the top over my head, I straightened the bows over my bra straps and looked in the mirror. When she was right, she was right. The light green next to my pale blond hair looked great, and the shirt did just what I needed it to.

Smiling, I looked behind me at her in the mirror. "It's great, Gemma. And best of all, it makes my boobs look great."

She twirled the back of my hair again and rested her chin on my left shoulder to look into the mirror with me. "Your boobs look great all the time. This just makes them even better. Now how do the top and pants feel? You need to look confident in the interview, so I don't want you having to fidget because you're uncomfortable."

"They feel great. I think if I wear my own shoes it'll be okay, right?"

"I think so. They're pretty nice and have that good platform heel action that we tiny girls need. Other than that, just remember to stress your time as a Storm cheerleader and knowing me and you'll be fine."

I nodded and wished I could feel as positive as she did. From the neck down, I looked great. From the neck up, well, that was an entirely different story. How we were ever going to cover up that horrible bruise just under my eye I had no idea.

Gemma must have been reading my mind because she set to work digging through her makeup bag on the back of the bathroom sink, pulling out tubes of concealer and every possible kind of cosmetics to make me look like a normal job applicant and not some girl who'd been used as a punching bag just a few days before.

By the time she finished applying all that makeup, my face had been transformed from bruised and spotty to nearly flawless. Only a tiny hint of Aaron's handiwork could be seen on my cheek, and for the first time since Gemma had mentioned the chance at a job with her at Club X, I honestly believed it could happen.

She turned me around to study her creation and

smiled. "You look gorgeous! Now show them the you I know and you'll be a shoo-in. Once you get the job, I'll ask Kane if he'd be willing to schedule us together for a while so we can drive to work together."

I took a deep breath and exhaled slowly, the pain in my ribs stabbing at me. "Okay, sounds good. What time is it?"

"Nearly quarter after six. Let's get going so we're not late."

"Okay. I just have to brush my teeth and I'll be ready to roll."

"Great! See you outside!"

Gemma closed the bathroom door, and as I began to brush my teeth, I really looked at the woman staring back at me. Twenty-two years old, I needed to get my life together. No more boyfriends who took more than they gave. No more making excuses for the mess my life had become. If Gemma could put in a good word for me with the owners of Club X, the least I could do was be someone who deserved that effort.

That woman in the mirror could be more than just some man's punching bag.

✕

GEMMA SQUEEZED MY HAND AS she opened the door to Club X and moved up to fuss with the hair around my face. "Just remember how terrific you are, okay?"

I plastered a smile on my face. "Got it. Terrific."

"Now let's go in and get you a job!"

Following her into the club, I looked around at the huge space that was Club X. She'd described the upper floors but not the nightclub itself. Even empty, the bar looked impressive. I wouldn't be working in this area, but I was still impressed with the size of the place and the huge glass bar.

"Cassian's office is in the back, so that's where you'll have your interview. I can't go in, but I'll be right out here when you get done. Just walk straight back and look for the door on the left."

Gemma squeezed my hand again, and I walked away to meet the three owners of Club X. She'd given me all the ins and outs of each man, so I knew what to expect. Cassian was the businessman. Stefan was the bar manager and still a flirt, despite being with someone now. And Kane was the one I had to impress, even if at first he scared the hell out of me.

Oh, and they were all drop dead gorgeous.

The door to the room I suspected was Cassian's office was open a crack, so I knocked gently. A male voice told me to come in, so I pushed the door open to see three large men staring at me. The one behind the desk waved me in, and as he introduced all of them, I saw Gemma had been right on the money with her descriptions of the Club X owners. Cassian wore a dark grey suit and definitely looked all business, even if he was knockout good looking in a cool way with his dark hair and stunning blue eyes. Stefan stood next to him in jeans and a T-shirt that showed off the tattoos covering his muscular arms. He had a real good time vibe in his deep brown eyes, tussled light brown hair, and friendly smile.

Kane stood off to the side of them, much larger than both the other men and staring at me almost angrily with his striking blue eyes. Dressed in black pants and a dark red long sleeved T-shirt, he had an intimidating look to him, but the tattoos peeking out from under his sleeves across his wrists and the top of his hands made me think there was more to him than the menacing man in front of me now. One thing was certain. He may have looked like Cassian, but one glance told me the two of them couldn't have been more different.

"Please take a seat, Abbi," Cassian said as I gingerly sat down in the leather chair in front of his desk, pain shooting through my left hip. "I do all the general managing of Club X and Stefan handles the bar, so we'll only be involved in the first part of the interview. Kane will take over the second part because you're interested in being a dancer."

I nodded and smiled nervously. I'd never had an interview like this before. Waitressing jobs didn't really require getting dressed up or answering a whole lot of questions.

"Tell us about yourself, Abbi."

Oh, God. I couldn't do this. Nothing about me would make anyone want to hire me. If I was lucky, they'd want me in spite of the fact that everything about me was a mess. My legs began to shake, and I stammered out in a soft voice, "Wha…what would you like to know?"

Cassian smiled, instantly calming my nerves. "Tell us how you heard about Club X."

I swallowed hard. "My friend Gemma works here as a dancer. She told me how much she likes working here, so when she said she'd try to help me get a job here too, I said yes."

Cassian seemed to like my answer, if his warm smile was any indication, and Stefan flashed me a smile too as I finished my answer. But Kane only grimaced as he had from the moment I walked into the room.

Thankfully, he wasn't conducting the interview or I'd have been sent home after the first time I opened my mouth. Instead, Cassian continued to ask me questions, and with each answer, I knew I was winning him and Stefan over.

Two out of three wasn't bad, but Gemma had warned me I had to win Kane over most. I smiled at him, hoping he'd warm up to me, but all I got in return was the same gruff expression and angry glare.

"Abbi, do you have any experience dancing in a club?" Cassian asked after looking at a sheet of paper that sat in front of him.

"No, but I was a Tampa Storm cheerleader and I know how to dance."

My answer seemed to please the two men I'd already impressed, but once again Kane simply frowned. Why did he dislike me so much even though we'd just met?

After a few more questions about me and my background, Cassian said, "Okay, Abbi. Give us a few minutes and Kane will be out to join you when we're done."

I stood from my seat and extended my hand to shake Cassian's and Stefan's hands. Both men thanked me for coming in, but when I turned to shake Kane's hand, it was like he dreaded touching me. Reluctantly, he took my hand in his and I noticed how large his was compared to his brothers'. Rougher too, it felt hard against my skin. For the briefest moment, he shook mine before turning away to speak to his brothers.

No thank you. No nothing. Just more grimacing.

Gemma came toward me all smiles as I entered the bar. "So how did it go? Aren't they as nice as I said?"

Workers began to come in past us, and I struggled to hold back my tears as my disappointment settled in. "Cassian and Stefan were very nice, but I don't think Kane liked me. He didn't ask one question and didn't even say thank you to me for coming in like his brothers did. I don't think I did very well."

"Oh, sweetie. Maybe you're just judging yourself

too harshly. I bet they loved you. Don't worry about Kane. Sometimes he goes entire shifts without saying a word to any of us. He's going to watch you dance now, so you still have a chance to convince him."

Terror raced through me. "You didn't tell me I'd have to dance tonight, Gemma! How am I going to do that? I'm not dressed for it, and every muscle in my body still hurts."

She held me by the shoulders and stared into my eyes. "Don't worry. You'll be fine. It wouldn't matter if you were wearing a burlap sack. Just listen to the music and dance. You can do this. I know it will hurt, but this can be the start of a new life for you."

"It's a big jump from cheerleader to dancer, Gemma. What if he doesn't like me? What if I'm not good enough? I've never even seen you dance." I hung my head as the tears began to well in my eyes. "This was a mistake."

As I stood there with Gemma, my emotions began to run away with me. Between the knockdown drag-out with Aaron and my body still aching like a bus hit it, I couldn't handle this. Kane obviously didn't like me—or maybe he didn't like Gemma helping me get an interview? I had no idea. All I knew was I couldn't do this.

"…you'll be fine. Abbi? Abbi, talk to me. It's going to be okay."

I looked up behind Gemma and saw Kane leave

Cassian's office. Still wearing the same deep frown, he walked toward us in all his miserable, hulking glory. Whoever he was with Gemma, this guy definitely wasn't a fan of mine.

"Gemma, come here."

His deep, husky voice resonated around us, and Gemma obeyed immediately. I imagined most people reacted that way to his voice. It hit me like one of Aaron's punches, sending fear tearing through me.

Straining to listen to their conversation, I leaned toward them and heard him say, "Gemma, you've always been a good employee, so I trust you. Can she even do this job? She looks like she's afraid of her own shadow. What's going on with her?"

Gemma whispered, "She's a good person who needs a break, Kane. I'll give my word on it she can dance as well as anyone here. She thinks you don't like her, so she's unsure of herself. That's why she looks so frightened."

He looked past her directly at me and twisted his face into an expression even more miserable than before. Then our gazes met and for a moment he didn't look so terrible. I saw a gentleness in his eyes that made all my fear ebb away. Unfortunately, that moment passed quickly and he knitted his brows as he turned back to Gemma.

"I don't need some frightened bird working for me. She needs to be able to handle herself. Right now, I don't think she can."

"Kane, give her a chance. She's much tougher than you think. Trust me. I know. She's a survivor."

"Fine. Give me a couple minutes and send her up."

With that, he stomped away toward the stairs on the far side of the room, never even speaking a word to me. Gemma walked back and gave me what could only be described as a forced smile. Even she knew this was a mistake.

"Okay, I guess I should admit that Kane can be a little grumpy."

"Grumpy? Grumpy's a dwarf who's a little cranky, Gemma. Your boss hasn't done anything but frown since he first looked at me. He won't even speak to me."

"I know. I don't understand why he's acting like this. Maybe he's having a bad day. Don't pay any attention to that. Just go up to his office on the top floor and show him your stuff. I'll be down here waiting for you, okay?"

"Okay, but if this goes like I think it's going to, I want you to know I appreciate you trying to help me."

"None of that talk." Gently pushing me toward the staircase, she added, "Just ignore his mood and show him the real you."

With each step, the real me felt like she was going to throw up, either from nerves or the pain in my hip. The knot in my stomach that had begun to form during the interview tightened into a ball of fear so intense I almost turned around as I hit the last step on the top floor. I didn't, but as I searched for Kane, I wanted to. I just didn't want to let Gemma down.

"Hello?" I tentatively called out as I walked down the dimly lit hallway.

"In here," he barked from a room behind me.

Turning around, I made my way to where his voice had come from and found him sitting behind a wooden desk that seemed too small for someone his size. For the first time, he didn't frown when he looked at me, and those blue eyes of his didn't seem to shoot daggers in my direction.

"Come in."

I stepped into his office and stood there as he had no chairs in front of his desk like Cassian had. He continued to stare at me, and while I wanted to break my stare, something inside me told me not to. He didn't need to think he scared me as much as he really did.

"You don't say much, do you?"

"I could say the same," I answered, suddenly accepting that if this wasn't going to end up with me getting a job at least I'd be myself. Gemma had said to show him the real me.

"Do I frighten you?" he asked, never taking his gaze off my face. I'd expected him to be more interested in my body.

"You did for a little while, but I've had to deal with much worse than you."

For the first time, his eyes trailed down my body and then made their way back up to my face. With the frown he'd worn for nearly every minute since meeting me, he said in a low voice, "I bet you have."

I had no idea how to respond or if I was even supposed to say anything to that, so I stood there in his office as he sat behind his desk staring back at me. I'd had some odd interviews, but this definitely ranked high on the bizarre meter. Even worse, I doubted I'd get the job after all his weird behavior.

"I need to see your body, and I can't in those pants. You look fine otherwise, but you'll have to put a skirt on."

Confused as to where I'd produce this necessary skirt from, I opened my mouth to explain I didn't have one, but he cut me off and handed me a black skirt I instantly knew would barely touch the middle of my thighs.

"Where do you want me to change?" I asked, worried about that bruise on my leg.

"Go out into the hallway and go in the first door on the right. Change and then go through the back door of that room into the hallway and look for the room with the light on."

Still confused but sure I had nothing to lose, I followed his directions to the letter and when I had changed into the skirt, I walked toward the room with the light, noticing the glass on the left wall of the hallway. This was how the dancers appeared in the rooms behind the windows.

Stopping when I reached the light, I turned to see him sitting on a couch in the room, his long legs casually spread in front of him and his arms fully extended out to the sides. For the first time, Kane looked appealing, even sexy. He said nothing and made no movement to instruct me on what he wanted me to do. Unsure of what he expected, I simply stared out through the window at him. He stared back, locking his gaze on mine, and I thought I saw the hint of a smile.

Just as I opened my mouth to ask what I should do, soft music began playing. Still, he made no movement to let me know what he wanted me to do, so I closed my eyes and listened as the sensual rhythm washed over me. Then I did as Gemma had told me to and danced for him.

Chapter Three

Kane

As soon as Abbi showed up in front of that window, I knew what I'd suspected was true. The reason she seemed so frightened became clear. Gemma had done a great job hiding the bruise on her face, but I'd seen enough girls in this job to know when makeup was being used to conceal instead of enhance. Then when I saw Abbi standing there in that skirt, the huge purple bruise on the inside of her knee told me all I needed to know.

I watched as she danced for me, easily better than any of the dancers I already had. As she moved, her body seduced me, and I knew she'd be a favorite of club members. Petite, she possessed a gracefulness that reminded me of a swan, delicate and soft. She was beautiful like an angel in the soft light of the room with her long blond hair gently flowing over the pale skin of her shoulders.

Just watching her behind that window made me want her.

But for all that, I saw things in her that signaled trouble. The bruises told me the ugly secrets of her private life, and I didn't need a dancer who brought that to my work. Beneath the telltale signs of abuse were the more subtle signs, like the wince that marred her beautiful face when she moved the wrong way and likely hurt already painful ribs.

Somebody had beaten her and recently too.

It wasn't that I hadn't seen this before. My line of work involved more of this kind of behavior than I preferred to see. That someone much bigger than she had laid their hands on her body in anger sickened me. No matter what she'd said or done, she didn't deserve that.

The music began to fade away, and even as I regretted that she'd stopped dancing for me, I knew it was for the best. I couldn't help her, no matter how much I wanted to.

When she finished her audition, I forced myself to wave her away, and she left, her expression one of confusion and rejection. I saw her minutes later after she'd changed out of the loaner skirt into the pants meant to hide the evidence of what some boyfriend had done to her. Looking up at me, she waited for me to tell her she'd gotten the job.

"One of us will let you know," I said flatly, unable to tell her I'd already made my decision as she stared at me with hope in her big blue eyes.

I watched her walk away as I tried to convince myself I'd done the right thing. If only the twinge in my chest didn't make me feel like shit for doing it.

By the time I reached the first floor, I'd pushed aside whatever she'd brought out in me. Entering Cash's office, I found him and Stefan still there.

"How'd the girl work out?" Stefan asked in his usual enthusiastic tone. "She seemed perfect to me."

Eager to take the attention off myself and my decision, I said, "I thought you'd given up on molesting the help since you and Shay got together. Back to your old tricks?"

A look of hurt crossed his face. "No. I just thought she'd be a good dancer. She has a great body, and she's cute. Nice eyes. The members who like the dancers would love her."

Leave it to Stefan to hit the nail perfectly on the head. The members would love her. She'd probably make a killing every night she worked. Too bad she'd never get the chance.

Cassian looked at me and shrugged. "So? Can she dance or not?"

"Not really," I lied. "I don't think she'll work out."

"Are you fucking crazy? How bad was she?" Stefan asked, instantly pushing my buttons.

I sat down in the chair next to him and shook my head, trying to remain aloof. "She's just not right for what I need up there. I'll let her know tomorrow."

"Forget that. I'll take her. She may not be able to dance, but I bet she can serve drinks like a champ. My regulars will love her. Those big blue eyes will have them throwing money at her and us. Give me her number and I'll call her. Better to hear good news from me instead of your bad news from you."

Stefan's interest in Abbi bothered me. It shouldn't have, but it did. He'd seemed to have turned over a new leaf since Shay, but was it possible that was all an act? Was he back to fucking the women who worked under him? I knew almost nothing about Abbi, but she didn't need someone like the old Stefan in her life.

I couldn't let him or Cash see I cared one way or another, though. "Whatever. I'll get you the number when I go back upstairs."

"Great! Maybe she can start tomorrow."

Cash seemed to not notice Stefan's enthusiasm at the prospect of Abbi's becoming a bartender or my apprehension over her working at the club at all. "Well, now that that's settled, Mason called me for a meeting. I think I'm beginning to miss Shank."

"He saved our asses, Cash. Mason can't be that bad," Stefan said quietly.

"What he is is demanding. I'm worried one of these days that councilman of ours is going to make a demand we can't meet. Then we'll have problems."

The three of us sat silently as the thought of someone even worse than Shank made me worry about the future of our club. Every night it became harder and harder. Hopefully, the deal with Mason to secure Club X wouldn't turn out to be a deal with the devil.

"You and Olivia going to Mom's tomorrow?" Stefan asked in an effort to change the subject.

"Of course. You'll be there? I'm sure she wants to hear all about what's going on with you and Shay," Cash said with a chuckle. "How is she?"

"She's good. She'll be back in a few months and maybe I can even convince her to come back to bartend while she's here."

Cash moved around his desk toward the door. "As long as she's not going to sue us for sexual harassment, I'm fine with whatever she wants to do here."

"She loves me, so it can't be sexual harassment. I'm a changed man, gentlemen."

I rolled my eyes at Stefan's remark, secretly hoping it was the truth. I might not be able to hire Abbi, but I wanted to believe she'd be okay bartending for him.

Standing to follow Cash, I felt Stefan jab me in the shoulder. "What the hell was that look for?"

"No look. Just hoping we don't have to shell out any more money on bartenders who aren't as in love with you as you think."

He walked beside me as I headed out into the club. "I'm not the one Cash should be worrying about. I saw the way you looked at that girl, Kane. I get the feeling she's just your type."

"Shut up, Stefan. You don't know what you're talking about."

"Yeah, yeah. I know what I saw. You can put that miserable guy face on all you want. You liked her. Not that I blame you. I like my women a little feistier, but whatever floats your boat. All I know is you liked her."

I stopped and turned to face him, hating that he could goad me like this. "If she was my type, wouldn't I have hired her to dance for me?"

He gave me a sneer. "I never claimed to understand how your mind works. I just saw the way you reacted when I said she could bartend for me. You can fool Cash since he's not paying attention because his head is full of all that wedding business, but I saw that look in your eyes. You don't have to worry. I told you. I'm a changed man. She's safe with me. I can even make sure nobody gets a chance with her, if you want."

"I don't care what you do, Stefan. What that girl does or doesn't do is none of my business. Now if you don't mind, I have work to do upstairs."

I quickly got away from him before he saw how much it bothered me to think of Abbi with him. I didn't know why, but it did and it had nothing to do with him being unfaithful to Shay.

"Hey, don't forget to give me her number," he yelled as I hit the stairs. "I want to get her in here as soon as possible."

Waving him off, I headed back up to my office to

bury myself in work and forget about Abbi, her big blue eyes, and the ugliness of her life I couldn't seem to get out of my mind.

✕

I KNEW FROM STEFAN'S NIGHTLY reports to me that Abbi learned her job as a bartender pretty easily. Much to his amazement, she was a quick study. After he'd gotten over his surprise at her being more than just a gorgeous outside, he saw her as someone who could handle the highly coveted position of front bartender.

Even as he told me these things night after night, I tried to convince him I didn't want to know about her or how great she was at her job. Standing in front of me at my usual post on the top floor, he yammered on about her, and I held my hand up to stop him.

"Why are you telling me all this?"

"Because I know you like her, Kane. I don't know why you didn't hire her, but your loss is my gain. She's a natural down there. Men love her. Hell, even women seem to like her serving them. You should come down and say hi."

"Thanks, but she and I aren't friends."

I busied myself with paperwork, hoping to give him the clear hint that I wasn't interested in what he had to say. Unfortunately, that's not how Stefan worked. He'd gotten it into his head that I liked Abbi, and until that thought was proven wrong, he'd continue with these reports every night.

"Kane, what is it with you? You never touch the dancers, and even though we have some gorgeous women working as bartenders downstairs, you never bother with them either. You live in that tiny apartment at the back of the building like some weird hermit. For the first time since we all began this thing, you like one of the girls. Why won't you admit that and do something about it?"

Stefan may have been my brother—or half-brother, to be more accurate—but he knew little about me. I'd made sure of that from day one, even as we'd hung out together as drinking buddies in the beginning. As different as night and day, he and I had few things in common. I was closer to Cash, maybe because we were almost the same age, but probably because his temperament was closer to mine. You could talk to Cash and trust him with what you said. Stefan was an entirely different story. Even if I wanted to admit that Abbi had moved me in some strange way, I could never say it to my younger brother.

"There's nothing to admit, and as far as I'm concerned, you can quit telling me this shit every fucking night."

Frustrated, he shrugged and shook his head. "Whatever. Just keep in mind that you can always stop down and say hi. She might like that. Maybe you could try to smile too. It might help."

Stefan turned and headed back down the stairs, disappearing into the darkness of the club. The truth was as much as I tried to act disinterested in his nightly rundown on Abbi, I began to look forward to hearing about her progress behind the bar. I didn't understand it, but there it was. I couldn't put my finger on how, but in just those few minutes with her she'd made me feel something I hadn't felt in years.

And that's what it would remain. A feeling and nothing more. Whatever spark she'd ignited in me as I watched her dance couldn't be fed. It, like any other feelings I could have for her, needed to be extinguished for the good of both of us.

Fate, or at least the people around me, seemed to have other ideas, however. Just as I got rid of Stefan, Gemma appeared in front of me for the first time since I hadn't hired her friend. One of my favorite dancers, she wore an expression that told me I wasn't one of her favorite people at the moment.

"It was the bruise on her leg, wasn't it? That's why you didn't hire her to dance," she said as she stared up at me with anger in her eyes.

"She got a job bartending, Gemma."

Her hands landed on her waist as her right hip shot out. "You know it's not the same, Kane. You promised me you'd give her a chance and you didn't. I think it's because you thought she'd be a problem. Stefan doesn't seem to have any problems with her, though."

I tore my gaze away and looked down at my paperwork. "Then it's a good thing he wanted her to work for him."

Gemma tapped her finger on the papers I pretended to study. "I think there's something else going on here. She told me how mean you were to her from the moment you met her. You've never been that way with me or any of the other girls. Why were you like that with her?"

I lifted my head to see her stare boring holes in me as she waited for an answer. I had none to give her. I didn't know why I'd reacted that way to Abbi, but from the very first moment I saw her, the need to push her away warred with an intense desire to protect her. I couldn't explain either feeling.

"Don't you have somewhere to be, Gemma? You still have three hours left on your shift."

Unsatisfied with my answer, she turned to leave, but stopped and turned back to face me. "I want you to know something. Three nights before her interview, Abbi's boyfriend beat the hell out of her. When I brought her to my house, she offered me every last cent she had to thank me for helping her. That person you so easily dismissed because you saw a few bruises needed a break, and you refused to give her that. Thankfully, Stefan, of all people, isn't like you. I thought you were better than that, Kane. Now you can fire me or do whatever you want for saying this, but it's the truth."

The thought that Stefan had chosen to be a better person than I had bothered me almost as much as Abbi working under him. "Go back to work, Gemma."

She marched away, still angry with me, as I reeled from her words. She'd struck a nerve. That she didn't understand why I'd refused to give Abbi a job didn't matter. That I'd done what I did for Abbi as much as myself didn't matter either.

Fuck! Why did this girl get under my skin?

After catching Samson as he headed off on his break and lying that I needed to handle something with one of the members, I found myself walking down the stairs toward the bar. I had no idea why, but something inside me pushed me to see her. Maybe it was the guilt trip Gemma had laid on me. Maybe it was Stefan's suggestion I stop down to see how well she was doing.

Whatever it was, ten minutes later I stood just a few feet away from the bar watching Abbi serve drinks to half a dozen men falling over themselves to talk to her. Her long blond hair tumbled over her shoulders down to her elbows, and she casually pushed it off her face each time it fell into her eyes. The movement made her seem awkward and innocent, and the men in front of her loved it. Just in case that didn't make them fall hard, her big blue eyes focusing on them as she pretended to listen to every word they uttered did the trick. She looked like an angel, and with each smile she flashed the customers, I saw Stefan's quarterly income column swell along with every cock in the room.

"Nice to see you took my advice and came down," Stefan said in a loud voice next to me.

I turned to see his shit eating grin and knew whatever I felt for Abbi was crystal clear, at least to him. "Don't make this something it's not, Stefan. I just decided to come down to see Cash."

Raising his eyebrows to show me he knew I was full of shit, he said, "As you well know, Cash and Olivia are down on Gasparilla Island until next week. He told us two days ago at our meeting. Remember?"

Nabbed.

"Let's get a drink," he said as he walked toward the section of the bar where Abbi stood.

I followed him, secretly hoping the music would stop for long enough that I could at least ask how she liked it down here. The crowd of men scattered as I edged my way to the bar to stand next to Stefan, and for the first time since she'd danced for me my eyes met hers. She smiled at her boss and then me, making me think her friend had taken her not getting hired upstairs far worse than Abbi had.

Leaning forward, she smiled even broader at Stefan and said over the music, "Hey, Stefan! What can I do for you, boss?"

He turned toward me and said, "I brought someone down to say hi."

Abbi looked at me and in an icy voice that belied her sweet smile said, "Mr. March."

As I tried to keep the disappointment off my face, I heard Stefan laugh. "Oh yeah, I'll leave you to it."

Surprised by the cold reception, I leaned forward toward her and said, "Jackson. My name's not March. I'm only a half-brother."

As if the music stopped just in time for her to respond, suddenly it went quiet and she said, "I can see that. You're nothing like your brothers. They're sweet and friendly, Mr. Jackson."

Mr. Jackson. Obviously, Abbi hadn't taken my rejection as well as I'd hoped. She leaned back to focus on the guy who'd pushed his way next to me, but I slid my hands out to the side along the bar to give him the clue that I wasn't done yet. Much smaller than I, he understood my body language immediately and backed off.

"Abbi, I hear from Stefan you're doing well down here."

Her smile faded just enough to let me know she didn't appreciate my comment. If I hadn't understood that, what she said next made it perfectly clear. Placing her hands on the bar, she leaned in toward me and said, "I would have done fine up there with you too, but you decided not to give me that chance. Now do you need a drink, Mr. Jackson, or may I pay attention to paying customers?"

Gemma hadn't lied. Abbi certainly was tougher than she looked. Feeling defensive, I blurted out, "Jack neat" and worked to keep my expression from showing how her words had affected me.

She flashed me a forced smile and turned back toward the wall of liquor bottles. Grabbing the Jack Daniels off the shelf above her, she pounded it down onto the bar. "There you go. Enjoy, Mr. Jackson."

I didn't take my eyes off Abbi, but I saw in the mirror behind the bar the guy next to me looked stunned. Sure I didn't want to stick around for any more of her anger, I grabbed the neck of the bottle and stormed off toward the stairs to head back to where I belonged to down as much Tennessee whiskey as it took to forget I'd ever had any ideas about this woman.

Stefan caught up with me before I got away and pulled me aside, no doubt to rub my nose in it after watching Abbi reject me. His grin told me he'd enjoyed the show. "Planning on drinking tonight, Kane?"

"Fuck you, Stefan."

"I've always wondered what it would look like when you actually tried to seduce a woman. Now I know why you don't do it."

"Enjoying yourself? Is this why you wanted me to come down here?"

"No. I thought since she mentioned you a few times that she might like you too. Guess I was wrong, huh?"

"Fuck off, Stefan. And just in case you plan on coming up to tell me any more about your bartenders, don't. I'm not interested."

I left my half-brother and headed upstairs where I belonged. It had been a mistake to think I should make an effort to be something I wasn't.

Chapter Four

Kane

EVER SINCE I WAS A kid, the surest way to make me want something was to tell me I couldn't have it. Once an idea made its way into my mind, it was there for good until I did something about it. The problem was with Abbi I couldn't do anything. Fuck, I didn't even understand why I wanted to do anything about her. Yes, I liked her from the minute I laid eyes on her, but I'd done the right thing and made sure any temptation from her ended when I didn't hire her.

Then why the fuck couldn't I get her off my damn mind day and night? Two weeks of avoiding the bar and her, and each night as I sat alone with a bottle after everyone had left the club, I thought about her. No matter how drunk I got, all I could think of was her.

It was wrong. I knew it. But it didn't matter. For every time I told myself nothing good could ever come of her and me together, my mind went back to when I watched her dance, my body coming alive with each moment she was in front of me.

I needed to forget her, but everything I tried only made me think of her more. I'd been successful in avoiding this because I knew how me being with any woman ended. For years, the memory of how I'd hurt the one soul I'd ever cared about had been enough to convince me I had to be alone.

I'd accepted it.

Some people shouldn't love because all they caused was pain. I'd brought pain since the day I was born. Pain was all I was. My mother knew it. Holly found out too late.

And if I didn't find a way to fight whatever this was that Abbi made stir inside me, she'd be hurt too.

I knew all of this but still it was her face in my dreams every night.

I made my way down to the bar before the crowds of the evening and the music made talking to another person impossible. How Stefan worked in this every night escaped me, but he seemed to love it. All that noise and all those people packed in like sardines weren't my ideas of a great workplace.

The ruler of the bar stood at the end talking to three of his bartenders. Tapping him on the shoulder, I wanted to find out if Abbi was on the schedule for that night. I'd try once more to speak to her before I had to devise another way of getting her attention.

"Where's Abbi, Stefan?"

He looked to his left and right and shrugged. "I

don't see her."

"Is she scheduled for tonight?"

"I don't know. Let me look." He scanned the papers in front of him on the bar and shook his head. "She's supposed to be here, but she called off."

"Why?"

He twisted his face into a ridiculous expression. "How the fuck would I know? All I know is she called off."

Stefan stomped off toward his office, so I walked back upstairs to find Gemma. Hopefully, she knew where Abbi was. Alone in the dancers' break room, she sat at a table playing on her phone.

"Gemma, why isn't Abbi at work tonight?"

At the sound of my voice, she turned to face me. Narrowing her eyes, she shook her head. "Why?"

"I want to know."

"Why? What does it matter if she's here or not?"

I leaned against the doorframe, already tired of getting no answers from Stefan and now her. "Gemma, I'm asking you why she isn't here. I'd like a straight answer."

"Are you going to tell me why you want to know?"

"Gemma!" I bellowed, scaring her. Struggling to keep calm, I lowered my voice and tried to get through to her. "Please tell me why she isn't here. That's all I want to know."

She looked down at the floor and then back up at

me. "I told her I wouldn't tell anyone, Kane. She'll be furious if she finds out I told you."

"I won't tell her I found out from you. Just tell me why she isn't here."

"Who else would you find out from? I know she didn't tell Stefan the real reason why she called off."

"Jesus Christ, Gemma! Just tell me. It's not like I'm going to do anything to her."

She hesitated and then in a tiny voice answered, "She's at The Carousel Club."

A hundred thoughts, each one uglier than the one before, tore through my mind. The Carousel Club ranked as the city's worst strip club. Some of my dancers had spent time there before coming to Club X, and I'd heard horror stories about the place. Negligent owners, patrons who were allowed to grab and fondle the dancers against their will, and a club that stunk of stale beer and desperation couldn't equal the money that could be made.

"Why is she there?"

"She needs money, Kane. That's why I asked you to help her out with a job. She thinks you didn't hire her because she doesn't have experience, so that's what she's getting."

Gemma continued to explain why Abbi had taken a job dancing at the nastiest club in town, but I wasn't listening. My mind raced with all the horrible things that could be happening to her at that place. She'd gone there because I refused to hire her here, and now God only knew what they were doing to her over there.

I stormed out to my office to find Samson to watch the floors while I left to head over to The Carousel Club. Pushing the Mustang's gas pedal to the floor, I tore through the streets over the mile or so to where Abbi was and hoped she hadn't been hurt already.

The Carousel parking lot teemed with cars, even though it wasn't even nine o'clock at night. Jesus, these guys liked it early and easy. No membership fees, no background checks, no discerning taste. Just skin and a lot of it at all hours of the day.

I opened the front door and the stench of cigarette smoke and cheap booze smacked me right in the face. Nausea crept up into my throat as I stepped into the club, but I needed to forget that and find Abbi. 80s metal music blared from the low budget sound system, and I scanned the room looking for her face. The lights trained on the center stage, and as the first chords of some Motley Crue song began to fill the room, she shyly walked out onto the catwalk in just pasties and a pink G-string.

The word NO filled every inch of my brain. She shouldn't be up there with all these pathetic middle aged men leering at her. She was too beautiful, too innocent to be in all this depravity. I couldn't stand there and watch her dance for these men.

My feet seemed to move before my brain made the

decision to take her away from this place. I marched down to the front of the stage and stared up at her. She looked beautiful, even surrounded by all the ugliness. Her eyes closed, she was an angel right there in front of me.

And then she opened her eyes and looked down at me in shock. She stopped dancing and yelled over the music, "Kane? What are you doing here?"

I could have explained that I felt guilty for being the reason she had to work at this shithole. I could have told her how wrong I'd been and how if she wanted a job dancing at my club, it was hers.

I didn't, though.

Instead, I reached up and wrapped my arms around her legs, throwing her over my shoulder before I turned to walk back up the aisle to the front door. A guy with a greasy comb-over and a cigar hanging out between his yellow teeth who sat at the door simply grinned at me as Abbi kicked and screamed for me to let her go. Something told me this wasn't the first time he'd seen a woman carried out of there.

"Kane, put me down! Why are you doing this?" she yelled as she pummeled my back with her fists.

She could scream and punch all she wanted, but I wasn't going to put her down until I got her safely to my car. I reached the Mustang and lowered her to her feet, realizing she still wore only pasties and a G-string. As a carload of young guys spilled out into the parking lot, I quickly took off my shirt and held it out to her so she could at least cover herself.

Abbi yanked the shirt out of my grip and threw it back in my face. "What is this?"

"Put it on and get in the car."

"You can't just drag me out of there like a goddamned caveman. Who the fuck do you think you are?"

I wrapped my arms around her shoulders and struggled against her fighting me to cover her with my shirt. "Abbi, I need you to put the shirt on and get into the car, please."

Planting her hands on my chest, she tried to push me away, but I was too big for her. Frustrated, she gave up, even as she continued bitching me out. "Fine, I'll wear the shirt, but I'm not going in that car with you. You're kidnapping me! This is kidnapping!"

She looked adorable in my shirt angrily pointing her finger up at me, those beautiful blue eyes so full of fire. Buttoning the second and third buttons, I tried to calm her down. "I'm not kidnapping you. I just don't want you to dance for those men. Please get in the car and I promise we can talk then."

I didn't know what I said to make her stop fighting me, but she sighed and climbed into the car without any more hassle. Half expecting her to jump out as I drove back to the club, I slid my arm behind her seat and held my finger on the door lock, just in case.

"Kane, you and I aren't close enough for you to pull the knight in shining armor thing. I needed that job to make more money, so after we do whatever this is, I'm going back."

As I drove, I tried to make sense of what I'd done. She was right—this could technically be called kidnapping. Not that I hadn't crossed over to the wrong side of the law before, sometimes for far less honorable reasons. If this is what it took to ensure Abbi's safety, then kidnapping was fine with me.

She didn't see it the same way. Out of the corner of my eye, I saw her flash a look of pure rage at me as I drove. I stopped at a light and turned to face her, knowing I'd probably get more of that Abbi anger. "I'm not letting you go back, so even if you try, I'll find you."

"Just who do you think you are? You didn't hire me, and last I checked, my boss was Stefan, not that he'd ever be crazy enough to track me down and drag me out of a club all the way across town. I don't need you to save me, Kane, so turn this car around and take me back."

"No."

Her eyes grew wide. "That's it? No? What makes you think I'm not going to jump out of this car at the next light?"

I pulled over and jammed the car into park. Turning my body in the driver's seat, I hung my head in frustration. This woman was the most infuriating soul I'd ever encountered.

"Abbi, you don't belong at a place like that. I made a mistake not hiring you to dance at Club X. I'm trying to fix that mistake. That's all this is."

She narrowed her eyes to slits and stared at me for a long moment before she spoke again. "Nobody does anything out of the goodness of their heart. I've spent enough time on this earth to know that. So what do you want? I have no money. In fact, the only thing I have to trade is what you insisted I cover up in this enormous shirt of yours. So what do you want?"

"Nothing but to see you dance at my club where you won't be touched and treated like a piece of meat."

"I don't believe you."

"Maybe that's because you're not used to people being nice to you."

"You mean men, not people. I see what this is. You think I'm some broken bird who needs a big, strong man to save her. You think because you saw a few bruises that I can't handle myself. Well, you're wrong."

I reached out and gently pressed my fingertips to the inside of her leg where the bruise had been the night I met her. "A man who cares for you wouldn't hit you, Abbi."

Pushing my hand away, she squeezed her legs together tightly and turned her face from me. Quietly, she said, "I'm not stupid. I know that."

"Do you also know that not everyone wants something from you?"

She looked at me with an expression of complete disbelief. "That's a lie. Everyone wants something. Even you, Kane. I don't know why you're doing this. Maybe it is to make up for your mistake. Maybe it's something else. But whatever it is, I know this. You want something. Everyone does."

"Right now, I want you to sit there until we get back to the club. Can you do that?"

She studied my face, likely for the answer to the question of what I really wanted from her, and then sighed. "Fine. My purse and clothes are back at The Carousel. Can we go back and get them at least?"

Sliding the car into gear, I began driving again toward my club. "I'll make sure you get them."

"What is that on the radio?" she asked with a tone of disgust.

"Led Zeppelin."

"Jesus, how old are you?"

"Twenty-nine, not that my age has anything to do with knowing what good music is. How old are you?"

"Twenty-two."

Out of the corner of my eye, I saw her slip her feet out of her shoes. She began to raise them to place them on the dash, and my hand shot out to stop her. "Keep your feet down. This is a '69 Mustang, not some POS car."

Lowering her feet to the floor, she snorted in anger. "Fine. I won't hurt your precious car, which is so quintessentially you, by the way."

"Really? Why?"

"A '69 Mustang Boss, one of the most badass cars there is? It fits you perfectly. Big, tough, and definitely you."

I pulled into a spot behind Club X and turned off the car. Easing my arm from behind her, I smiled. "That's nice of you to say. I'll take that as a compliment."

"Take it any way you want. I'm out of here."

And in a flash, she opened the door and ran from the car. Thankfully, my much longer legs made catching up to her easy, and by the time she hit the road that ran alongside the club, I had my arms around her in a hold much tighter than I'd normally use on a woman so much smaller than me.

"Damnit, Abbi! I can't trust you, can I?"

She flailed in my hold but got nowhere. "Let me go!"

I leaned down and whispered in her ear, "No. I didn't want to do it this way, but you've made it necessary. Stop fighting or I'll carry you in."

Pushing against me to get away, she growled, "Don't you dare pick me up again!"

Her fingernails caught my cheek, and I reared back in pain as she scratched the full length of my jaw.

"Fucking woman!"

Scooping her up, I threw her over my shoulder and walked toward the back entrance of the club, all the while feeling her hit my back with her fists.

I marched up the four floors to my apartment and sat her down hard on the bed, making sure to block the door so she couldn't run away again. Abbi sat there with a hurt look on her face, but when she opened her mouth, I couldn't help but be hurt myself.

"Just in case you think you're different from any of the men who hit me, they all said I made it necessary for them to act the way they did too."

Jesus, she had a way of being able to cut me to the quick. I couldn't have this conversation right now, though. I walked to my closet, never taking my eyes off her, and grabbed a new shirt. As I dressed, I explained the best I could, even as I fought the defensiveness she so skillfully brought out in me.

"There's no point in running, Abbi. I'll find you and just bring you back here. I'll be back in a few hours, and hopefully by then you'll be calmed down."

Her hurt expression morphed into one of shock at my words. "You can't just keep me here. I promise I won't go back to The Carousel Club. Gemma's working tonight, so she'll make sure I get home."

I walked to the door and shook my head. "No. You're staying here. You've shown me you can't be trusted to stay put. You're free to eat all my food, drink all my liquor, and watch TV until I get back. Don't bother screaming or yelling because you're in my part of the club and no one will hear you. The door will be locked from the outside, and you're on the fourth floor with no way to get to the street even if you squeeze out the bathroom window, so don't try because you'll hurt yourself."

"Kane, you can't do this! You can't keep me prisoner here," she said with a sob in her voice as she walked over to stand in front of me. Looking up at me with her big blue eyes, she asked, "Why are you doing this to me?"

Christ, I wanted to take her in my arms and never let her go when she looked at me like that. And I didn't know why I was doing any of this since I knew being with her would bring nothing but bad, but I'd gone too far to turn back now.

"I'll be back later."

Before she began to cry, I got the hell out of there and locked the door from the outside. Turning to head back up to my post on the top floor, I heard her call my name, but it didn't matter. I hadn't lied. Nobody would hear her there.

I found Samson waiting for me at the top of the front stairs where I'd left him. Barely ten o'clock, it was still early and I hadn't missed anything important other than some problem between two of the dancers. Nothing new.

"You have a few rooms to handle tonight, but I'm going to need you back here to stand in for me by one. I have something I need to take care of."

"Whatever you need, Kane. I'll be here anyway."

"Thanks, Samson. Oh, by the way, we'll have a new dancer soon. She's good."

The news of an addition to the dancer ranks made him smile. "Good. For a moment there, I thought you might mean a new guy. I thought you were nicely telling me I was going to need a second job soon."

Samson was too important to the success of the fantasy part of the club, and I wasn't a fool. Slapping him on the back, I assured him of his status at Club X. "No worries, man. I know this business, and you bring in a lot of customers with a lot of money. I'd call that job security. Plus, I can trust you to take care of my business when I need you to."

"Thanks, Kane. I appreciate that. I'll be back by one."

He left me standing there alone, and even though I had a full night of members' fantasies to handle, my mind was one floor down with Abbi. I had no idea what I planned to do about her. All I knew was every fiber of my being wanted to protect her from all the men who'd hurt her.

Chapter Five

ABBI

I DIDN'T KNOW HOW LONG I pounded on the steel door and yelled for Kane to let me out, but I finally gave up when my voice went hoarse. Who the hell did he think he was kidnapping me and keeping me hostage in his shitty apartment? Exhausted, I threw myself on his bed and let the tears finally fall. I cried for what Aaron had done to me. I cried for how fucked up my life was. I cried for being stuck in these tiny rooms of a man who was basically a stranger to me.

I cried until there was nothing left in me.

When there finally were no more tears, I wiped my face and looked around at my prison cell for the night. Kane owned part of Club X, and he lived in this cheap three room apartment? Why? Was he a lesser owner than Cassian and Stefan? Or maybe the club didn't make much money.

The white painted cinder block walls stood bare of any pictures of family or friends or even cheap wall art people hung up to give their homes some feeling of warmth and hominess. Looking down, I saw the wood floor looked old and beat up, like something heavy had been dragged across it, leaving deep scratches and dents, and hundreds of feet had trampled over it when the building was a factory.

Kane's metal twin bed with its single pillow sat in the corner against two walls, making me feel like this place was a prison even before he'd locked me in here. No knick-knacks sat on shelves. Only a single dresser stood on the wall opposite the bed, but even that had nothing sitting on top of it.

My curiosity about Kane and all of this made me want to snoop, so I opened the top drawer of the dresser and looked inside. All I saw were the usual socks and men's underwear, although the guy seemed to like black a lot, if this drawer was any indication. I opened the second drawer and found shirts neatly folded. The drawers below that one were very similar, with both of them filled with Kane's long sleeved T-shirts I'd seen him in at work. Lifting one to my nose, I inhaled the fresh smell of laundry detergent.

I headed toward the closet, hoping to find something to tell me more about the man who I now considered my jailer. Opening the door, I found just a few dress shirts like the one I wore and maybe a half dozen pairs of jeans and pants. It was the least cluttered closet I'd ever seen in my life. But on the floor sat a box, and crouching down, I saw it contained old records like the kind my parents used to love listening to. I thumbed through the albums and saw all those bands from the 60s and 70s the classic rock stations liked to play.

Nothing about his clothes told me much of anything about Kane, other than he definitely wasn't like his brother Cassian. There was a man who knew how to dress to impress. Always in expensive suits and silk ties, he looked powerful.

Not that Kane didn't look powerful. I doubted I'd ever forget the moment as I stood up on that stage and opened my eyes to see him staring up at me and then the next minute him throwing me over his shoulder and carrying me out of The Carousel Club.

Thinking about Kane as some rescuer would only get me into something I didn't need. Angry at how easily I could forgive him for basically ruining my only chance at that club, I slammed his closet door shut and stalked away toward the bathroom. He wasn't a rescuer. He was just like every other man.

Not to be trusted.

I stared at the tiny bathroom window he'd mentioned as he listed all the rules of this prison and saw he hadn't lied. Squeezing through the space would be difficult. I could probably do it, but it would take some work. I stood on the toilet lid and looked out to the street below. Four floors would be a drop to my death without anything to hold on to, and I saw nothing to help me down the side of the building.

I was trapped.

For a moment, I stood there staring at that tiny window and wanted to cry. It was like a symbol for my life. I could see a way to escape, but I couldn't get out. I felt like the punchline of some cruel joke. Would I never find the way out of my life? Was I destined to spend every day trapped in one way or another?

I walked back out to the kitchen hoping I wouldn't find the typical bachelor refrigerator filled with milk past its expiration date, some kind of rotted meat, and too many bottles of alcohol. If I was going to be stuck in his crappy apartment, I planned on eating what he had. Feeding me was the least he could do for keeping me here.

To my surprise, I found food—real food like normal people ate. In fact, I found the kitchen stocked with everything needed to make practically any meal I'd want. There in that tiny apartment that looked more like a jail cell than a home he had a place that felt warm and welcoming. Not the décor, which consisted of the same boring white painted cinder block walls and old wood floor, but what he hid in the refrigerator and behind the cabinet doors.

The image of Kane as someone who'd care enough for anyone to feed them lingered in my mind as I made myself a meal of spaghetti. What was this guy's deal? He didn't even try to hide his dislike for me in the interview, making up his mind about me not dancing at Club X before I even hit the top floor. Then weeks later, when he stopped down at the bar, he seemed to want to talk to me like we were friends, but why?

"I'm good enough to bartend but not good enough to dance," I muttered to myself as I washed my dirty dishes and placed them in the dish rack next to the sink to dry.

That must have been it. He didn't think I had the right stuff to dance at his precious club. But why then had he come to The Carousel and taken me from that place like he felt bad about not hiring me to dance for him?

I couldn't figure him out. He hated me from our first meeting and then one night he decided he needed to save me from the ugliness of some strip club across town where he didn't think I deserved to be.

Why did he care at all?

The question rolled around in my head as I returned to snooping around my captor's apartment. Did he have a girlfriend? I imagined he must. The man may have been strange, but he was stunning. Well over six foot with jet black hair and piercing blue eyes that seemed to stare right through you, he was the type of man women noticed. Add to that the tattoos on his arms, which gave him a badass look, and the fact that he said practically nothing, even when he was being nice, and I couldn't imagine how women didn't fall at his feet.

If he did have a woman in his life, she didn't spend a lot of time at his apartment. The place showed no sign of any feminine touch at all, and I found no clothes a woman would wear stored anywhere in his dresser or closet.

So if he didn't have a girlfriend, did he rescue me because he wanted me? No, that couldn't be it. I'd worked at his club for weeks and only once had he even bothered to speak to me. Not that I gave him much reason to after pulling my nasty bitch routine on him.

Jesus Christ! I must be suffering from Stockholm syndrome. I'm sitting here locked away in the guy's apartment wondering if he wants me to be his girlfriend and actually thinking I like him!

Like him would have been a stretch. I barely knew him, and what I knew I wasn't too sure I appreciated. Sullen and brooding most of the time, he definitely had a domineering thing going on. Not that I didn't like a man taking charge, but driving across town to yank me off the stage at another club and carry me out of the building was definitely a bit much.

Plopping myself down on his couch, I tried to figure out what all this was with Kane. The guy was a puzzle. Hated me from the minute he met me but rescued me. That didn't make sense. He had seemed nice part of the time on the drive there. Well, when he wasn't chasing me down and carrying me to this place to be kept prisoner for God knows how long.

I didn't want to think about this anymore. Turning on the TV, I sat watching an MMA wrestling show for about three minutes before I began desperately searching for the remote. I didn't need to see people beating the fuck out of each other. My life had enough of that, thank you.

Ten minutes later, I hadn't found the remote to change the channel and some poor guy was lying on the floor bloody on the screen in front of me, so I just turned the TV off. Kane was part owner of the most exclusive clubs in town and in these shitty rooms he didn't even have a remote for his fucking television. Did he just watch MMA shows whenever it was on?

As I sat there in the silence of Kane's apartment, the memory of the last time I lay in a bloody mess after Aaron beat the fuck out of me came back with a vengeance. I hadn't thought of it since that night he found me at the grocery store. Sliding the wig off my head, I ran my fingers over my chopped hair, unable to stop the tears.

I stood outside the store with my arms full of bags to wait for the cab to take me to Gemma's house and felt someone brush up against my back. Immediately on edge, I had no way of getting away as he wrapped his hand around my neck and whispered, "I've been looking for you, Abbi."

I wanted to cry out, but I knew it was no use. With all the bravado I possessed, I turned my head and said quietly, "Let me go. I won't let you do this to me."

His dark eyes narrowed and he tightened his grip on my throat, his fingers pressing hard into my skin. Low in my ear, he said, "You don't get a say in what I do, Abbi. Now come with me and keep your mouth shut or the beating you get when we leave will be even worse. You know that I'll do it."

I let him lead me to his car and jumped as I sat down and heard the automatic locks click shut. I was trapped there with Aaron, the man who'd promised to kill me if I ever left him. Covered in the bags after he'd thrown them on top of me, I thought about anything I could use to fend him off. Cans of soup and boxes of breakfast cereal wouldn't stop him. As he talked about what he planned to do to me, I retraced my steps through the supermarket to remember if I'd grabbed anything that could help me.

"You thought you'd just leave me, Abbi? You've had your fun, but now it's time to come home. No more hanging out with Gemma, that fucking whore. The next time I see her I'll show her what I think of her taking you away."

I knew better than to defend Gemma. If I did, both of us could get hurt. As it was, he might forget about hurting her if he could take his rage out on me enough.

He continued to rant about my leaving him, and I continued to mentally walk through the store. I'd passed up buying too much junk food because Gemma warned me if I was going to dance, even at The Carousel Club, I needed to make sure I kept at my best weight, so I'd spent most of my shopping trip in the fresh fruit and vegetables section. But hitting Aaron with the asparagus I'd gotten a great deal on wasn't going to help me much.

Then I remembered the scissors Gemma had asked me to buy for her to cut food up. Fuck! What bag had the guy packed them in? Quietly, I slid my hand along the outside of the bags, feeling for the outline of the scissor package. If I could find it and get them out of the plastic before we got back to the apartment, I could use them. I wasn't above stabbing someone to get away from having my skull crushed in.

Aaron stopped the car at a stoplight and turned to face me. I froze as he ran his hand through his blond hair and gritted his teeth in anger. "What are you doing over there?"

"I was looking for an apple. I'm hungry."

"You can eat when we're done," he snapped. "Until then, you'll listen to me tell you how stupid you were to leave me."

God, I needed to find those scissors! The image of me jamming them into his neck made listening to his threats and insults even possible, and I slowly went back to feeling for the scissors package.

He jammed the car into park and jumped out of the car in a picnic area surrounded by trees, angrier than I'd ever seen him. As he stormed around to my side of the car,

I grabbed wildly at the plastic grocery bags. Just as he opened my door, I wrapped my hand around a rectangular plastic package I knew contained what I needed and stuffed it down the back of my pants.

"Time to go, Abbi. We have some things to work out, and since you brought all this food with you, I'm thinking after we're done you can make me a nice meal to make up to me."

I held on to two bags and stepped out of the car to stand behind Aaron. As long as I could stay out of his line of sight, I might be able to get the scissors out of the package before he started hitting me. I followed him for a few steps knowing I couldn't outrun him, my right hand clutching all the bags as my left hand worked to get the scissors out of my pants. I needed my right hand to open the plastic, though, but when I moved to tear at it, the bags made a rustling noise.

He quickly turned around, and in an instant, all my efforts were exposed. The rage in his eyes terrified me, and any thoughts of fighting back rushed away as he yanked me into the bushes. I fell onto the ground, scattering the groceries everywhere around me when they flew out of my hand as I held tight to the scissors package, my last hope.

I stared up at him as his anger exploded out of him. "Planning on cutting me, Abbi? Let's see how it feels."

He grabbed the package from my grip and ripped open the plastic with one tear. Scrambling to my feet, I made it two steps toward the clearing when he grabbed my hair *and sent me flying back down to the ground. In a flash, he was holding me down, his body covering mine so I couldn't move. He pressed the point of the scissors to my neck and ran it down to my shoulder, and I was sure at any moment he'd stab me.*

"I got a better idea. Just in case you were thinking anyone else would want you, I'm going to make sure they don't."

"Aaron, please don't kill me. Please!"

He laughed the way he always did when he was going to hurt me. "I'm not going to kill you, Abbi. I'm just going to make sure no one else wants you."

I cowered in fear, sure any second I'd feel the point of the scissors blades cutting into my face, but he didn't go for that. Instead, he slowly opened the scissors and winked. With his knee pressed into my chest and his left hand holding my wrists, he began hacking into my hair, scraping my scalp with the points as he carved into my favorite part of me.

"Aaron, no! Don't cut my hair!"

My pleas did nothing to stop him. He just continued hacking away at my long blond hair as I struggled to get free, twisting my head left and right to try to end his attack. Finally, he stopped and looked down at me. Spitting into my face, he said, "There. Now see if you can get anyone to fuck you looking like that."

I lay there on the ground surrounded by chunks of my beautiful hair and unable to even cry. I'd done everything right, and still he'd gotten to me. He stood over me laughing for a few moments and then stormed away, jumping into his car and leaving me there. I guess I should have been thankful he didn't beat me, but what he'd done was worse. I'd lose my job bartending because no one would want to see someone so hideous serving them drinks. I'd have no way to make enough money to even try to start a new life.

Slowly, I got to my knees and stood up. He'd left me with my cell phone, so at least I could call Gemma for a ride and not have to be humiliated by having to walk or take a cab. I knew by the horror in her eyes when she found me that Aaron had succeeded in what he wanted to do. Now nobody would want me.

I stood in front of Kane's bathroom mirror and stared at my reflection. My hair, the part of me I'd always loved the most, lay flat against my head in uneven layers. Gone were the long blond waves that had framed my face, and in their place was a mess perfectly suited to who I really was. I touched the ragged ends and looked away, saddened by the reality of me.

A mess of a woman abused by one man and now imprisoned by another.

Chapter Six

Kane

G EMMA STOPPED AT MY POST on her way out for the night, her expression full of worry. "Do you know where Abbi is? I've tried to call her half a dozen times tonight and she never answers. Did you see her?"

I looked down at my monitors to avoid her stare. "She's fine. Don't worry about her."

"Fine? Don't worry? Did something happen at The Carousel Club?"

"She's safe and sound. No need to worry."

Unwilling to take my curt answers for what they were worth, she tapped on the desk in front of me. "Kane, where is she safe and sound? You left here after I told you where she was and she's not answering her phone. I want to know what's going on."

I took a deep breath and looked up at her. "I brought her back here. She's in my apartment."

"You brought her back? As in took her out of The Carousel Club and brought her here? She was okay with that?"

I returned her stare with one of my own. "Have a good night, Gemma."

A smile slowly spread across her lips. "You like her. That's why you were so difficult from the moment you met her, isn't it?"

"Goodnight, Gemma."

She caught my arm in her hold and squeezed gently, getting my attention. "I need you to promise me something. Don't hurt her. I'm not talking about physical hurt. She's tough. She's learned to handle that kind of pain. But she can't take you breaking her heart, Kane."

"I just brought her back here to make sure she didn't get hurt at that club. She didn't belong there. That was it."

"I've seen the way you are with the women here, Kane. You're distant and cold at times. As a boss, it's not hard to deal with. It's actually okay since you leave us alone. That iciness outside of work can hurt, though. I need you to remember that with her. She's sweet, and men want that. You want to protect her. I get it. But if you can't take care of her heart, don't do this knight in shining armor thing. She can stay with me as long as she needs to."

"Gemma..."

"Just promise me, please. I can't leave here unless you promise you're going to take care of her."

"Okay. I promise I'll take care of her."

"I'm trusting you, Kane. You've never been a bad man in my mind. Don't do anything to change that opinion."

Gemma left me standing there feeling confused. I didn't want to admit to myself that I wanted to protect Abbi. All that would do is end up with us making a mess of our lives. I couldn't let her go back to that club, though. At the very least, I had to make right what I'd done when I didn't hire her to dance for me.

I OPENED THE DOOR TO my apartment slowly and cautiously looked in, just in case Abbi lay in wait for me, still furious about my leaving her hours earlier. I heard nothing and stepped in to look around but didn't see any sign of her. Spying her lying on the bed in the next room, I walked in and saw she still wore my shirt but her long blond hair was gone. In its place was short hair that looked like it had been chopped off.

What had happened?

My hand hovered over her head to touch her roughly cut hair, but instead I just pulled the sheet up to cover her naked legs. She moaned softly at the touch of the fabric against her skin and curled her arms under her before going back to sleep. I'd prepared myself for more of her anger, but I hadn't been ready to see her like this—so vulnerable and innocent there in my shirt and lying in my bed.

Quietly, I stripped down until all I wore were my

boxer briefs. Leaving my clothes in a pile in the corner, I grabbed an old blanket from the closet and spread it out on the floor next to the bed. Abbi mumbled something in her sleep, and I stood silently watching her delicate mouth move, my body suddenly very aware of her nearly naked body just a few feet away.

What was I doing? All the bells had gone off in my head from the moment I met her, but still there I stood watching her innocently sleep in my bed. Why hadn't I just done the same thing I'd done for years?

My cock ached as I stared down at her. I'd known that first night she'd make me want things I couldn't have. Things I shouldn't have. But there I was standing over her, my hands itching to touch her hair and her skin just to know what they felt like as she lay next to me.

She looked so small there in my twin bed, the sheet tucked up near her chin and her legs pulled up under her. How could anyone want to hurt someone so small and helpless?

I lowered myself to the floor and lay back against the hard wood beneath me. Staring up at the ceiling, I tried to focus on anything but Abbi lying just two feet away. I ran through the reports I had to complete and send to Olivia by the end of the week, but the numbers got lost among thoughts of Abbi's soft perfume filling the air around me. It smelled like baby powder and some kind of summertime flower mixed together.

As the minutes ticked by, everything about her preoccupied my mind until all I wanted to do was crawl into bed next to her. What was I thinking bringing her back here? These rooms kept me away from the rest of the world, and now here she was in my bed wearing my shirt and a G-string.

Fuck. This was a mistake. How could I have thought I could have her so close and still stay away? I should have just left her at The Carousel Club, but I couldn't. Just seeing her on that stage with those men leering up at her made me sick to my stomach.

Just like I'd felt that first night when I knew someone had hurt her. The rage had filled every part of me, making me want to beat the hell out of the man who'd put his hands on her body. I knew then I couldn't be around her without wanting to protect her.

She sighed in her sleep, and an ache in the pit of my stomach pinched at me. I wanted to touch her, to hold her in my arms and listen to her gentle sighs for the rest of my life. That even having me in her life would be the biggest mistake she could make hung over my head like a truth so ingrained there was no way to deny it.

I didn't want to think that way, though. I wanted to think she could be mine and I could be hers, and we'd protect each other from the world outside these rooms.

I knew differently, though. The man who'd hid away in these rooms—in this club—would bring nothing but bad to her life. My demons made that certain. They'd rear their ugly heads and show me for the man I really was.

A monster. Violent. Ruled by my rage.

Maybe this time could be different. I had been able to love once, a long time ago. Didn't that mean I could be the kind of man I needed to be to love again?

But that had been before I let my demons take hold and control me.

I closed my eyes and tried to remember a time in my life when I wasn't this person. Had I ever been anything but filled with anger? From the minute I could understand her words, my mother had told me the story of what I was. Why she'd named me Kane. Then later when I first showed signs of my demons, she pulled me close and urged them on, welcoming them when she should have been chasing them away.

My mother held my hand and smiled down at me as she led me from the school principal's office. The anger of a third grader had horrified him, but she simply used the same old reason to excuse my behavior.

"Boys will be boys, Mr. Truesdale. It's just his nature."

He'd shaken his head in disagreement, disturbed by my hitting a classmate until he bled and my mother's easy dismissal of it, and given me three days detention. Almost as if the punishment was a badge of honor, my mother simply smiled and took my hand to lead me out to our car. I knew there would be no reprimand when we got home.

"Kane, what did that boy do to deserve what you did to him?" she asked in the same pleased tone she always used when I got in trouble for hurting others.

I looked down at my hands in my lap and saw his blood under my fingernails. "He said I didn't have a dad so I'm a bastard."

Never turning to face me, she kept her eyes on the road and asked, "Did you do as I said to?"

"Yes, mama. I said nothing. I just hit him until they pulled me off him."

"No words, right? There's no point in speaking, Kane. People don't listen to words. They listen to fists."

"Yes, mama."

We drove home saying nothing else, but she took my hand again as we walked up to our house and led me to the kitchen. "Sit down and I'll get you a bowl of ice cream."

Still in her black and white waitress uniform, she served me three large scoops of my favorite treat, cherry vanilla ice cream, in my favorite blue plastic bowl. I'd done what she'd told me to do, and now she rewarded me.

Placing it in front of me, she kissed me on the forehead and smiled, her happiness going all the way to her blue eyes. "That's my big boy. Principal Truesdale doesn't understand you. Do you know what he thinks you should do when someone says cruel things to you, Kane?"

With the sweet taste of cherry vanilla on my tongue, I swallowed a spoonful of ice cream and nodded. "He says I'm bigger than everyone else, so I have to be careful I don't hurt them."

"No!" she screamed, scaring me. "He's wrong, Kane. Your being bigger has nothing to do with how you should treat people. When someone hurts you, you hurt them back. Do you understand me?"

"Yes, mama."

"When I was carrying you, I knew who you were. I chose your name the same night your father left me after I told him about you. Kane, like from the Bible's Cain and Abel. I knew you'd get what you deserved in this world, but you'd have to fight for it."

I listened to her tell the story of Cain and Abel and how I was like the son of Adam who killed his brother with his own hands. Not a day had gone by since I'd been old enough to understand her words when she didn't tell me that story. I was Cain. My name may have been spelled a different way, but I was him.

Cain. The first murderer on Earth.

"When someone hurts you, they deserve to be hurt, Kane. You did nothing wrong today. You understand that, right?"

Scraping the last of my treat from the sides of the bowl, I smiled and nodded. "Yes, mama. I did just like you tell me to all the time."

She kissed me on the forehead again and leaned back in her seat. Tired from a long day at the restaurant she worked at waiting tables for tips, she smoothed her brown hair back from her face and closed her eyes. "You're going to have people tell you that what you do is wrong, Kane. As you get older and bigger, they're going to say you shouldn't be who you are. They're going to want to change you. They won't be able to, though."

"Okay, mama."

She opened her eyes and cupped my cheeks in her palms. "This is who you are, Kane. Don't let them tell you it's bad. Your demons are the only protection you have in this world because no one else will take care of you."

"You will, won't you, mama?"

"I won't always be here for you, baby. When I'm gone, I want to know I've done all I could to make sure you're ready because the world is a harsh place where no one will care about you more than you care about yourself. Remember that always."

"Even my father?" I asked, hoping the answer would be different this time.

"Especially your father. He's what you need to watch out for in this life. Look at us. While he and his precious wife and sons live in that big house, we live here in this tiny shack. Why? You're as much his son as those two are, but you have my name instead of his because he's too ashamed to claim you so we get to live like this."

"I like our house, mama."

She pulled me into her arms and held me close so the smell of other people's food she wore on her clothes filled my nose. "We deserve better, Kane, but the only way you get better in this life is if you take it, by force, if necessary. Remember that."

I'd never forgotten that, even if I'd wanted more than anything else to believe it wasn't true. Years later, just a few months before she died and after years of living with her hate, she used one of the last times we'd be together to make sure her lesson had been learned.

My mother sat in her favorite red chair in our living room after working a twelve hour shift at the diner while I laced up my boots to go out for the night. Her blue eyes looked dimmed, as if the light in them was gradually going dark. Years of working long hours and not taking care of herself had taken their toll, but I wondered if it was more the anger and hatred she kept alive inside her that was slowly killing her.

"I know you met with him last week. Why didn't you tell me?" she asked in a voice full of bitterness.

I tugged my laces, pulling them tightly away from my boot. "Because I knew it would bother you."

"What did he say? What excuse did he have for waiting until you're seventeen years old to finally want to see you?"

"No excuse. He just wanted to see how I was."

"I bet he thought he could buy your love, didn't he?"

I looked up to see her eagerly waiting for my answer. Shaking my head, I told her the truth. "He didn't seem to think anything. Just wanted to meet me."

"Don't believe what he says, Kane. His words are all lies. Remember how we've had to live all these years while he lived in that big house with the sons he loved."

Her words registered in my mind, but I felt no anger at the thought of Cassian and Stefan March at that moment. After years of her trying to school me in hating them and me being the willing student, I felt nothing for my father or his sons. He called them my brothers, but they weren't my brothers. They were his sons.

I remained what I'd always been. My mother's son. Kane.

"When I'm gone, he'll want to know you more. He'll want you to suddenly be his son. Don't forget all the birthdays when it was just the two of us. Don't forget every Christmas with not even one gift from him under the tree."

I wanted to tell her those were the things I wanted to forget. That even though I tried, I couldn't hate him and his family like she wanted me to. I said nothing, though.

"Do you remember that school counselor when you were in fifth grade who told you that you had to fight against your demons? Do you remember what I said to him that day in his office with him and the principal sitting there passing judgment on you like you'd done

something wrong in acting in your nature?"

"Yes, mom."

"What did I say, Kane?"

I swallowed hard and repeated the words she'd said in my defense as those two men glared down at me like I was some animal to be hated and feared. "His demons are what he is. That he doesn't act like you think he should doesn't mean who he is needs to be fought against."

"Exactly. I worry when I'm gone you'll forget who you are because your father will swoop in and show you a world where someone like you wouldn't fit in if he didn't change."

My demons were as much a part of me as my black hair and blue eyes, so her fear that I'd become a different person without them was just useless worry. No matter how much I wanted to shed them, they were who I was.

I finished tying my boots and stood from the couch to walk to where she sat. Leaning down, I kissed her goodbye like I did every time I went out. "I'll never be anyone but your son, so don't worry."

My words sounded dismissive, but I'd meant them more as a simple truth. Those demons would never leave me, and no matter what happened, all that she'd taught me would stay with me forever.

Abbi stirred in the bed, and I looked up to see her gazing down at me. Those big blue eyes that made her look so innocent had fear in them. She should be frightened. Even now, my demons made me want to take her in my arms and bury myself in her.

Bringing her back here was a mistake.

CHAPTER SEVEN

ABBI

I LAY ON MY SIDE and stared down into his almost hypnotic blue eyes. "What do you want, Kane? You must want something or you wouldn't have brought me here."

He said nothing but shook his head, even as he never took his gaze from my face.

"Do you do this with a lot of women? I still think this is kidnapping, by the way."

The corners of his mouth hitched up slightly, but still he said nothing. It was like having a staring match with a cat. Kane merely looked up at me from his place on the floor, which confused me even more. This was his home, yet he chose to sleep on the floor?

Not much of a captor. That was a good thing. Maybe he wouldn't hurt me.

"Please talk to me. You have no idea how strange it is to be in some man's bed with him silently staring up at you when you ask him question after question."

He opened his mouth, but nothing came out at

first. Pressing his lips together, as if to stop himself from saying something, he finally smiled and said, "I don't say much. I think you noticed that the first time we met."

As he spoke, what I noticed was how perfect his mouth looked. Lips just full enough to be sensual, they made me think of what they'd feel like if he kissed me.

"You seemed to say a lot earlier when we were in the car."

"Uh huh."

The mention of our time together after leaving The Carousel Club made me remember I hadn't returned to get my things there. "I didn't get my purse and clothes! They'll be gone by now. The last of my money was in my purse."

He said nothing as I began to sob but pointed at a chair near the door where my purse and clothes sat.

"You got my things?"

Another nod but nothing more.

I couldn't figure out what he was up to. He'd said he didn't want anything from me, but who acted like this without wanting something? I was basically his prisoner here in this tiny apartment he called home, yet he was the one sleeping on the floor.

I looked back at him, this time noticing his gorgeous body above the blanket that only covered his legs. Tattoos covered his muscular chest and arms, and a single line of words crossed his lower abs just above his hipbones. As I studied it, I realized the words read DO NO HARM.

What an odd thing to tattoo there.

"Do you want to come up here instead of sleeping on the floor? That can't be comfortable."

"No. I'm fine here."

Something made me want to comfort him, even though he'd given me no real indication anything was wrong. It just made me feel selfish to let him sleep down there on the hard floor alone.

I slid out from underneath the sheet covering me and lay down next to him, pulling the blanket over me. In the dim light of his bedroom, I saw the confusion in his eyes. His skin felt heated to the touch as I curled up against his body, resting my head against his shoulder, and everything about him felt hard against me.

Looking up at him, I asked quietly, "Is this okay or do you want me to go back up there?"

He said nothing, but shook his head. Unsure if that meant no it wasn't okay or no he didn't want me to go back up into the bed, I stayed right there next to him, loving the feeling of safety he gave me.

"Kane, are you going to make me stay as a bartender or will you let me dance?"

I felt his chest expand beneath my head. He held his breath for a moment, and then let the air out slowly. I waited for him to answer, to say something, but he remained silent next to me.

"It's just that…I really need the money. That's why I went to The Carousel Club. I'm staying with Gemma, but I can't expect to stay there forever. I need money to get my own place. If you let me dance, then I'd be able to afford an apartment."

Stopping for a moment, I gave him a chance to speak, but he said nothing. He wasn't going to let me dance. I knew it. Why couldn't he have just left me at The Carousel Club? I'd been sure that he'd want something from me, but it seemed like he had no interest in that either.

If meeting my basic needs wasn't a good enough reason, then maybe a more sentimental excuse could work. "I want to make enough money to help my mom too. She's sick and lives on what the government gives her, but it's not enough. If I had more money, I could give her some so she'd have a better life."

I looked up at him, afraid he'd fallen asleep, but his eyes were open and watching me. Did he want me to come right out and say I'd do anything he wanted to dance at his club? Was that it?

Sitting up, I gathered all my courage and quietly said, "Kane, I'll do whatever you want to dance here."

His blue eyes widened for just a moment at my offer, and I waited for him to tell me what he expected in return for hiring me. Instead, he simply stared, making me even more uneasy than I'd been before.

"I mean it, Kane. Whatever you want, I'll do."

Still not a word from him. He wasn't going to make this easy, was he? At least I didn't get the sense that he was a violent man, even with his size. Closing my eyes, I began to unbutton his shirt and finally blurted out the truth. "I mean, if sleeping with you is what you require for me to dance, just tell me. I'll do it."

As the seconds ticked by, he didn't move. I looked down to see him staring up at me with hurt in his eyes. What had I done to make that happen? I didn't know what to say. I couldn't figure this man out. So much bigger than me, he made me feel protected instead of frightened, like I was used to with men. He said next to nothing, and now after I'd offered to sleep with him, thinking that's what he wanted since he'd dragged me back to this place and held me here, he looked hurt by my offer.

What the fuck was with this guy?

Reaching out, he pulled me down next to him and wrapped his strong arms around my shoulders, silently holding me as the purest feeling of security washed over me. Unsure of what was happening, I whispered, "I'm sorry if that offended you. I didn't mean to. I just assumed since you brought me here…"

"I brought you here because you deserve better than The Carousel Club."

"Not everybody can get better, Kane."

He tightened his hold around me, pressing my

body to his. "You can."

We lay there for a long time saying nothing until he broke the silence with a question. "What happened to your hair, Abbi?"

I hid my face in his muscular chest, embarrassed by how I knew I looked. My long blond hair, the part of me I loved the most, was gone, and all that was left in its place was a hacked up mess. I'd forgotten that, but now I cringed at how terrible I must have looked to him. I struggled to find the words to explain what Aaron had done to me, but then I felt the light touch of Kane's fingers slowly stroking my hair. Closing my eyes, I let the gentleness of his caress into me.

"My ex-boyfriend did this," I explained, ashamed that I'd let Aaron hurt me like that. "He was angry that I left, and he held me down and cut off my hair. I bought a wig so I'd look like I used to since I knew no one would want me to work for them looking like this."

In a low voice that made me think he was angry, he asked, "Why do you let men treat you like that?"

Fuck. I began to think I liked it better when Kane didn't talk since when he finally said something, I had no idea how to answer. I didn't know why my boyfriends hit or why I let them. I just knew men always hurt.

"I told you. Some people can't get better."

His fingers slid down to the ends of my hair and

across my neck over and over, like he was trying to smooth away the anger that had caused me to look like this. It made me feel safe and loved. I closed my eyes, but somewhere in the back of my mind I waited for it to stop as all good things did in my life. He'd stop and then he'd become hurtful and angry with me. I'd do something that upset him, and he'd hit me or choke me.

As I waited for him to get to that point, I felt him press his lips to the top of my head in a soft kiss. Then he whispered, "People will continue to hurt you as long as you let them. Don't let them."

I pulled away and leaned on my elbow. Staring down into his eyes, I asked, "Are you going to hurt me? You basically kidnapped me and brought me here. And look at you. You're over twice my size and much stronger than me."

"I don't hit women," he bit out angrily.

His anger unnerved me, and I quickly moved to change the conversation. "So no girlfriend? I expect if you had one she wouldn't like you keeping me here."

"No girlfriend," he said quietly in his raspy voice that now sounded unbelievably sexy.

"Why not? You're a good looking guy, and I bet lots of women here at the club would love to get their hands on you."

"Haven't found anyone I want, I guess."

I couldn't tell if that was a lie or the truth. All I

knew was he didn't seem interested in me. I could understand that. I wasn't blind. I knew what he saw. All the better. I didn't need a boyfriend now anyway, no matter how much I liked the feel of his arms around me.

Since we were going to be just friends, I pushed further with my questions. Even though he'd basically kidnapped me, as he lay there next to me, I had a feeling he wasn't all that bad. As bizarre as that seemed. I might as well know the guy a little better.

"Did it hurt to get those piercings?"

"Which ones?"

Pointing at his nipples, each pierced with a silver barbell, I said, "Those. Do you have more? I don't see any others."

"No, they didn't hurt. I got my lip pierced a long time ago. That hurt a little."

"So now you only have the nipple ones?" I asked, more curious about piercings than I thought I could be.

He gave me a sly grin. "No. I have one other piercing."

I turned my head and scanned his body for any others. "I don't see it. Where is it?"

After a long pause, he said in a low voice, "My cock."

He said that word in a voice that made an ache form deep inside me. Never before in my life had I wanted to see something as much as I wanted to see his cock piercing at that moment. A rush of heat flooded my cheeks, and I looked away, inadvertently focusing on his crotch. Quickly, I looked back at his face and blurted out, "Can I see?"

What was I doing? I didn't know, but the words were out so there was no putting that genie back in the bottle. Like when I offered to sleep with him, his eyes grew big for just a moment and then he smiled.

"If you want."

In for a penny, in for a pound, as my grandmother always said. Nodding, I mumbled, "I've never seen that before. I'm just curious."

For the first time since I'd met him that night of my interview, Kane looked completely sexy and not the least bit scary. Licking his lips, he stared up at me. "Okay."

His hands slid his boxer briefs down to reveal his pierced cock. Long and thick, he wasn't even hard and I knew I'd never met any man so big. The head was pierced twice, and two silver barbells sat on each side.

I couldn't take my eyes off them or his cock, but I squeaked out, "Did that hurt?"

"A little."

"Why did you get that pierced?"

"Long story. Some women don't like it, though, so I can understand if you don't."

I couldn't help let my mouth hang open slightly as the thought of that gorgeous cock fucking me settled into my brain. Licking my lips to moisten them, I said, "I don't know why. It's hot."

Holy fuck! I'd just said to him that I thought his pierced cock looked hot! I wasn't lying, though. I suddenly wanted more than anything to know how it felt when he was sliding it inside me. It was insane, but I couldn't help it.

Thankfully, he slid his underwear up again before I did anything I'd regret later. A few seconds more and my brain might have thought it was a good idea for my hand to touch his piercing.

God, I was a mess. Barely out of a relationship with Aaron and here I was ogling Kane's cock.

Quietly, Kane said, "Abbi, I didn't hire you to dance for me because I wasn't sure you could handle it."

I turned to face him and shook my head. "Why?"

"Because I knew someone was hitting you. You have to be tougher to dance for men, even here. If I had left you at The Carousel, you would have gotten hurt."

"So that's why you took me out of there?"

"Yeah. I didn't want to see you hurt."

"Why? You barely know me. Why would you care if I got hurt?"

"I don't know. I just know that from the moment I met you I wanted to protect you."

"So you kidnapped me and brought me here. I guess that's technically protecting me, but it's more like holding me hostage."

His blue eyes grew softer as he looked up at me and said, "I couldn't think of another way. I'm sorry."

The way he said those words made my breath catch in my chest. I couldn't remember the last time a man had apologized for doing anything to me.

"Well, of all the things I've had done to me, I guess this isn't the worst. I mean, you even let me sleep in your bed while you took the floor." I stopped for a moment and then looked away. "And you don't seem even interested in sex with me, so…"

"I don't force women to sleep with me to dance here."

The tone of his voice told me I'd hurt his feelings again. Jesus, the guy was just trying to help me and I'd offended him twice already.

I turned to face him and saw that hurt settle into his eyes. Reaching out, I touched his hand. "I didn't mean that. I'm sorry, Kane. I just don't know what to say here. I'm not used to people doing nice things for me without expecting something in return. I keep thinking you must want something from me." I lowered my head and tugged on the sprigs of hair near my nape. "I get why you wouldn't want to sleep with me, though. I mean, I know what I look like now."

"My not sleeping with you has nothing to do with how gorgeous you are. It's just not something either one of us wants me to pursue. Trust me."

The only thing I really heard was that he thought I was gorgeous. No man had ever told me I was gorgeous. Pretty. Hot. Sexy. But never gorgeous. But if I was that wonderful to look at, why didn't he want me?

I stared down at this strange man who'd shown me his piercing but wanted nothing to do with sex with me. Who had come to The Carousel Club and had taken me out of that place to protect me. And who lay there gazing up at me like I was some kind of angel or something, even as I sat there next to him with the proof of Aaron's rage all over me.

Kane lifted his arm and wrapped it around me. "Come here. Time for us to get some sleep."

I snuggled up next to him, loving the hardness of his body next to mine that made me feel safe and secure. With my head in the space between his shoulder and his neck, I closed my eyes and breathed in the clean scent of soap on his skin. No fancy cologne or body spray. Just soap.

Then I felt his fingers gently slide through my hair, and for the first time since Aaron had hacked it all off, I felt beautiful.

Gorgeous.

"Thank you, Kane."

He remained silent for a long time and then whispered in his raspy voice, "For what?"

"For making me feel beautiful again."

Squeezing me tighter to him, he pressed his cheek to the top of my head. "You're welcome, Abbi."

I tenderly ran my fingertip down his jaw and over the red scratch I'd given him earlier. "I'm sorry I scratched you. I shouldn't have done that."

He said nothing but kissed the top of my head again, like a sign he'd forgiven me.

I lay there on the floor with him in that surreal situation that strangely felt so right, unable to sleep as everything I'd learned about Kane danced in my mind. The man who'd frowned from the moment I'd met him held me in his arms, protecting me even though he barely knew me. I didn't know what would happen when we woke up, but for the first time in my life, I was in the arms of a man who made me feel safe and beautiful.

A twinge of sadness settled into my heart at the thought of all this going away once the sun came up. I'd never believed anything could be worse than a man's fists hitting me, but as I listened to Kane's breathing above me, I was sure him being that silent man he'd usually been with me would be more devastating.

To know that here, in these tiny rooms he called home, he cared for me yet in front of others I'd be just another Club X employee made me sadder than any beating I'd ever gotten.

Chapter Eight

Kane

I LAY WITH ABBI IN my arms as she drifted off to sleep, my body yearning for more than just cuddling on the floor of my crappy apartment. Every fiber of my being wanted to make love to her, but that was a mistake neither one of us could afford. I should have never gone to The Carousel Club.

Fuck, I should have never let myself want her after that first time we met.

Two fucked up people didn't make a good couple. All we'd make was a mess of each other, something neither one of us needed.

But now, as I played with the ends of her soft hair and enjoyed the feel of her warm breath gently drifting across my chest as she slept next to me, I wished more than anything in this world that I could be the kind of man she needed.

Then in a split second, my mind switched gears from wanting to make her mine to wanting to kill every single man who'd ever hurt her. The idea of someone holding her down as he hacked away at her hair made my fists close into angry balls until my fingernails dug into my palms. I imagined her crying, helpless as he punished her and she feared for her very life. I wanted to find him and make him suffer like he'd made Abbi suffer.

This couldn't happen. I knew this, and still there I was with her in my arms as my brain wrestled with the need to beat the fuck out of the guy who hurt her. She didn't need someone like me in her life. It was already fucked up enough for two lifetimes.

Yet with every moment that passed, she felt more right in my arms than anyone ever had. I closed my eyes and tried to push away the truth that never went away.

I'd only end up hurting her.

✕

"KANE, YOU UP?"

I opened my eyes to Abbi sitting up next to me and smiling. "Yeah. What time is it?"

Shaking her head, she lifted my arm to look at my watch. "A little after ten."

"Okay. Guess it's time to get up," I said as I stretched the sleep from my limbs.

Abbi's eyes opened wide and I followed her gaze to where my morning hard-on had poked out from under the sheet. A blush covered her cheeks and she stammered, "Where…um…can I take a shower?"

Scrubbing the night from my face, I struggled to think of anything but rolling her on her back and taking her right there. Looking away toward the bathroom, I said, "Uh, in through there. Feel free."

Nearly jumping up from her place next to me, she trotted off toward the shower as I watched her gorgeous ass as she walked away. I squeezed my eyes shut and told myself fucking Abbi was the worst idea I'd had in a long time. Unfortunately, my cock didn't agree with me, growing harder than it usually did most mornings. Even as I ran through every reason why I shouldn't even think about wanting her, somewhere in my mind a little voice murmured that she was right there in the next room, naked and wet and…

Fuck! What was wrong with me?

I lay back down and covered my eyes with my forearm, needing to get my head back to where it should have been. Abbi would only get hurt if I acted on the ideas marching through my mind. I knew this. Now I just had to tell myself that over and over again until every cell in my body didn't want her more than anything else in the world.

Ten minutes later, Abbi stood over me pushing my arm with her toes. I looked up at her standing there in just a towel looking fresh and clean and entirely too sexy.

"What's up?"

"I don't have any clothes. Remember? All I was wearing when you threw me over your shoulder at The Carousel Club was a G-string, pasties, and my shoes. I can't go around wearing your shirt, and the t-shirt and shorts I wore there aren't exactly good for daytime," she said with a chuckle.

"Hmmm…"

I had no clothes a woman could wear, but I had an idea. Rolling over to hide my still raging hard on, I stood and walked over to the kitchen table to grab my phone. After a few rings, Cash picked up.

"Hey, Kane. What's up?"

"I need to speak to Olivia, Cash. Is she there?"

My half-brother remained silent for a moment and then quietly in a skeptical voice said, "Yeah. Here she is."

Thankfully, he didn't ask why I'd need to speak to his fiancée before work started. Olivia and I had become closer after that Ciara Danson business, but no guy wanted men calling their girlfriends about borrowing some of her clothes.

"Kane? What's up?" she asked with more than a little curiosity in her voice.

"I need you to let me have some of your clothes."

"What?"

"I have a friend here who needs clothes and I don't have any for her. You're the only female I know well enough to ask."

"Oh, okay," she said sweetly. "What do you need?"

I looked over at Abbi standing across the room from me in my towel and tried to imagine her in anything Olivia wore to the club. "How about something casual that you wouldn't wear to work?"

"How about one of my sundresses? Would that be okay?"

"Great. Thanks, Olivia. Can you bring it with you this morning?"

"Sure. I'll be there in a few minutes. Do you want me to bring it up to your office?"

"No, that's okay. I'll come down for it. Thanks again."

I took the phone from my ear, but I heard Olivia say, "Kane, wait!"

Pressing it next to my head, I asked, "What?"

"Is everything okay? Does your friend need anything else?"

"No, everything's fine. Just the dress. Thanks."

"Okay, I'll be there in a little while. Just tell her to hang on for a few more minutes."

I placed the phone back on the table and looked over at Abbi. "Olivia's bringing you something to wear. She usually gets to work by eleven, so it'll just be a few minutes."

"Olivia, Cash's girlfriend?"

"Yeah."

"That's nice of her. Why is she doing that?"

I'd forgotten how little Abbi knew of kindness other than Gemma. "Because I asked her. Olivia's nice like that."

A strange silence settled in between us, but I didn't know what to say, so I escaped into the bathroom, leaving Abbi there. I didn't need to be around her when she was only wearing a towel.

And then halfway through my shower, she poked her head into the bathroom. "Kane, can I eat that cake in the fridge?"

I looked out through the clear glass shower door and saw her standing there staring at me as she waited for my answer. There was no way she couldn't see every inch of me. Christ, she was making it next to impossible not to want her.

"Yeah. No. Wait for me and I'll make you breakfast. I have some eggs, I think."

"Okay." She didn't say anything else but stood there staring at me for a few moments more before she left.

Damnit, she wasn't going to make this easy. She had no idea how much she shouldn't want me.

Olivia's clothes fit Abbi awkwardly, but I couldn't help but notice how cute she looked in her pink sundress, even though it covered more of her than it should as it hit near her ankles. Abbi fussed with the fabric while I made her breakfast, and even as she ate her scrambled eggs, she couldn't stop touching it.

I finished my eggs and asked, "Are all your clothes at Gemma's?"

She dropped her gaze to her nearly empty plate and shook her head. "I don't have any clothes."

"None?" I asked, confused since I'd seen her show up for work behind the bar dressed every night for weeks.

"No. I've been wearing Gemma's until I have enough money to buy some."

"Haven't you gotten paid yet?"

She looked up at me and nodded. "I told you. I need money to pay for more important things. I'm trying to save up for an apartment, and I helped my mom a little with the money I've made so far."

I didn't know why but the idea of her not having clothes bothered me. Taking her plate, I put it in the sink with mine and said, "Then we have somewhere to go this morning. Get ready."

"For what?"

"Shopping."

Turning around, I saw the surprised look on her face. Or maybe it was confusion. Whichever it was, it quickly changed as she shook her head.

"No. I don't want you to buy me anything."

"Whether you want me to or not, I'm going to, so it would probably be better if you're there. If not, I might get the wrong sizes."

My attempt at humor didn't work, and she frowned. "I don't want to owe anyone anything. I've done that before, and it never got me anywhere good."

"Then accept whatever I buy as my apology for basically kidnapping you last night. Then neither of us will owe the other person anything."

Abbi considered my idea for a minute and smiled. "Okay, it's a deal. I don't wear anything expensive, so you're getting off easy for kidnapping and holding me hostage."

Her comment about being held hostage bothered me. It was stupid, but it did. I forced a smile at her joking and led her to my car for our shopping trip, her comment nagging at my gut.

"KANE, WOULD YOU BE WILLING to take me to my apartment?"

I turned to see Abbi staring at me with those big blue eyes that made me want to do anything she asked. "Yeah, I guess."

"It's just that my boy—I mean, ex-boyfriend might be there and…"

Looking away, I thought about what I wanted to do to this ex-boyfriend of hers who'd done all that shit to her. Beating the fuck out of him would be the first thing. Then I'd figure out what to do from there.

"Sure. You can't be getting clothes, so why do you need to go there?"

I stopped at a red light and looked over to see Abbi's head hung and her tugging on the ends of her hair. "My mother gave me a ceramic bell and I want to get it back. I don't think it was broken when he—" She stopped talking and then quietly said, "I didn't remember to take it when I left."

Jesus, I wanted to fucking crush this guy's skull. Not only had he done everything he could to hurt her physically, but he'd taken everything else from her.

"Just point me in the right direction."

Abbi told me how to get to her place, and I pulled up in front of an apartment house in the middle of a block filled with rundown houses and empty, torn up lawns. She didn't seem to want to get out of the car, instead staring down at her hands as they lay in her lap, so I opened my door and walked around to her side to show her she wasn't alone.

She looked up at me with the purest expression of fear I'd ever seen. What else had this fucker done to her?

"It's okay. I'm here. I doubt your ex could do anything to me."

"I guess. I'm just wondering if this was a bad idea."

I held my hand out to take hers. "C'mon. Show me where you used to live."

She took my hand and we walked up to the front door. Her hand shook as she put the key in the lock, and as she pushed the door open, I felt her squeeze my fingers tightly. Whoever this guy was, he terrified her.

We entered the apartment and found nothing. The place had been emptied out. She walked into the middle of the room and slowly turned as she looked for that bell, but there was nothing left. He'd made sure to hurt her to the last.

"Oh, my God," she sobbed as she collapsed to the floor. "It's gone. He took it. He took everything."

Tears rolled down her cheeks as she sat there so tiny, her body heaving from her crying. My heart felt like someone was squeezing it in their fist. That feeling I'd had the minute I met her rushed through me again, and I crouched down next to her to put my arms around her shoulders. "Abbi, come with me."

She looked up at me, so helpless, and dried her eyes. "I have nothing left, Kane. All I have are the clothes you bought me today. Everything I had all those months I lived here is gone."

"Come with me. We can go back to the club and get you set up with the costume designer. You're going to need something to dance in."

"Really? You're going to let me dance for you?"

I nodded and forced a smile, even though the idea of Abbi dancing made my chest tighten. "Yeah, so let's go."

She stood and threw her arms around me, hugging me tightly. "Oh, Kane, thank you! I promise you won't be disappointed. I'll be the best dancer you have."

All Abbi could talk about on the way back to the club was how much she looked forward to showing how she could dance, but with every minute that passed I regretted my offer. Club X may have been a hundred times better than that shithole I found her dancing in, but I still didn't like the idea of her dancing, even for my club's members.

I LEFT ABBI WITH THE costume designer for the dancers and headed back to my room to clear my head. Something about this woman made me think things I shouldn't, and I had to try to push them out of my mind before we went further into something neither of us needed. The sight of my shirt she'd worn last night laid out on my bed made all those ideas about how much I wanted her rush back, but I needed to fight the urge to let myself want what I shouldn't have.

By five o'clock I'd talked myself into believing I could have her dance for me and not need to be with her. That the idea of other men watching her dance, even fully clothed, wouldn't drive me out of my mind with jealousy.

Then she walked into my rooms and reality crashed down on me, forcing all those ideas out of my mind. There, right in front of me, she stood in the costume members would see her in. A white dress that accentuated every sensual inch of her body and was meant to make her look sexy and innocent both at the same time. The costume designer Janie knew her stuff, and one look at Abbi made me want to grab my shirt again to cover her. It wasn't pasties and a G-string this time, but the effect was the same.

"What do you think? Isn't it gorgeous? Janie said she'd been waiting a long time to make a costume like this. Do you like it?"

Abbi twirled around to show me the back of the dress, and my cock stiffened at the sight of her perfect ass filling out the costume in a way meant to make men go out of their minds with desire.

She spun around again to face me, those blue eyes looking up at me filled with hope. "You don't like it? She said it would be perfect."

"It is," I said quietly. "It looks great."

"Are you angry at me? You look just like you did the day you interviewed me. You haven't changed your mind, have you? I really need this job, Kane."

I shook my head slowly. "No, I haven't changed my mind. If you want to be a dancer, the job's yours."

Abbi smiled, lighting up my dingy rooms with her genuine happiness at my gesture. "I have something to ask you. I hope you say yes to that too."

"What's that?"

"Gemma has a new boyfriend, and I don't want to be in the way at her house. You know how it is at the beginning. Nobody wants a third wheel around. Would you be okay with me staying here until I get the money for my own place? From what Gemma said, I should be able to make enough in a week or so since I'm only looking for a one bedroom or even a studio."

She wanted to stay with me there in my tiny rooms I kept to hide away from the world. Unable to say no, I mumbled, "Sure."

Again, she threw her arms around me and hugged me close. "Thank you! I'll sleep on the floor so you don't have to give up your bed anymore. It wasn't too bad last night, so don't worry."

For the first time since we'd gotten up that morning, I held her to me, loving how she felt against my body. When she looked up at me, I loved seeing the happiness in her face. Pressing my lips to her forehead, I kissed her softly, closing my eyes to enjoy the warmth of having her next to me.

As I let myself get lost in the quiet joy she gave me, I felt her lips gently touch mine. Opening my eyes, I looked down to see her mouth open slightly in a kiss. My body came alive, reacting to the softness of her lips as they caressed mine, and my cock grew hard against her. Just a small kiss and everything I feared I'd want raged inside me.

She was so close, so tender, so willing…

And so not someone I should be kissing.

Pulling away, I pressed a smile onto the lips she'd just thrilled with a kiss and tried to calm myself. "I left your clothes on the table there, so feel free to hang them in the closet since you'll be staying."

She looked confused by my reaction, but after a moment she nodded and gave me one of her sweet smiles. "Okay. Thank you. I promise it won't be long. I'll make sure to work as many shifts as you'll let me so I won't be intruding for too many days."

Abbi moved toward the table to gather her new clothes, leaving me there wanting so much more than just a mere kiss and knowing even desiring her was wrong. As she made herself at home, I wondered how the hell I was going to deny what my body already craved and my mind was quickly becoming obsessed with.

How would I spend night after night with her right there next to me and not give in to what would undoubtedly end up hurting us both?

CHAPTER NINE

KANE

I WATCHED AS ABBI AND the other dancers readied themselves in their dressing area to perform their first dances of the night, most of them calm and almost bored, except for her. She and Gemma stood next to one another laughing and smiling about something, and only Abbi seemed truly eager to enter the hallway to go her first room.

Of all the costumes they wore, Abbi's alone seemed sexy to me now. Even the dancers who wore just pasties were nothing next to her. My gut knotted up thinking about her dancing for some of our members even as she seemed thrilled to begin her first night of work.

All my people filed into their break room, and walking in, my very presence there made everyone go silent. All eyes focused on me, as they did every night, but all I could see were Abbi's blue eyes staring at me from the corner of the room.

"We've got some new dancers here tonight, so you veterans keep an eye out for them. If they have any questions or run into any problems, help them out. I'll be out there like always keeping an eye on things, so those of you who are new I want you to know I won't let you get hurt. Anyone have any questions?"

One of my dancers who'd been with me for nearly three years raised her hand. I nodded in her direction, and with a silly grin Simone, the dark haired beauty with a body all our members loved asked, "When did you get so nice, Kane? I'm just wondering since last week you didn't speak to any of us for two days straight and the best we could get from you was a grunt anytime we asked a question."

A few of the dancers who'd been with me almost as long as Simone laughed and repeated her question.

"Simone, just for that, I'm going to make sure you get stuck in every freaky room," I said with a smile.

Batting her eyelashes at me, she said in a syrupy voice, "Oh, Kane. You always say the nicest things."

"Just have a good time tonight, ladies and gentlemen. Remember if you run into any problems, I'm never far away."

The dancers filed out one by one until the only people left in the break room with me were Gemma and Abbi. Walking toward me, Gemma winked at me, whispering, "You did the right thing. Thank you, Kane."

Abbi stopped in front of me and looked up with fear in her eyes. "I hope I don't mess up and make you regret this."

"Don't worry about that. You'll be great. I knew you would from the first time I saw you dance."

Reaching out, she gently squeezed my forearm right above my wrist, sending a rush of heat over my skin. "Thank you. It's nice to know you're watching over us making sure we're okay."

"You'll do fine, Abbi."

She flashed me a sweet smile and headed out to where Samson had their first assignments as the knot in my stomach tightened its hold on me. Every jealous need to protect her screamed not to let her dance, but I couldn't stop her now. As long as I watched and made sure she was okay, I could handle this.

Her first room was right down the hall from where I stood every night. Just a few yards away from me a middle aged man with a penchant for young, beautiful blondes sat on a chair he'd dragged close to the window separating him from where she'd dance. I saw in his face how eager he was tonight and instincts normally reserved for the dancers who worked inside the rooms kicked in to high gear. I wanted to grab him by the collar and throw him out of that room before he saw her. I'd met this member before and knew what he used the rooms for.

I watched as the wall lifted and Abbi appeared before him. A pale light washed over her, and the combination of that and her white dress made her look like a goddess. As I watched her, I wanted her. I knew he did too.

Soft music flooded the room, and she began to dance just like she did that first night I sat in a room just like that one and fell in love with how her body moved. Her eyes closed, she looked gentle and innocent and with each moment that passed I got lost in her all over again.

A sudden movement jarred me out of my fantasies, and I saw the man yank his cock out of his pants and begin stroking it. I'd seen this on my monitors thousands of times. Never once had it bothered me before. Now I could barely hold myself back from charging into his room and beating the fuck out of him to show him jerking off as Abbi danced wasn't okay.

Her first assignment and already I was barely able to contain my jealousy. Fuck. This was a mistake.

But I couldn't tear my gaze away from the monitor, even as the guy went to town on his dick. Abbi never noticed anything, entirely consumed by her desire to dance. She was pure and sweet, and the man watching her fed on that as he jerked off, no doubt fantasizing about fucking someone just like her.

For fifteen minutes he slid his hand up and down his small cock as he licked his lips at the sight of her so close to him, separated by just a pane of glass. I'd watched people fuck nearly every night for years, and never once had any of it seemed wrong or dirty. This was what my part of Club X was. Sex. Lust. Fantasy. But now as he masturbated to Abbi's dancing, all I could think was how much I hated watching him do it.

He came with a rush and a long groan, covering the front of his pants and his hand in cum and sickening me, but as I moved my gaze to see if she'd noticed, I saw her eyes still closed and her dancing as if the simple movement of her body to the music made her happier than she'd ever been in her life.

The man's time in his fantasy room ended, and he cleaned himself up before leaving without a glance more in Abbi's direction, his fantasy fulfilled. I watched her finish her dance and saw her open her eyes just as he closed the door behind him. For a moment, she looked around the room but then she left, never knowing anything had happened other than she'd danced.

I caught Samson as he walked past me on his way toward the dancers' break room. "The room you had Abbi in needs to be cleaned before the next person scheduled."

Looking down at his schedule, he nodded. "Okay. I have a fantasy scheduled in there at the top of the hour, so I'll get the crew in there. They're down on the third floor cleaning up after a couple got a little wild with Simone."

"Wild? She okay?"

"Yeah, nothing she can't handle. You know her.

She likes to get her freak on. They had a thing with flavored oils and some toys, I think. She's fine. Just needs a shower. The place was a little greasy after them. Thank God they only had a short time. A few hours and we'd have to hose the place down, you know?"

Samson smiled at his joke, and I pretended not to suddenly hate what I did every night. "This is why they pay us the big bucks, right?"

"You know it, Kane. How's your new dancer doing on her first night? That whole innocent Lolita thing is a huge favorite for a lot of our members. Great recruiting on that. She's going to have them lining up around the block to get a room with her."

Samson's all-too-accurate description of exactly the vibe Abbi gave off made me hate my life even more. "Yeah, she's doing fine. I'll keep an eye on her for a while."

"Good idea. She's close to Gemma, though, so I bet she's tough."

As I tried to pretend I didn't care about Abbi any more than I did for the other dancers, Samson got to work getting the room cleaned and handling some security issue down at the front door. Normally, I took care of the bouncers. Not tonight, though. Tonight I planned on staying put right where I was in front of my monitors.

I fought the urge to go back to the break room to see Abbi and waited for her to appear in Room 12 for her second assignment that night. Just before midnight, I saw a man and woman stumble into the room and collapse onto the couch. Obviously drunk, they had their hands all over each other, so they'd likely fuck right there as Abbi danced. At least it wouldn't be some sad old guy jerking off to her.

The music began playing, a far more sexual piece than in her first room, and I watched as the screen lifted to show Abbi standing there with one of the male dancers. I hadn't paid attention to the list Samson gave me at the beginning of the night because I'd been too preoccupied with Abbi. Quickly, I found it next to where I stood and scanned the schedule to see this assignment was exactly what I hadn't wanted her doing on her first night.

Reservation: male and female dancers—basic package with erotic dancing

Who the fuck was I kidding? I didn't want her doing that any night. At least these members only reserved the basic level so they wouldn't want anything but dancing.

Behind Abbi, Rhett stood with his hands on her shoulders as she leaned back against him. Nearly six foot, he had short brown hair and brown eyes, but what members loved about him was his body. The man looked like he lived in the gym, and while I'd always appreciated how much in demand he was, especially for bachelorette parties, at that moment I hated him, his look, his fucking abs that made me money whenever he danced, and every inch of muscle that now pressed up against Abbi.

Eyes closed, she slid her hands up to circle his neck, and I watched as his hands slowly crept over her breasts down to her hips. He nuzzled her neck and looked out to flash a predatory smile at the couple in the room who'd stopped mauling one another to watch with rapt attention the scene in front of them.

Rhett knew how to sell sex without actually having it, but that didn't make the scene in front of me any easier to watch. Turning Abbi around, he began to do something I'd seen him perform hundreds of times before. Sliding his hands under her dress, he slowly lifted it to the tops of her thighs and pulled her into his body.

For the first time, Abbi opened her eyes and looked up at him, clearly surprised at what he'd done. She searched his face for reassurance, no doubt frightened at her first time dancing with Rhett. Why the fuck had Samson put her in there with him on her first night?

Always the professional, Rhett gave her a smile and winked to let her know everything would be okay. Her blue eyes still showed how unsure she was, but I doubted the couple watching them noticed any of what I was seeing. All they likely saw was two dancers giving them exactly what they'd asked for as Rhett knelt before her and lifted her leg onto his shoulder to simulate him going down on her.

If Abbi's first assignment had made me want to march into the room and beat the hell out of the guy, this one made me want to grab her and take her back to my rooms and never let her dance again. I didn't know how I was going to make it through the night watching her like this.

Engrossed in the torment of seeing her dance with Rhett, I didn't notice anyone standing in front of me until I saw out of the corner of my eye a hand tap on the counter. Looking up, I saw Cash standing there.

"Hey, what are you doing up here?"

"Nice to see you too. I work here. I used to know one of the other owners, a guy named Kane who used to come to our meetings."

"What's up, Cash?"

"I just figured I'd come up and see how things are with you these days. You don't seem to come downstairs anymore."

Glancing down at the monitor, I saw Abbi slowly lower herself to her knees in front of Rhett and looked away before the urge to yank her out of there took over.

"I've been pretty busy. You know how it is."

My vague answers might have put Stefan off, but Cash was different. He was like me, so while he might want to respect my desire to keep whatever I was hiding private, his need to make sure I was okay took precedence.

"I do. I've been involved in the whole wedding thing, so I understand being busy. I'm just wondering if you're okay up here."

"Yeah, why wouldn't I be?" I asked as my gaze trailed back to the monitor with Abbi and Rhett.

"I don't know. Because you're acting strange?"

I folded my arms across my chest and sat back on the barstool behind me. "Nothing strange here. Just me and my people doing our thing like every other night the club is open."

"I guess I'm just used to you coming to the meetings. It's strange when Stefan shows up and you don't."

"What meeting are you talking about?"

"The one we had scheduled for this afternoon. I know it wasn't a weekly meeting, but it would have been nice to have you there."

Had I known about this meeting? When the hell was it? I drew a blank and shook my head. "Sorry, Cash. I didn't remember. What did you have to tell us?"

He began to explain about the councilman wanting more perks at the club, but I couldn't help looking at the room Abbi was dancing for. The couple had moved on from watching her and Rhett to fucking. Obviously, the dancing had done its job, which didn't make me feel any better about it. The fact that Abbi and Rhett's erotic dance had been convincing enough foreplay made me more jealous than I thought I possibly could be.

"Kane, did you hear a word I said?"

I looked up to see Cash staring at me with frustration written all over his face. I was used to seeing that look when he talked to Stefan, but not me. Quickly, I tried to guess what he'd said, but I merely stammered out a few words before admitting I hadn't been listening.

"Sorry, Cash. I'm a little distracted tonight."

"What's going on? Who are you watching?"

"Nobody. Just want to make sure everything's okay in the rooms."

"Are you expecting a problem?"

"No. Just like to keep on top of things."

Whatever I thought I looked like, Cash saw right through my act. "What's going on with you, Kane? Is there something I should know?"

Below on the monitors I saw Rhett's lips slide down Abbi's neck and I couldn't help but stare. Cash came around the desk and followed my gaze to see what I was looking at. Quietly, he asked, "Is that the girl you didn't think could dance?"

I nodded as I continued to watch her lean back in pretend ecstasy as Rhett slid his hand over her breast. "Yeah. That's her."

Cash stood there watching for a few more moments. "Wasn't she bartending for Stefan?"

"Yeah."

"So other than the fact that you've never been that wrong about a dancer, what's going on here?"

I tore my eyes away from her and shrugged. "Nothing."

"Kane, this is Cash you're talking to. Remember? We're brothers and partners here, and I like to think we're friends."

Letting out a sigh, I hung my head so I didn't have to face him when I said the words. "I'm doing my best here not to fuck everything up, Cash."

"Fuck everything up? What are you talking about?"

"She was dancing over at The Carousel Club and I brought her back here to dance for us. I can't explain why I gave a damn about her, but I did. From the first time I laid eyes on her. I never do this with any of my dancers. You know that. I don't know why, but I couldn't let her dance at that shithole."

Cash smiled and looked over at the monitor before looking back at me. "I don't think that's the problem, Kane. You can't take your eyes off her, and if you clench your fists any tighter, your fingers will be coming out the tops of your hands."

I realized he was right and slowly opened my hands from the tight fists they'd been in since Abbi had begun dancing with Rhett. Stretching my fingers, I felt an ache travel up through both my palms.

"I thought I could handle it, but this is only her second room and I'm fighting myself from marching down there and carrying her back to my apartment. I'm acting like a jackass. She's no more mine than anyone else's, even if she is staying with me."

"Ah, so that's what borrowing Olivia's clothes was about."

"Don't worry. I won't do anything to fuck up the club. I think she has a boyfriend or something anyway. Some asshole who beats the hell out of her."

My hands balled into fists again, and I slowly eased my fingers out of my palms.

"And she's staying with you? Sounds like that boyfriend is an ex-boyfriend."

"She doesn't need me in her life. It's already fucked up enough."

Cash patted me on the shoulder and walked toward the stairs. "I think she could do a hell of a lot worse than you, Kane. Don't sell yourself short."

"What did you want to talk to me about anyway?" I asked as I watched Abbi and Rhett disappear behind the screen.

"Mason wanting more extras here. He's becoming more demanding by the day."

"Well, just let me know if you need anything from my area. We aim to serve here."

Smiling, he nodded. "That we do. See you later,

and don't forget what I said. You're part owner of a business that makes millions each year. Remember that."

"What happened to the idea of not fraternizing with the people who work for us?"

My brother gave me a sly smile. "I'm pretty sure that went out the window when Olivia and I got together, don't you think? Anyway, you're not like Stefan used to be. I know we won't end up at some lawyer's office because of this." He stopped for a moment and then said, "She must be someone pretty special for you to take a shining to her, Kane."

Cash left me standing there at my usual post, but no matter what he said, I couldn't believe Abbi would be better off with me in her life. Whatever I was now because of Club X, my past hadn't changed and neither had I.

And she didn't deserve to have to deal with that.

Chapter Ten

Abbi

I RETURNED TO KANE'S APARTMENT feeling like I was walking on air. Never before in my life had I experienced anything like how I felt when I danced for the first time. I'd performed as a cheerleader, but that didn't compare to the exhilaration of standing behind that glass and knowing the men and even some of the women watching me dance were there just to see me. For the first time in my life, I was the center of attention for those few minutes each time. I, Abbi Linde, was the reason they were in those rooms.

Kane had already gotten back before I arrived. Seated in his tiny living room, he looked angry about something. Or maybe that's how he usually looked and I was just finding that out.

Still excited from my first night of work, I twirled around in my costume and wished he wasn't so miserable. I'd expected him to say something about what he saw of my performing, but he seemed not to care.

I stopped in front of him and smiled. "Did you see any of my dancing tonight? Did I do okay?"

Looking up at me, he shot me a look that made his crystal blue eyes look so cold. "You did fine from what I saw. I got a little busy for a while there."

Unable to keep my feet still, I twirled around again. "I bet you think it's silly that I'm so happy about tonight, but it really did mean a lot to me. The members seemed to like me too. I made a bunch of tips, and that's with all my clothes on. I wonder what I'd make if I was like Shana and could do the kind of dancing she does."

He stood from his seat and walked past me without saying a word as I thought about how much Shana made dancing nude. If I could pull in nearly two hundred dollars dancing fully dressed behind a window, she must have been making three or four times as much in the rooms right there with the members.

I watched him head into the bathroom and heard the water run for a shower, and I had to fight the urge to walk in on him like I had the day before. I wanted to see him like that again.

In truth, I wanted him to want me like I wanted him.

So far, the way he thought of me seemed to range from being overprotective to being entirely disinterested. There didn't seem to be any in-between with Kane. I would have taken the overprotective him over whoever this man tonight was, though. This Kane didn't even seem to know I was in the same room with him.

Closing my eyes, I relived my first night of dancing, reenacting each move and feeling I experienced as the wall raised and I peeked out to see people waiting to watch me move my body for them. I'd hoped the one person I wanted to watch had seen he'd made the right decision, but it didn't seem like he'd seen much of my dancing at all.

I couldn't figure him out. He took me from that strip club to protect me and held me all night long in his arms. Then he took me shopping for all new clothes and even went to my old apartment with me, all the while knowing Aaron might be there. I'd thought after all that and after he'd made me so happy by saying I could dance for him that he'd be even nicer to me, but since the moment he saw me in my costume he'd been cool toward me, as if he didn't like me as much anymore.

Maybe that was it. Maybe because I was dancing at his club his interest in me had disappeared.

The problem was mine hadn't. The more time I spent around him, the more I wanted him. As I thought about the man who'd showed me his piercings and then made no move on me at all, a disappointing realization came to me. What if he never had any interest in me and I was just some charity case for him?

Kane came out of the bathroom wrapped in a white towel that hung low on his hips, and I stopped my dancing, unable to keep myself from staring. For the first time, I really looked at his body. Tattoos covered his arms from his wrists to his shoulders, black and grey images of animals, skulls, and crosses that created sleeves on both arms. The intricate design across his chest contrasted with the simple tattoo across his lower abdomen. Stretched from one hipbone to the other, DO NO HARM was written in heavy black letters that appeared so ominous just above what I knew was hidden beneath that terry cloth towel.

As if his tattoos and piercings weren't sexy enough, his body rippled with muscles. Every inch of him appeared hard and unyielding, from his bulging shoulders and biceps to his six-pack cut abs, but I knew better. When he held me in his arms, that hardness faded away to reveal a gentleness he kept hidden beneath his tough exterior.

He seemed oblivious to my staring at him as he stood drying his cropped hair with a towel. Throwing it over one of the kitchen chairs, he closed his eyes and cracked his neck twice, all the while saying nothing to me.

I couldn't stand the silence, and I blurted out the first thing that came to mind. "Did you have a nice shower?"

Practically dismissing me, he nodded and mumbled, "Yeah, it was fine."

God, the man didn't even like me enough to try to have a conversation. There I was standing in his home still in my dancer's costume from the sexiest club in town while he stood in just a towel, and it was like we were strangers waiting for a bus. I snuck a look at that towel and saw his cock had as much interest in me as his mouth and brain did in talking to me.

"Since you didn't get to see me dance much tonight, can I dance for you now?"

His eyes widened like they always did when I said something that interested him, and his pupils seemed to take up his entire eyes, blocking out the gorgeous blue color. He said nothing but stared at me with a look that conveyed a longing for something.

Was that something me?

I closed my eyes to shut out my doubts and began to dance, rolling my hips slowly as I moved toward him. With my arms raised, I turned away from him and leaned into his body, loving the feel of his muscular chest against my back as I slid my hands up toward his neck. The damp towel brushed up against my legs as I swayed back and forth to the music in my head, and I sensed his cock harden with every time I touched him.

Each moment that passed made me want him more, but his silence told me my feelings weren't returned. Rolling my hips in bigger circles, I pressed my body to him, praying he'd do something to show me this made him happy.

I should have stopped, but I couldn't. I wanted him. I wanted him to want me.

"Take the wig off," he said in a deep voice meant to let me know that wasn't a request.

I stopped my dancing and turned to face him, unprepared for what I'd see. The impassive man who so often seemed disinterested had disappeared, and in his place stood one with wild eyes full of need.

"I said take it off, Abbi."

The stern look in his eyes commanded me as much as his voice, so I lowered my hands to my head and slipped off my blond wig to once again reveal what made me ugly. Holding it in my hand, I hung my head, unable to hide my unhappiness and insecurities, and whispered, "There. It's off."

"Why do you want to tempt me like this?" he groaned above me.

"I can't now. Now I'm just me, messed up me," I said quietly as I tugged on the ragged ends of my hair.

He cupped his hand to my cheek and lifted my face so I had no choice but to see him. His face strained, as if he was in pain, and he closed his eyes, wincing. "I've tried so hard to fight my desires, Abbi. All we're going to do is hurt each other if we do this."

"You would never hurt me, Kane."

His eyes opened and in them all I saw was that pain

I'd seen in his expression. "Everyone I get close to gets hurt. The last thing in the world I want to do is hurt you."

"I can't believe you'd hurt me. Not the man who drove all the way across town to protect me."

Those beautiful blue eyes that so often seemed so cold flashed the purest emotion I'd ever seen. "Every demon I have inside me wants you. They scream your name day and night, and I've been fighting them because I'm terrified what will happen if I give in. Leave here and never look back. Take all the money I have in my wallet and run, Abbi. Leave me alone with them and be happy."

Cradling his face, I shook my head and smiled. "I don't want to leave. I'm not afraid of bad things. Every man I've ever been with had bad in them, but none of them cared for me like you do. I don't believe you're a bad man."

Kane leaned down and gently kissed me. Pressing his forehead to mine, he said in a voice filled with anguish, "I'm sorry if I hurt you. I swear it's the last thing I want to do."

I didn't know what demons he had in him, but I wasn't afraid of them. The only thing I was afraid of was losing him. I didn't know what it was about him, whether it was how he walked into that club and rescued me from that awful place or how he held me in his arms all night long after, but I didn't want to think of my life without him, demons or no demons.

"Kane, you never hurt me."

He kissed me deeply and whispered against my lips, "I will, and for that, I'm sorry."

His hands slid down to cup my ass, and he lifted me so my legs easily wrapped around his waist. Clinging to his neck, I felt his muscles thick against my calves as I pressed my heels to his powerful lower back to bring him closer to me. His towel still hung across his hips, but I wanted what was underneath that towel.

Kane kissed me hard as he pushed me against the wall, like he couldn't hold back how much he wanted me anymore. His tongue snaked into my mouth, searching for mine, and I met his need with my own, softly mewing my desire for him.

Pulling away, he looked down at me. "I want to be inside you so fucking bad it hurts."

With my heel, I pushed down on his towel, and it fell to the floor. Licking my lips, I stared into those gorgeous eyes and said, "Please...no more waiting."

He lifted me higher and covered my mouth with his in a kiss that took my breath away. I felt the head of his cock press against me, and then he stopped, making me want him even more. "I don't wear anything because of my piercings. Are you...?"

I nodded and kissed him. "Yes. Don't worry. Please don't stop."

Kane's hands cupped my ass and squeezed as he slid

into me, those piercings grazing my sensitive skin and making my nerve endings come alive. The feeling was the most exquisite I'd ever experienced.

"I tried to stay away, Abbi," he groaned as he thrust the last few inches hard into me. "I did. Ever since that first night, I tried."

His cock stretched me until I couldn't imagine being able to take any more of him, and then as soon as my body adjusted to his sweet invasion, he left me, making me feel emptier than I'd ever been before. I clung to him, crawling up his body as mine begged for more of him. Pulling away from his kiss, I whispered, "Don't stay away, please, Kane. Don't leave me alone."

He slammed back into me with a deep grunt and moaned, "Never. I can't do it. I don't want to stay away."

His cock slid up into me until we were joined completely, my body needing what only he could give me. Each stroke into my pussy sent a string of sensation from his piercings caressing against my flesh. And with each time he pushed deep into me, I was sure I'd come, but then his cock would retreat from my body, leaving me wanting at that point just before he gave me any release.

With each moment, he edged me closer to my orgasm, so close and then he'd back off just enough to keep me needing him. Never before had I craved a man like I craved him.

I watched his face as he fucked me, those blue eyes so intent as they stared into mine. This man who so often had seemed to not even notice me now made me feel like he looked down into my soul with his gaze.

His hands moved up to cradle my face, and he whispered in his raspy voice, "Don't let go, no matter what I do."

"I won't. I promise."

Clinging to his neck, I pressed my heels into his back to hang on as he stroked in and out of me. Grunting, he fucked me hard and slow, taking my body over. The icy façade and aloofness he nearly always wore disappeared, replaced by a level of passion no one had ever shown me.

"Abbi," he whispered hoarsely in my ear. "Tell me to go away. Tell me you never want to see me again."

"No! Don't stop," I cried as my body willingly surrendered to his like it never had with anyone else before.

He looked at me and rasped, "I'll only end up hurting you. Get away from me before I do."

I cradled his face and pressed my forehead to his as his thrusts slowed. The pain in his eyes tore at my heart. Why did he keep saying he would hurt me?

"Don't make me go, Kane. Whatever you're afraid of, I'm not. I want you. Don't you want me?"

He stopped and smiled so sweetly, like he only did when we were alone. "The last thing I want to do is hurt you. Since the moment I met you, I haven't been able to think of anything else. I've been alone for so long that I thought that was the way it was supposed to be. Alone in these rooms hidden away I couldn't hurt anyone."

"I'm tougher than I look, I promise. But do you want me or is this because I'm just here with you?"

Closing his eyes, he said softly, "You're all I can think of, Abbi. I was ready to be alone for the rest of my life, but now I can't think of living another day without you."

I caressed his face and said, "Look at me, Kane. I'm not afraid."

His eyelids slowly lifted and he shook his head. "I hurt everyone I touch. I have these demons inside me that make do things I shouldn't. I'm just afraid they'll make me hurt you someday."

"No, I can't believe that. You wouldn't do that."

He slid out of me and lifted me up in his arms to carry me to the bedroom. Placing me on the bed, he gently caressed the ragged ends of my hair and kissed me so sweetly, I couldn't imagine him ever hurting me.

We made love no less intense than we'd started just minutes before, but now something had changed in him. In his powerful hands, I felt worshipped and cared for. The hardness that surrounded him faded away, and as he wrapped his arms around me, I sensed his loneliness that had been masquerading as coldness begin to disappear.

His body invaded mine and took over, but I wasn't afraid. With each thrust into me, I felt more than just the physical ecstasy he gave me. In his care, I felt secure and loved.

When I came, I gave myself over to him believing he'd protect and take care of me. As we lay there in each other's arms, I placed my head on his chest and whispered, "I trust you, Kane. Of all the people in this world, I believe in you and that you won't hurt me."

His fingers played with the ends of my hair and he kissed me on the top of the head. Hugging me tighter, he whispered to me in those little rooms he hid away in, "I won't ever hurt you on purpose, Abbi. I swear."

Chapter Eleven

Kane

I HELD ABBI CLOSE TO me as my heartbeat returned to normal, never wanting to let her go. I'd fought what she brought out in me from the first time I laid eyes on her, but now I couldn't imagine ever being without her. Her head on my chest, she sighed as I squeezed her to me and we lay there in silence while she traced her finger over my skin.

After a long while, she said quietly, "Tell me why you wanted to help me."

I closed my eyes and remembered the moment I knew I couldn't just forget her. "Have you ever just known something deep inside—like a truth you can't deny? That's how I felt when I first saw you in Cash's office. You were beautiful and I knew someone had hurt you, and even though we'd just met, I wanted to find that person and make them pay for what they'd done. I'd only felt that once before."

"Tell me about her. I want to know everything about you. Who you loved. Why you loved her. How she lost you."

Taking a deep breath, I told her what I'd never told another soul. "Her name was Holly. She was sixteen and I was seventeen. I lived to make her happy, and she loved me more than I'd ever been loved before in my life. I needed her. I wanted her. I couldn't live without her."

"Why did you love her?"

I thought about the moment I realized I loved Holly. That night she lay in my arms just like Abbi did now. "She made me happy like I'd never felt before."

Abbi looked up at me and smiled. "Back to not saying much?"

I kissed the top of her head and chuckled. "I loved her because for the first time in my life, I felt at home with someone. I'd never felt that before Holly."

"Never?"

"Never. All I'd known before was hate. My mother hated my father for not leaving his wife and sons. It's why she named me Kane. My life before Holly consisted of her hate for him and by extension, for me."

"I can't believe your mother hated you," she whispered almost reverently, as if the truth of my life needed to be kept secret.

"She named me Kane after the Bible's Cain and Abel. She wanted me to kill Cash, the child she believed kept my father from us."

"Really kill him?"

"I don't know. I just know from the moment I could understand, she told me the story of my being named after the son who killed his brother."

"But you didn't. You and Cash seem close even."

"We are. Now. But before our father died, we weren't. I grew up hating him because of my mother. Then I met Holly, and there was no hate to feel."

"What happened to her? Why aren't you with her now?"

The terrible events of the night that changed my life flashed through my mind. "She's dead. A drug overdose when I wasn't there to keep her safe."

Abbi's eyes filled with tears and she looked up at me. "I'm sorry, Kane. I didn't mean to bring up things like that. I didn't know."

I smoothed her hair under my palm and kissed her gently on the lips. "It's okay. You didn't do anything wrong. I should have been there to protect her, but I didn't have a choice."

"Why?" she asked in a tiny voice filled with fear.

Swallowing hard, I confessed to her all that I'd done, knowing that I might lose her because of it. "One night, she and I were out and four guys jumped us. I offered them everything I had thinking it was a mugging, but that's not what they wanted. While the three of them held me down, the biggest one raped her as they forced me to watch. I swore to every one of them that I'd find them and make them pay, even as they were beating the hell out of me. I came to and saw Holly in a bloody heap next to me, barely conscious. When I could finally move without every bone in my body aching, I found every single one of them and beat the hell out of them. The one I'd watched rape her I went too far with and beat him to death. I didn't mean to, but I wasn't sorry."

Abbi cradled my face and kissed me. "Oh my God, Kane. I had no idea."

"Nobody knows. I've never told Cash or Stefan. Or anyone before you. They tried me for manslaughter and because I was a minor and he was an adult who'd raped Holly, they sentenced me to juvenile detention until I was twenty-one. So for four long years, I lived in a cell like any other prisoner. When they let me out, all I could think of was returning to Holly, but she was gone. She was never able to handle what that fucking animal did to her or what I did to him to make them take me away."

"I'm so sorry. I didn't mean to bring all this up."

I pushed the hair out of her eyes and looked down at her. "You needed to know the kind of man you're with. I'm not sorry I killed him, just like I wouldn't be sorry if I killed your ex-boyfriend for hurting you. I've got this rage inside me that takes over."

Abbi stayed silent as the truth of who I was settled into her mind and then said, "I've never had anyone defend me. Maybe I should think it's wrong for you to want to kill someone who hurt me, but I don't. Every man I've ever been with hurt me, and never once did anyone step up to help me."

I leaned forward to kiss the spot near her eye where he'd hit her right before I met her. "I will never let anyone hurt you again. I promise you that."

Snuggling up against me, she said quietly, "You have this club, your car, and so much, and I have nothing. Why would you want someone like me?"

"I didn't know why or how, but I knew from the moment I saw you that night in Cash's office that I'd never live another day without you in my mind or in my arms. I didn't think I deserved someone so gentle and kind, so I did everything I could to keep you away all the while unable to think of anything but you, but it was no use. I couldn't go on like that. Then when Gemma told me you were at The Carousel Club, something inside me snapped. I had to take you away from there."

"Do you still love that girl?"

I thought about that for a minute. "In some ways, I'll always love her. She was the first person to show me love. But I'm not in love with a ghost."

"I don't know what to think of all this, Kane. I'm sure you've noticed I don't seem to do slow and easy when it comes to relationships. I just broke up with Aaron, and here I am naked in your arms. You told me about you, so I want to make sure you know who I am."

"I know everything I need to know, Abbi. You're beautiful and sweet and gentle. You make me feel something I was sure I'd never feel again. I don't need to know anything more."

She sat up and shook her head. "No, I want you to. You believed in me to tell me about who you are, so I want to tell you who I am."

"Okay, but it doesn't matter what you tell me. To me, you're my Abbi."

She closed her eyes and took a deep breath before she began to speak. "I had the perfect family. My mother and father loved me, and I was their only child. And then one day it was all gone. My father died when I was ten, and my mother was devastated. She was so lonely. All she wanted was what she'd had with my father, so she looked for someone to fill that emptiness from my father's death, but no one was ever enough. Her boyfriends came and went, each one spending just enough time in my life for me to get attached before they left or she left them. All she wanted to find was what she'd had with my father, but she never could."

I watched a tear slide down Abbi's cheek and wiped it with my knuckle. She flinched and opened her eyes. Just seeing her this sad tore at my heart. "I promise you'll never be alone again, angel."

"Everyone's said that, Kane. And then everyone left. When I started dating boys, I went for all the wrong kind—the bad boy—and every one of them was bad. I've been beaten unconscious, and I've done some things other people might not think are right because I couldn't see any other way. You called me angel, but I'm no angel."

I pulled her down on top of me and whispered against her lips, "You're my angel."

"Then I'm a fallen angel, Kane. I may not have killed anyone, but I've done things that were almost as bad."

"Then we belong together. Two people who've done terrible things and had terrible things done to them finally deserve happiness, don't you think?"

"I want to believe that. I do. I've just never seen that before."

"I'll have to make you happy then."

"I need to know something. Will you promise to tell the truth?"

"Yes. Always."

"Why didn't you watch me dance tonight? It meant so much to me that you would watch me, and then you said you didn't even see much."

Smoothing the hair from her face, I looked into her eyes and told her the truth I knew might frighten her away. "I did watch you dance tonight. I stood in front of those monitors and watched every second of it, even though my gut hurt just seeing you dance for other men. I wanted to rush into each room and beat the fuck out of every one of them for watching you. I wanted to tear Rhett in half each time he touched you. I know it's wrong, and I know I have to fight what I feel, but I wanted to hurt them."

"They weren't hurting me. I like dancing. It makes me feel beautiful."

"I know. That's why I didn't do anything. I just stood there and watched the most beautiful woman in the world dance for strangers."

She closed her eyes and frowned. "I can't bear to think what I'm doing makes you so unhappy. That's not what I want. I won't dance anymore. I can go back to bartending downstairs, if you'll let me stay here a little longer."

"Abbi, open your eyes and look at me." She did as I ordered and I continued. "No. You want to dance, so that's what I want. And I don't want you going anywhere else. I want you to stay right here with me."

"But I can't stand the thought of you standing there so angry as I do something that makes me so happy."

Her willingness to give up what she loved made me want her even more. I slid my hands down over her back and cupped her ass to pull her up against my cock. "You're going to dance and you're going to stay here with me, and that's final."

Abbi bit her lower lip as my cock touched her clit. "Oh, okay. Is there anything else you've decided?"

"Just one more thing."

I slowly pushed inside her and groaned, "God, you feel so good around me. This is why I get jealous. I know those men want to be inside you too."

Rolling her hips, she took me as deep as I could go. "I don't want them. I only want you. All you need to do is remember that. I only want you, Kane."

The demons inside me who wanted me to possess her slowly began to uncoil, like a snake, and I slid out of her and turned her on her stomach, needing to claim her. In her ear, I groaned, "I want every man who sees you to know you're mine."

She turned her head and whispered softly, "Yes."

Pulling her up to her hands and knees, I felt her body open up for me and I slammed into her until my cock had reached its hilt. "I want every man who sees you to know your body craves only me."

Abbi arched her back as I reared back to thrust into her again. "Yes," she moaned, her answer punctuated with a tiny whimper.

I leaned forward and pressed my palm to the front of her throat. "I want every man who sees you to know only my cock belongs inside you."

"Yes," she said, her voice pleading for me to fill her up again.

Barely able to control myself, I pushed my hips forward and buried myself balls deep in her wet cunt. "Feel that? Feel when those metal studs on my cock touch you? I want every man to know when they look at you that deep inside, you bear my mark on your skin. That every time my cock slides into your pussy, that mark is made fresh again."

She strained against my hold on her throat and groaned, "Yes. Please, yes."

The monster inside me took over, and I pounded into her body like a wild animal, fucking her from behind until her legs were barely able to hold her. She came once, twice, her body shaking from her orgasms, but my release lay waiting inside me still.

The beast hadn't gotten enough yet.

She never wavered, even though I knew her body must have been exhausted. Every time I pushed my cock into her, she pushed back against me, wanting me to fill her up as much as I wanted her. Her cunt clung to me, and each time I pulled out of her, she moaned a tiny noise that made me need to be back inside her again.

As I fucked her, my mind replayed every moment of her dancing and those who watched her. I became obsessed with her knowing she belonged to me and me alone. That she wasn't theirs to have or love. They could watch her, but only I could feel her as she surrendered to my hands and my cock.

I needed her. I adored her. I hated the men who watched her excite them. The thought of the man jerking off while she danced, defiling the sweetness of her, drove me wild, and I squeezed my hand around her throat. "I want every man who sees you dance to know you don't dance for them. You dance for me."

She arched her back and in a pleading voice said, "You. Only you."

Sliding my free hand around her body, I pulled her upright, my other hand still circling her neck. My teeth sunk into her earlobe, biting down until she cried out my name, and I slid my finger over her swollen clit, teasing it as my cock continued to fill her.

"Tell me you aren't afraid of me. Tell me you know I would never hurt you, angel."

Her answer came out in tiny pants. "I know you'd never hurt me. You take care of me."

My fingers parted her folds as they pressed toward her opening, and I felt my cock filling her. "Does this hurt?"

Her hand covered mine. Stretching her finger to reach, she stroked the underside of my cock, sending jolts of desire through me and I eased out of her only to thrust hard back into her. "It feels like you're ripping me apart, but I've never felt so good in my life."

The thought of hurting her tore at my heart. Suddenly, the demons inside me weren't in control anymore. Gently, I bent her over and eased out of her body to take her pain away. "I'm sorry, angel," I said softly near her ear. "I didn't meant to hurt you. I'm sorry. I'm a fucking monster. Leave me before I do something that I can't apologize for."

Abbi leaned back against my chest and hung her head. "You didn't hurt me. How can you say you're a monster?"

"I am and now you've seen the real me."

She turned to face me and shook her head. "That's not the real you. The man who rescued me from that horrible club is the real you. The man who gave me his bed and got me clothes to wear is the real you. Kane, I don't know what kind of monster you think you are, but with me, you aren't that."

"I can't control what I feel about you, Abbi. I've tried from the moment I met you, and every day my need for you gets worse. I'm afraid what I'm going to do if the demons inside me have their way. Every time I think of someone hurting you I want to kill them. It's an overwhelming urge I have to fight constantly. If they can't get their way, the demons will make me do something that hurts you."

"I can't believe you'd hurt me. No. The way you are with me when we're together like this doesn't hurt me. I want to feel your desire for me. Don't hold back. Show me how I make you feel."

I pulled her onto my lap and slowly slid inside her until our bodies joined completely. "I only feel whole when I'm inside you and your body is giving in to me. What if that won't be enough someday? I worry my demons will turn on you."

Abbi kissed me, her tongue sliding over mine and sending waves of need straight to my cock. I lifted her off me until only the head of my cock teased her and slowly lowered her again, loving the sensation of her body gripping me like a glove.

"I've known bad men. You aren't them. Whatever this demon or beast is inside you makes you afraid you'll hurt me. Don't listen to it."

She rode me slowly, almost torturing me with the need to come, her body tenderly inching me closer until finally I exploded into her, filling her with my release. With her arms wrapped around my neck, she pressed against me and whispered, "I was beginning to doubt you wanted me you took so long."

Cradling her face, I looked into her eyes and saw she'd told the truth. "Never doubt that. I want you so bad it hurts. It's like an ache inside that only wanes when you touch me. I've felt it since that first night when you danced for me."

"I only dance for you, Kane. When the music comes on, I close my eyes and think about you watching me. I think about your touch making my body come alive. I think about the feel of your piercings as they slide up inside me, sending strings of sensation through my body that make me never want to be with another man again."

"No one has ever liked that the way you do."

Abbi bit her lower lip and moaned, "Good. I want to be the only woman who feels you that way."

CHAPTER TWELVE

ABBI

KANE CARRIED ME INTO THE bathroom to wash me, as if cleaning me would get rid of any memory of whatever fears he had about hurting me. I'd never felt so wanted as when he was inside me, his hands caressing my body and his words telling me how much he cared. I couldn't let him think he'd done anything wrong. He deserved to be as happy as he made me.

Taking the soap from him, I ran my hands over his skin, loving the muscular ridges and valleys of his body. There, standing under the water, he looked down and watched me wash him like my very touch was something sacred to him.

I gripped the base of his thick cock, still semi-hard from our lovemaking, and slowly moved my hand up to the head where those four metal studs sat. Caressing the velvety skin, I cleaned each piercing and slid my hand back down his shaft, loving the look of ecstasy that came over his face. Backing him up into the stream of water coming from the showerhead, I let it rinse him clean and pulled him back toward me.

His eyes rolled back into his head and he groaned, "Don't stop. God, don't stop."

I loved seeing him like this. I wanted to make him happy, so I lowered myself to the floor of the porcelain tub and knelt in front of him. He stared down at me with pure need in his eyes, and I wanted to fulfill that need.

Tracing the ridge of his hip, I touched my fingertip to a vein running next to it and followed my mouth along that path. I loved the feel of it against my tongue, raised from the skin like some beautiful roadmap to his cock.

"Angel, wrap your lips around me."

He gripped his cock to direct it to my mouth, but I wanted to tease him a little more. Flicking my tongue over the base, I slid up to the swollen crown and sucked gently, tasting the pre-cum that seeped from it.

I felt his hands in my hair and looked up to see a wild look in his eyes that told me his control was slipping away. His demons wanted more than just my teasing. I braced myself for the sweet pain that came from him pulling my hair as I went down on him, anticipating the first rough tug of his hands to guide me down on his cock.

But it didn't happen. Instead, he eased his fingers from my head and quietly said, "No more playing.

Suck my cock, angel. I can't control myself for long."

I knew by the soft look in his eyes that for the moment he had reign over his demons, so I wrapped my lips around him and slid my mouth down his shaft until the short hairs at the base tickled my nose and his piercings touched the back of my throat. My knees ached and my jaw hurt, but none of that mattered when I stared up at him and saw pure pleasure on his face.

His clean and masculine taste danced over my tongue as I slid him out of my mouth, leaving only the pierced head against my lips. I cupped his balls and gently squeezed at the same time I sucked him back into my mouth, and from above me I heard a groan of pleasure echo against the tile walls.

I bobbed my head up and down, all the time watching how my actions thrilled him. But soon I saw that same wild look in his eyes, and they narrowed to make his expression almost angry. His demons were gaining control.

"Angel, if you don't get me off soon, I'm going to bury my hands in your hair and fuck your mouth hard and raw. I'm barely holding on here, baby."

"Maybe I like it that way," I said with a smile before flicking the tip of my tongue up his shaft. "I'm not afraid of your demons, Kane."

I saw the change in his eyes as they grew dark, and then he buried his hands in my hair and yanked it tight in his fists. "You should be. Please, angel. I need to come."

He guided me down onto his cock until every inch had disappeared into my mouth. I didn't know what he'd be like hard and raw, but I secretly loved the power that emanated from him when he was like this. I wanted to test those demons and show them they could do their worst but I wouldn't be scared off.

Kane pulled back out of my mouth and I stared up into his beautiful eyes looking down at me and pleading for me to save him from what they were pushing him to do. He pressed his hips forward with a low groan and said, "Jesus, Abbi. Don't do this. I don't want to hurt you."

He fucked my mouth, not hard and raw but like a man who had a woman who loved pleasing him. As I went down on him, he caressed my cheek and moaned my name like a prayer. He possessed all the control, but I didn't want it any other way. To see him tower over me thrusting his hips forward to fill my mouth made my pussy ache with need. When he came, I swallowed every ounce that flooded down my throat, loving the look on his face as I sucked him dry.

Kane pulled me to my feet and kissed my lips still wet from him. "You make my fucking legs go weak, angel. I didn't hurt you, did I?"

I hugged him to me and pressed my cheek to his chest to hear his heart hammering away. "You didn't hurt me. I loved seeing you like that."

The truth was I didn't fear the beast inside him like he did. I loved that part of him as much as I loved the man who gently stroked my back now as we stood together with the water pouring down over our heads washing away all the doubts that lingered between us.

STILL GROGGY FROM SLEEP, I stretched my legs and felt Kane's muscular thigh push between them. Opening my eyes, I looked up into his face and saw him still asleep, his beautiful lips parted ever so slightly showing his straight white teeth.

I couldn't help but study him as he lay there next to me. His jaw and cheekbones were angular, and I reached out to run my fingertip over his early morning dark stubble he'd shave off before he started his day. Everything about him exuded strength and power. Even now as he slept, I felt protected with him by my side.

He stirred as my fingers stroked his short black hair he kept cropped close to his scalp. Slowly, he opened his eyes and I saw their stunning blue color. Crystal clear even first thing in the morning, they focused on me immediately.

"Morning. I didn't mean to wake you up. I'm sorry."

"It's all right. Everything okay?"

That was why even though I hadn't told him, I was already falling madly and completely in love with him. No sooner were his eyes open and he wanted to know if I was okay. Not why I'd bothered him or woke him when he still wanted to sleep. Not what I'd do for him. He wanted to know how I was.

"I'm fine, Kane."

A slow smile spread across his lips. "Good."

"I love it when you smile. A real smile. The kind you give at work are nice, but when you smile like this I know it's real."

His hand moved up my arm until it came to rest on my shoulder. Just like the first night I slept next to him, he slid his fingertips over the ends of my hair and over the back of my neck as we silently lay there on the floor together. It was a small gesture, but it meant the world to me.

It showed me I was beautiful in his eyes.

Squeezing me close to him, he pressed his lips to the top of my head and whispered, "Are you happy, Abbi?"

I lifted my head off his chest and looked at him. "Why? Aren't you?"

His hands pushed my hair from near my eyes and he leaned forward to kiss my forehead. "I asked if you were happy, and you want to know if I am. But you didn't answer my question."

Fear coursed through me as I thought about what

to say. I'd heard something like that from every man I'd ever been with. When I didn't give the right answer, every one of them had become angry with me.

"I don't know the right answer, Kane," I said quietly, avoiding his gaze and worried I'd already upset him.

"The only right answer is the truth. If you're not happy, you have to tell me so I can change whatever is making you unhappy, Abbi."

"I don't want you to get angry with me."

Gently, he pulled my chin so I had to face him. "Look at me. I'm not going to be angry with you if you're unhappy. I'm going to figure out how to make you happy, if that's the case. Are you happy?"

"Yes. I just worry that I'm going to do something to make you mad at me."

"Abbi, no matter how angry I get with you, I would never hit you. Never."

I believed him when he said that, but my past told me the different. "I believe you, Kane. I do. It's just that it always ends up the same with me. Some guy says he cares, and then one day I say something to make him angry and he hits me. They all say they'll never do it, but then they always do. It must be me. I must be the reason it happens."

"Don't ever think that. You aren't to blame because someone can't control themselves."

"Then why does it always happen to me? Other

women don't get beat up by their boyfriends. It must be me," I sobbed.

He cradled my face in his hands, stroking my cheek with the pad of his thumb. Looking at me with such tenderness in his dark blue eyes, he said, "I don't know, but I promise you'll never be hurt by my hands. I'll leave before I let my demons make me crazy. And if I ever see anyone lay a hand on you, I swear it's the last thing they'll ever do."

I lay my head on his chest and closed my eyes. As he gently ran his fingers over my nape, I whispered, "Promise me something else, okay?"

"Anything."

"Promise me you'll never do anything for me that could hurt you. I couldn't stand you being hurt because of me."

"Don't worry about me. I'm tough. I can handle a little hurt."

Looking up at him, I shook my head. "Please promise me."

"Okay, okay. I promise. But you don't have to worry about me. As long as you're safe and happy, I'm happy."

"Can we do something today?"

He slid his palms over my back and pulled me close. "I have an idea on how I want to start the day. Other than that, I have a surprise for you."

"A surprise? What is it?"

He smiled. "It wouldn't be a surprise if I told you."

"Then let's get up so we can go see this surprise!" I said as I moved to stand, eager to see what he'd gotten for me.

Kane pulled me back down on top of him and nuzzled the spot just under my ear. "Not yet, angel. We haven't started the day the right way."

When he pressed his lips to that spot and whispered his nickname for me in his husky voice, I couldn't help but practically melt in his arms. He slid his hard cock through my already wet pussy, grazing my clit with the metal barbells pierced through the head and sending waves of need through my body.

I rolled my hips and felt him nudge his cock up against my opening. Spreading my legs wide, I straddled him and slowly sat down on him, loving the fell of those metal balls gliding over the tender skin inside me. His cock stretched me until I didn't think I could take any more, but I wanted all of him.

Kane's hands sat at my waist guiding me as I rode him. I loved being on top so I could look at his expression as I made him happy. When we were like this—naked and open with nothing standing between us—his eyes ceased to look cold, like they often did, and the passion and need in him became clear as he stared up at me.

"You look so beautiful like this," he groaned.

I stopped for a moment and asked, "Like what?"

Kane slid his thumb up to my clit and began to draw tiny, slow circles. "On top with me inside you."

Tracing the thin line of dark hair that led to his cock, I said, "I love when you say things like that."

Arching my back, I heard him say, "Oh yeah?" in that deep voice that never failed to thrill me.

Leaning forward, I settled my gaze on his beautiful face and nodded. "I love whenever you speak, but especially now."

His thumb ceased its movement and Kane pulled me hard down onto his cock, grunting a guttural sound as he pushed his hips off the floor to bury his cock inside me. "Ride me, angel. I want to watch your body give in to me. I want to feel that snug cunt squeeze my cock when you come."

I pressed my hands to his hard chest and balanced as our bodies joined and separated over and over, his body marking me as his own with every thrust of his pierced cock. I gave myself to him willingly, wanting more than anything to give him the pleasure he gave me.

His cock swelled inside me as we raced toward our release, and he sat up and pulled my body to his, pressing me tightly to his chest as my orgasm began. Holding the back of my neck, he said gruffly, "Don't close your eyes. I want to see them when you come."

I obeyed his command and kept focused on him as wave after delicious wave rolled over me. My body surrendered completely, becoming his as each moment passed. His eyes looked deep into mine, into the depths of my soul as he came. In them, I saw need and safety.

And love.

I slid into Kane's Mustang and turned to face him as he started the car. "Will you tell me now what the surprise is?"

"Not yet. A few minutes more."

Pouting, I asked, "Where are we going?"

"That's the surprise. Just sit tight and be patient. I don't have to hold the lock down so you don't leave, do I?" he asked with tiny grin.

I blushed at his mention of how I'd behaved that night he took me out of The Carousel Club. Lifting his hand to my lips, I kissed it and quietly said, "I'm sorry I was so awful."

He put the car into gear and kissed me on the forehead. "You had every right. I was kidnapping you."

"No, you weren't. You were doing something nice and I acted like a bitch. I'm sorry, Kane."

"It's okay. As long as you don't still think I'm some kind of Cro-Magnon man," he joked. "Now close your eyes and wait for your surprise."

I shielded my eyes with my hand and closed them tightly. "I'm so excited! I haven't gotten a surprise like this since I was a little girl."

He drove over the streets of Tampa and joked

about how impatient I was until we finally came to a stop. I began to lower my hand, but he grabbed it. "No, not yet. I want you to keep your eyes closed. I'll come around and get you."

I waited for him to open my door, and he took my hand to lead me to my surprise. I heard children playing nearby and was sure I was walking on a sidewalk, but other than that, all I knew was Kane had my hand in his and I trusted him completely.

"There are three steps, so watch yourself so you don't fall."

Nodding, I squeezed his hand tightly and walked up the stairs onto a surface that made a creaking sound when my foot landed on it. "Can I look yet? Please?"

"Just a few seconds more."

I heard him open what sounded like an old screen door that needed to be oiled and then his hand pressed softly against my lower back to guide me. He stopped our movement and in my ear said, "Okay, you can open your eyes now."

Lowering my hand, I slowly opened my eyes to see we were in someone's house. Full of knickknacks, it looked like someone lived there but I didn't see anyone around. "Whose house is this, Kane?"

"Mine."

I looked up at him in total confusion. "Yours? Then why do you live in those rooms at the club?"

Kane smiled. "This was my mother's house. My

father bought it for her, but he never lived here with us. This was where I grew up. When my mother died, it came to me, but I never felt right living here alone. I figured now since you're staying with me, it might be time for me to come back here."

"You mean we're going to be living here?"

Looking around at the house obviously so full of memories, he said, "Yeah, if you want to."

I let go of his hand and walked through the living room to a kitchen at the back of the house. Kane followed and smiled when I squealed, "I love it! It's so cute!"

"Good. Then I'll have all your things brought here and we can start sleeping here tonight."

I sensed a hint of sadness in his voice. "Is everything okay? We don't have to stay here if you don't want to. I'm fine with your rooms at the club. I like sleeping on the floor. As long as you're next to me, I don't care where we are."

He wrapped his arm around me and pulled me into him. "No, that's not it. It's just strange being back here after all this time."

"How long has it been since you lived here?"

Kane seemed to think about it for a minute and answered, "It's got to be seven or eight years."

I stood on my tippy toes and kissed him. "Well, what do you say as a celebration I make us dinner in this wonderful house of yours?"

"Ours. I wouldn't be here if it weren't for you, and when you finally make enough money to move to your own place, I'll close this place up again and move back to my rooms. Unless you decide not to move."

I stared up into his gorgeous blue eyes and saw he was sincere. "You barely know me, Kane. Maybe you should wait until I make you angry and we have our first fight before you offer to let me live here with you permanently."

"Abbi, I have no idea what will happen tomorrow. I don't think about the future. Never could. I try not to think about the past. There's nothing good back there. The present is all I've ever been able to focus on, and right now, I can't think of anyone else in the world I want next to me every morning when I wake up."

The idea of the future being so vague scared me. "And I'm all about tomorrow, Kane, because my past and present have been bad for so long. The future's all I had to hope for."

He kissed me softly on the lips and pressed his forehead to mine. "Then it's settled. I'll worry about making your present good, and you worry about making my future good, okay?"

"Okay."

"Come with me. I want to show you the rest of the house."

I'd never seen Kane as happy as when he gave me the tour of that house. I couldn't imagine him having any good memories of the place after hearing about his childhood, but his whole personality seemed lighter just being there. The serious man who'd intimidated me when we'd first met beamed with every room he showed me.

The change was completely unexpected, but I loved it. I loved him. It was crazy and stupid and I only knew him for just over a month, but I loved him with every ounce of my being.

And the thought of a time when he and I didn't live in that little house with its squeaky door and the joyful sound of children playing outside made my heart hurt.

Chapter Thirteen

Abbi

I SAT WITH GEMMA IN the dancers' break room waiting for the night to begin, still nervous since it was only my first week of actually dancing at Club X. The other dancers sat around us, some fixing their costumes while others put on makeup instead of getting ready in the dressing room right next door.

A few of the dancers sat in the far corner of the room drinking as they did every night. Gemma had told me about them on my first night. They were some of the ones who danced in the rooms without their clothes on, and Gemma thought they had to get drunk just to do the job. All three women had gorgeous bodies—much nicer than any of us who danced with our clothes on—and one in particular, Simone, had the most beautiful violet colored eyes. I didn't know if they were real or contacts, but they were stunning.

Leaning over, I whispered to Gemma, "I wonder if they make a lot more than we do."

Unsure who I meant, she shook her head. "Who?"

"Simone and the others who dance naked in the rooms."

"I bet they do. They have to handle a lot more than we do. Why do you think they drink?"

"I guess," I said quietly, unable to take my eyes off their corner. Was it really so bad that they had to be drunk?

"I hear Victoria prefers a different kind of way to forget," Gemma said with a wink.

"Really? What?"

She didn't answer but sniffed to let me know she meant coke. I'd seen a bunch of the dancers at The Carousel do coke on that one night I danced there, but I was surprised to find out Kane allowed that kind of thing at Club X.

"I guess it's not that great if you have to do things like that."

Gemma nudged me with her elbow. "What do you care about making more money? Now that you're living with Kane, you have it made. The guy's a millionaire, not that you'd ever know it, but he is."

"Really?"

"Of course, honey! He's one of the owners of this place. He, Stefan, and Cassian all own Club X, so if the other two are millionaires, so is he."

"I didn't think about that," I said quietly.

Gemma continued to talk about something, but I wasn't listening anymore. My attention was on Kane who'd just walked into the room wearing jeans and a navy blue T-shirt that showed off his tattoos. He didn't act like he was a millionaire. He acted like every other guy I'd ever dated. Millionaires dated women who wore designer clothes and shoes that cost more than I made in a week. I wasn't exactly the type of female a man with money would want to show off to his rich friends.

He finished his nightly pep talk, and we all began to file out toward our first assignments. Suddenly self-conscious about everything I was and wasn't, I followed close to Gemma to try to sneak out past him, but he caught me by the arm and pulled me aside.

"Hey, angel. I'll be watching you tonight," he said in a sexy voice.

I avoided looking at him, instead looking down at my feet. "Cool. Thanks. I better get going."

Kane lifted my chin with his finger and looked down at me with hurt in his eyes that made me feel like shit. "What's wrong? Did something happen with one of the girls?"

I shook my head. "No. It's not that."

"Then what's wrong? I told you it's my job to make your present happy, but I can't do that if you don't tell me what's wrong."

"You're a millionaire."

"Yeah, I am. A few times over, in fact."

"What would you want with someone like me then?"

"Why would I live in those rooms on the fourth floor? Why would I drive a car older than me? Why would I wear T-shirts and jeans? Having money doesn't change who I am, Abbi."

"I'm sorry. You're mad at me now. I can tell because you called me by my name."

He gave me one of those wonderful smiles I only saw when we were alone. "I'm not mad at you. Don't think about how much money I have. It obviously doesn't change who I am. And as for what I'd want with you, it's exactly what I get from you. You make me happy."

"Okay. I just wondered when I found out you had all that money. I'm not what a millionaire would want in a girlfriend, Kane."

"You're what I want in a girlfriend, angel. Now go out there so I can watch the most beautiful woman in the world dance."

I hugged him tightly, loving the feel of his strength around me. "I'll pretend I'm dancing for you."

"Good. And later when we go back to the house, I have another surprise for you."

Another surprise? I stepped back in shock. "Another one? Let me guess. You got the front door fixed so it doesn't squeak anymore," I said with a giggle.

"No, and no more guessing. Now get out there so I have someone to watch tonight."

I DANCED THE BEST I could, my eyes closed and every moment pretending it was Kane sitting in those rooms watching me. I loved the idea of him standing out at his post at the top of the stairs looking at the monitors for my assignments. It meant so much to me that he liked what I did and I made him proud.

My rooms were only for solo dancing, likely because Kane had told Samson not to pair me with Rhett or any of the other male dancers. I could handle that. His jealousy made me feel loved and cherished, and I'd never want him to be hurt by anything I did. I didn't have to dance with anyone else. My dancing was for me and the man I loved.

The night flew by, and by three a.m. we were back at the house we now called home. He hadn't mentioned my surprise again, but I knew he wouldn't forget. Kane never forgot anything. He might not say anything about a problem or comment, but he remembered.

I opened the front door and heard it squeak. Turning to look at him as we entered the house, I joked, "Definitely not my surprise."

"No. Your surprise is waiting for you inside. I'd say close your eyes, but you'll probably hear it before you see it. Just be careful when you walk in and let me turn on the lights first."

Hear it before I saw it? And why would I have to be careful in the dark?

Kane flipped the light switch and there in the middle of the living room lay a tiny dark brown and white kitten curled up on a white pillow twice its size.

"Angel, meet Angel. Now it's the three of us."

"Oh my God! She's adorable, Kane! A kitten—" I couldn't hold back the tears and began to cry at how sweet he'd been to get me a kitten. "I've always wanted a cat."

He walked past me and crouched down to pick the kitten up in his hands. "I thought it would be nice to have someone here on the nights I have to work and you don't."

I knelt down next to him and petted her soft fur. "She's so gorgeous. I love the way she's all white except for around her nose and mouth and on her ears and feet. It looks like she was dipped in chocolate. And she has the biggest blue eyes I've ever seen!"

Handing her to me, he said, "Here. Hold her. She's obviously happy. She's purring."

She settled into my palms and opened her mouth wide to yawn. So small and so delicate, she made me feel like the luckiest woman in the world. "She's so beautiful. I can't believe you got her for me. Nobody's ever gotten me anything like this."

"As long as you're happy, I'm happy."

"Why did you name her Angel? Isn't that your name for me?" I asked as I rubbed her perfectly white belly.

"Because she's sweet like you. I walked into the store and she looked up at me with those blue eyes and all I could think of was how beautiful she was, just like when I saw you for the first time."

I could have sat in the middle of the living room floor and played with her all night. Angel was perfect and precious. I instantly fell in love with her.

When it was time to go to bed for the first time in our new house, I followed Kane up the stairs to a room with a queen size bed and other normal bedroom furniture, unlike in his room at the club.

Extending his arm, he showed off our new accommodations. "A real bedroom for us. You deserve better than to sleep on the floor or on that old twin bed of mine."

With Angel in my arms, I climbed on top of the white down comforter and closed my eyes, loving the feel of its softness under me. Lying back, I set the kitten on my chest and whispered to her, "A new home for you and me, Angel." Kane climbed into bed and as we fell asleep in each other's arms, he whispered those same words to me.

"A new home for you and me, angel."

✕

ANGEL AND I PUTTERED AROUND the house finding out about our new place after Kane left for the club just before eleven the next morning. I set up her food and water in part of the pantry at the back of the house and made sure she had a litter box too. Because she was a kitten, she slept a lot, so I busied myself with cleaning the first floor of a thin layer of dust before Gemma came by to see my new place.

Right before noon, she knocked at my door and peeked her head in. "Hey, you! Let me in to see your new digs!"

I opened the door and beamed my pride in the house Kane had given us. "This is it! Isn't it incredible? And wait until you see what else he got me!"

Gemma walked in and looked around with her mouth hanging open in amazement. I knew how she felt. I'd been amazed when I first saw it too. Angel came trotting in and stopped at Gemma's feet to look up at her with her big blue eyes as if to say, "Who are you?"

"Oh my, Abbi! She's adorable! Kane got you a kitten?" Gemma asked as she knelt down to scratch Angel between the ears. The kitten lifted her chin to let her know some scratches on her neck were in order too.

"Isn't she cute? Her name is Angel, after his nickname for me."

Gemma picked up the kitten to cradle her in her arms. "Kane and a kitten. I can't believe it. You must be the luckiest woman in the world."

I ushered her over to the couch so we could sit and talk. "I think I am. It's hard to believe just a few weeks ago I was living in that awful apartment with Aaron and out of a job and now today I get to live in a place like this with a man like Kane and my very own beautiful kitten."

Angel kneaded my leg and found a place to snuggle on my lap as Gemma told me all about her new boyfriend and how happy they were. As she spoke, I couldn't help but think we'd finally found the happiness we both had hoped for. Gemma might not have had a boyfriend who beat her, but she'd dated her share of losers and this new guy sounded like he treated her like she deserved.

"I'm so happy for you, Gemma. Billy sounds like a great guy. He's got a great girlfriend in you too, so don't forget that."

"Don't worry about me. I'm more concerned about you and all this. You and Kane certainly do move fast. One night he's taking you out of that club across town and the next he's moving you into a house and buying you a pet."

I sensed the caution in her words and knew she was probably right to be worried about how fast we were moving. "I know. I didn't have anything to do with this house, though. I only asked him if I could stay at his place until I made enough money to get a place of my own, but then things just happened between us. He's just so different when we're alone, Gemma. He's not that scary guy I met the day I interviewed or the quiet guy at work. He's gentle and sweet and when he smiles, I can't help but—"

Cutting off my sentence before I said the words I worried would get me a lecture, I switched my attention to Angel who had climbed up onto my chest and was now kneading on my collarbone. "And this little one is just too cute, isn't she?"

Gemma knew me too well to let my diversion work and knitting her brows, leveled her gaze on me. "Can't help but what? Are you falling in love with him, Abbi?"

I hung my head and quietly said the truth. "Yes."

"I don't want to put a damper on this for you. It's just that you're so open and vulnerable after the whole Aaron thing, which I totally get. He finally got his, though, so at least there's that."

I looked up at her, confused about what she meant about Aaron. "Got what?"

"Didn't I tell you? I heard from that lady who rented the apartment to you two that somebody beat the snot out of him. They found him on the sidewalk in front of your old place all busted up. He just got out of the hospital, but he's still a mess, Abbi. I'm guessing he crossed the wrong person finally."

"Someone beat him up?"

"Yeah. Broken nose, ribs, internal injuries and all that. He had it coming to him, honey. He beat you up enough times to deserve whatever the world dumps on him."

"Yeah, I guess," I said quietly, my mind drifting back to what Kane had told me about why he went to prison.

"What's wrong? You can't be sad about what happened to Aaron. He was a total asshole to you."

Shaking my head, I forced a smile. "No. I wouldn't wish pain on anyone, but I don't care what happens to Aaron. Whoever beat him up just gave him a dose of his own medicine."

"He'll be fine, but maybe he won't be so quick to smack women around anymore. I bet he got nasty with some girl and her brother and his friends found Aaron and let him know that's not the way to treat her."

Gemma and I moved on from Aaron and continued to talk about the wonderful house and how life had finally given us all the blessings we'd always dreamed of having, but I couldn't get the thought of someone attacking him out of my mind. I ran through every moment since Kane and I began spending time together and couldn't figure out when he would have found the time to do it, but I couldn't shake the idea that he had.

ANGEL AND I FELL ASLEEP on the couch, but at just after one a.m., I felt a hand shaking my shoulder and opened my eyes to see Kane kneeling down next to me. "How are my two girls doing tonight?"

The kitten jumped down onto the floor and

scurried away as I wiped the sleep from my eyes. "I wanted to stay up to see you."

"I left Samson in charge so I could come home early. It's only one."

Sitting up, I worked to focus my eyes. I needed to speak to Kane about my suspicions with Aaron's beating. "Gemma told me something today. I want to ask you a question."

He sat back on his haunches and slowly slid his hands up my thighs, smiling that sexy grin that never failed to make me want him. "Shoot."

His touch made my brain go foggy, and I couldn't concentrate. "I'm serious. I need to ask you about something."

Kane stopped his hands' movement. "Okay. Ask."

"Do you know anything about my ex-boyfriend getting beaten to a pulp?"

I watched his expression for any sign of his guilt, but his face remained the same as it had just moments earlier. Placid, almost stony. His eyes, soft and gentle as they usually were when we were alone, stared up at me and he said, "I don't know who your ex is, angel."

"Gemma told me someone beat the hell out of Aaron and he was injured bad enough he had to be hospitalized."

"Why would I know about that?" he asked with just a hint of sharpness in his tone.

Placing my hands on top of his on my thighs, I

stared down at their size. The hands that cradled my face when we made love and caressed my body to heights of ecstasy were powerful and nearly twice as big as mine. I ran my fingertips over their thick knuckles and imagined the pain they'd inflict when they hit another's cheek.

"I don't know."

"This man beat you, angel. Why would you care if someone did the same to him?"

I lifted his hands from my legs and brought them to my lips. Kissing one hand and then the other, I lay my cheek against his open palm. "I don't care about him. I care about someone getting in trouble for what they did. Gemma thinks it's probably his new girlfriend's brother who did it to let him know the girl had people watching out for her."

Kane kissed me on the forehead and smiled. "I'm sure she's right. I wouldn't worry about someone getting in trouble. Maybe it's just karma coming back to haunt him."

I wanted to think that. The thought of Kane harming someone seemed so foreign, even though he'd told me what he did to that man who'd raped the girl he loved. Part of me worried the anger that could make him beat someone so badly would someday be turned on me, but I couldn't believe that. Whatever he might be to other people, to me he was always kind and protective.

No one would ever be able to convince me he was like the others. Kane wasn't a bad man, no matter what he did to people who hurt those he cared about.

Chapter Fourteen

Kane

Cash sat in his office waiting as Stefan and I arrived and took our seats. The frown etched into Cash's face told me everything I needed to know about this meeting. Unless he'd somehow fucked everything up with Olivia, he was about to tell us something bad that would affect all of us.

"Jesus, Cash. You look like some disgruntled old bastard. What's with the face?" Stefan asked as he settled into his chair in front of Cash's desk.

"I'm not in the mood for your ass busting today, Stefan, so if we can just pretend this is a place of business for a few minutes, I need to discuss something serious with both of you."

Stefan looked at me for some clue what was bothering our brother, but I had nothing. He hadn't said anything to me. "Okay. Sorry, Cash. What's up?"

"Mason. He wants to come by to see what his help is getting him. As if the money we pay means nothing."

"This guy is a pain in the ass. I'm beginning to

think he's worse than Shank," I said, understanding Cash's frustration. We paid him each month. Now he wanted to check out what he was getting for his money? Fucking politician!

"I'm thinking it's no big deal, guys," Stefan said in a chipper voice. "We run a great place, so what's he going to find? I'll make sure my bartenders serve him the good stuff, and when he goes upstairs, Kane can make sure he gets the show of his life. He's already a member, so it isn't like he hasn't seen what we do. Nothing to worry about, I say."

Cash's frown stayed firmly in place. "It's the fact that now he wants to see about his investment, as he calls it. I just have a bad feeling about him. He mentioned he's bringing his brother with him, some guy who runs a bar in Bradenton."

"Manatee County's finest watering hole?" Stefan said sarcastically. "Maybe I'll tell the bartenders to forget the top shelf stuff. He probably wouldn't know the difference."

"I wish you'd take this seriously, Stefan. I'm worried."

I knew Cash wasn't exaggerating. I hadn't seen him this stressed out since the whole problem with Shank. "Don't worry. Stefan will do what he always does and Mason and his brother will love the club. Then they'll come upstairs and my people will make sure this backwater bar owner is blown away by their talents.

We'll take care of it, Cash. You just do your thing and we'll make Mason happy he's working with us."

Nodding, he sighed deeply. "Okay. I just have a bad feeling about this guy. Every week it's something else with him. Maybe it's what Olivia said. Maybe I did get too used to dealing with Shank. I hope so."

"Not to worry, big brother," Stefan said with a smile. "The March brothers own the best club around." Realizing what he'd said, he turned toward me and chucked me on the shoulder. "You're like a March, so it works. We all come from the same sperm, so that makes us brothers, no matter what your last name is."

I looked over at Cash, who didn't seem to know how to react to Stefan's declaration of brotherhood, and shook my head. "On that note about our father's sperm, I'm out of here. I have work to do so Mason and his brother have the time of their lives. Just give me a call when you're bringing them up."

"He said they'd be here around ten, so I'll keep them downstairs with Stefan's people to loosen them up for a while. I'm thinking between eleven and midnight."

Standing, I turned to leave. "Got it. I'll block out some time with my best dancers. Any idea what they'll want?"

"No, but I'm thinking girls in the room would be a good bet. Plan on that."

With a chuckle, I said, "It'll be the easiest dance

most of them have ever had, I bet. Small town guys are usually pretty easy on the girls."

"Let's hope so."

WHEN EVERYONE ARRIVED FOR WORK, I pulled Simone aside to let her know about the club's special guest for that night and explained how she'd be working with another dancer for him. Always a trooper, she jumped at the chance to show off her stuff and represent the club.

"Thanks, Simone. I knew you'd be a good choice. I'm going to put you with Abbi, so he'll have opposite ends of the spectrum."

"She's brand new, Kane. Are you sure?" Simone asked, her eyes studying me closely.

"You doubt my decision?" I joked.

"No. Just that she's never done anything in the rooms and she's really new."

"She'll be fine. I'll be watching on the monitors, so don't worry. It won't be a girl on girl thing. It's just the two of you dancing in the room."

Simone shrugged. "Oh, okay. So we'll just be doing our thing and that's it? Who's the guy?"

"The brother of someone we're working with, so I want him happy."

A sly smile spread across her lips. "How happy are we talking here, Kane? You're putting your girlfriend in the room with him."

"Not that kind of happy."

Simone's allusion to them servicing Mason's brother bothered me, and it was clear from her reaction that she knew. "It's kinda cool seeing you with someone, Kane. Everyone knows, but it's okay. You just broke a few hearts."

"Get to work."

I turned and walked out toward my post as she called after me, "I saw that smile. I want you to know I like this new Kane better than the cranky one."

Ignoring her teasing, I found Abbi milling around the fifth floor hallway with a few other dancers. "Ladies, you need to get yourselves ready, so head back to the dressing room. We've got a big night tonight and I want things to be great."

As they passed me, I caught Abbi by the arm and stopped her. "I'm going to have you dance in one of the rooms tonight."

Fear filled her eyes. "In a room? I've never done that, Kane," she said in a panicked voice.

"Don't worry. You'll be fine. Simone will be in there. Just dance like you always do, okay?"

Nodding, she tried to force a smile. "Okay."

"I won't let anything hurt you, angel. I'll be watching on the monitor the whole time."

"I know. I just worry that I'll mess up."

I ran my finger down a long blond tendril that touched her cheek and whispered, "I wish we were home right now and you weren't wearing that wig. I like it better when I get to run my fingers through your hair."

She instinctively touched her nape and frowned. "I wish I still had my hair."

"Shhh. You look beautiful no matter what your hair looks like. Now go get ready and when Samson comes to get you for that dance, don't worry. Remember, I won't let anything hurt you."

Abbi stared at me with a frightened look for a long moment and then said quietly, "Okay."

I saw a text right before midnight from Stefan telling me Cash was bringing Mason's brother up to his room, so I texted back *Room 1* and sent Samson to find Abbi and Simone. I didn't like the idea of them being two floors down, but that was the only big room empty for the night. I'd be watching the entire time, so if anything happened I'd be down there in seconds.

Cash brought Jethro Jennings up to meet me on the fifth floor a few minutes later. Not always a believer in first impressions, this time I couldn't deny they were usually right. I instantly disliked the guy. His look was too fucking slick, especially for a supposed small town bar owner. Well shorter than his brother, he came up to right above my shoulder and reeked of cheap drug store cologne like he'd taken a bath in the shit. One look and I knew he gave off a vibe that made me mistrust him as much as I'd ever mistrusted Shank.

As usual, Cash played his role as the consummate classy businessman with perfection, though. Even as his eyes watered from the smell of his guest, he introduced Mason's brother and I shook his hand, noticing how tight the guy's grip was. Only men trying to prove they're tough guys shook hands like that.

"Nice place you have here, Kane. Can't ever go wrong with tits and ass."

Asshole.

I may have been the guy who ran the darker section of the club that rarely kept on the right side of the law, but I did it with respect for my people. This guy in one sentence had diminished every person who danced for us to body parts.

Cash's eyes grew as big as saucers, probably because he thought I'd lay the guy out for saying that kind of shit about my staff, but I knew my role in this and simply smiled as I tried to forget how much this guy rubbed me the wrong way.

"I think you'll find my people are the best around, Jethro. Enjoy your time here. And as I always tell our members, remember no touching unless the ladies say so."

Quickly, Cash told him about the room we'd set up for him down on the third floor, and they left to head off in that direction just as Samson came running up behind me. "Small wardrobe malfunction. Simone must have had one too many pieces of Janie's chocolate cake the other night because she's busting out of her top. They're fixing it now, but she needs a few minutes before she can get to the third floor room."

"Is Abbi ready?"

"Yeah. She's good to go." Samson wrinkled his nose. "What is that disgusting smell?"

I rolled my eyes. "The guy she and Simone have to dance for. Cash just took him down there, but he's still with us in all his disgusting spirit."

"We usually get a better class of people here. Anyway, I'll get Simone downstairs as soon as Janie gets her sewn into her costume."

"All right. I'm sure Abbi will be fine. Just tell Simone to lay off the cake from now on."

"Got it!"

Samson ran back to get Simone ready as the fifth floor began to fill up with members waiting for their rooms. Booked solid all night, the fantasy rooms would be busy right up until closing, but my focus was on Mason's brother two floors down. Checking the monitor, I saw Cash close the door behind him, leaving Jethro on the couch to wait for Abbi.

Inhaling, I took a deep breath of the lingering stench of his cologne and watched as she entered the room. She'd never interacted with any of the members before—something I hadn't considered until that moment—but she gave him one of her sweet smiles and introduced herself. The first notes of music filtered into the room, and on cue, she closed her eyes and began dancing.

Her white dress flowed gently as her hips slowly swung left and right. Just as the first night I saw her perform, she enchanted me. The intoxicating mixture of innocence and sensuality never failed to take my breath away. She was beauty and sweetness, and I couldn't take my eyes off her. I saw Jethro respond to her just as every other member had, leaning back against the couch to stare up in awe of her dancing just for him. That she danced only for me was our secret.

Abbi turned her back to him to perform the section of her dance that involved her teasing members with her gorgeous ass and shy glances. Always a favorite part in the past, it seemed to make Jethro unhappy. Leaning forward, he frowned, but when Abbi looked back and smiled at him, he appeared to like what he saw.

Then as I watched her turn her back on him again, he lurched forward and grabbed her so quickly she cried out in terror. In a second, I was running down two flights of stairs, pushing people out of the way as my fear of what he was doing to Abbi took over. I tore down the third floor hallway, threw the door open, and what I saw made me go blind with rage.

Jethro's fucking hands grabbed at Abbi's body as she screamed for him to stop. I ripped him off her and tossed him across the room. She fell to the ground, but I followed him and slammed my fist into his face, crushing his nose as I held him down on the floor. Blood squirted from his face, covering my hands, and I reared my arm back again to smash my knuckles against his cheekbone. His jaw shattered beneath my fist, but still I didn't stop. Over and over, I pummeled him, governed by a singular need to hurt him like he hurt her.

I didn't know when he stopped fighting back—he'd landed a few punches but I didn't feel them—but at some point I realized he was little more than a ragdoll. Hands pulled at me to let him go. I couldn't. I couldn't stop even though his blood covered me and he'd stopped fighting back.

Finally, I heard Abbi screaming for me to stop. I turned to see her crying and instantly dropped Jethro's lifeless body to the floor to go to her. Cash and Stefan tried to hold me back, but I easily pushed their hands from my shoulders and took Abbi in my arms.

Sobbing, she sagged against my chest and whispered, "I didn't mean to do this. He just came at me."

Her words made my hands ball into fists again. She hadn't deserved what that fucking pig had done, and now she was apologizing. I ran my hand down her back, trying to comfort her. "You did nothing wrong, angel. Don't talk. Shhh. I'm here, angel. I'm here."

I felt a hand on my arm and turned my head to see Cash next to me saying something. His words sounded garbled, like he was talking underwater. Finally, they began to come through loud and clear. "Kane, what happened here?"

"He grabbed Abbi. I stopped him."

Mason entered the room and pointed his finger in my face, barking, "You'll pay for this and not just with this club!"

Lunging at him, I reached out to grab that fucking finger to break it off, but Abbi and Cash held me back while Stefan pulled Mason out into the hallway so I couldn't get at him too. Abbi begged me to stop, quietly pleading, "Kane, no more. Please no more."

"Cash, I'm taking Abbi home."

He looked back at Jethro lying all bloody and broken on the floor and then at me. "The cops are going to want to know what happened. Mason's not going to help with this."

"I don't care. I'm going home. Handle this."

Abbi buried her head in my chest, and I huddled close to her as we walked her out to my car at the back of the building. Blood ran off my hands and arms, covering her white dress wherever I touched her. At the car, I stopped and slid out of my shirt for her to wear so she wouldn't have to look at blood all the way home.

She stared up at me as I wrapped it around her shoulders. "Are you okay? There's so much blood, Kane. Are you hurt?"

Shaking my head, I smiled. "I don't think so. Wear

this. It has less blood on it."

I began to button it to cover her, and she stopped my hands. "You're always covering me with your shirt. I need to know you're okay."

"I'm fine, angel. As long as you're not hurt, I'm fine."

Abbi caressed my cheek with her palm and gave me a tiny smile. "I'm worried, Kane. I don't want you to get in trouble for this. I can't stand the idea of that."

"I'm fine. Cash will take care of it. Let's go home and get you cleaned up."

I knew that was a lie. If Mason's brother died, I'd be arrested and charged with murder. If he lived, at the very least I'd be charged with assault. Either way, there was little chance Mason could be bribed out of making sure I saw the inside of a prison again.

Abbi held my still blood-covered hand as I drove to the house, apologizing the entire way there. This wasn't her fault, and no matter how much I knew I should be sorry for what I'd done, I wasn't. He'd hurt someone I loved and gotten what he deserved. I wouldn't be sorry for that.

That's what a man was supposed to do. A man should protect the woman he loves, and that's what I did. I wouldn't apologize for taking care of Abbi.

She leaned her head against my shoulder and said quietly, "Kane, I'm worried. What's going to happen?"

I softly kissed the top of her head. "Don't worry.

No matter what, we'll be okay."

That promise I could live up to. Even if the worst happened and they ended up putting me away for what I did, Cash and Stefan would make sure Abbi was taken care of. When all was said and done, they were my brothers and whoever I cared about they cared about.

That's what brothers did, even half-brothers.

Chapter Fifteen

Abbi

KANE SAT AT THE KITCHEN table in only his pants, still covered in blood from his elbows to his fingertips. I'd cleaned off all the blood splatters on his face and neck, and taking his hands in mine, I slowly wiped each finger clean of blood and checked for any cuts, but all the blood was that man's, not his. He said nothing but watched me carefully, like what I was doing enthralled him.

Dipping the washcloth in the big bowl of water next to me, I rinsed out the blood and returned to cleaning his arms. Each stroke over his skin revealed another part of his tattoos. Within a short time, I'd cleaned him up and couldn't stay silent any longer.

"You say not to worry, but aren't the police going to get involved, Kane?"

"No more talking about that, angel. I want to spend a quiet night at home like other people do."

My fear at what would happen to him nagged at me, but why wouldn't he talk to me about it? I couldn't stand there and pretend everything was okay. I took the bowl full of bloody water to the sink and washed it out, letting the water dilute the dark red liquid until none of it was left. As if it was perfectly normal to clean some man's blood off the man you love after watching him beat him because of you.

Tears welled in my eyes as I thought about the police taking Kane away from me. Hanging my head, I quietly said, "I can't pretend like I'm okay with this. I need you to talk to me."

"There's nothing to talk about."

God, why wouldn't he talk to me? Frustrated, I turned the water off and slammed the bowl down in the drainer. Then I turned around and yelled, "Yes, there is! What am I going to do if they take you away from me?"

All the emotion drained from his face until he looked stark white. His eyes, usually so soft when he looked at me, hardened so he looked like he did that first night I met him. "You'll never be alone, Abbi. If I'm not around, Cash and Stefan will make sure you're okay until I get back."

"Why did you do it? Why didn't you just push him away?"

His eyes softened and he gave me that gentle look I loved. "Because he was hurting you. I protect the woman I love, no matter what."

All my fear and anger ebbed away at the sound of

those words. I protect the woman I love. I knelt down in front of him and looked up into that beautiful, tortured face. "You love me?"

He cradled my cheek in his hand. "More than anything or anyone else in the world. No matter what they do to me, it couldn't be worse than seeing you hurt."

"But I'll be hurt if you're not with me. I love you, Kane. I don't want to lose you."

"I promise you won't lose me. I won't let that happen."

"The police are probably on their way right now. They're going to take you away and all because of me," I sobbed.

"Let's go upstairs. Time for bed." Kane pulled me up to my feet and took my hand in his to lead me up to our bedroom. "No more talk about that. I don't want to think of anything but how your body feels against mine."

I followed him up the stairs, clutching his hand in mine. Still dressed in my costume and his shirt, I stood by our bed as he slid out of his pants and saw the mess I was. Suddenly, the reality of what I'd caused was too much to bear and I began to cry, knowing that whatever there was about me that made men want to punish me had hurt this man who had never done anything but care for me.

Kane pulled me close and held me, whispering,

"Are you hurt? Don't cry."

"I'm not hurt."

He slid my blood matted wig from my head and smiled. "Good. And I don't want to see you in this again. You're beautiful just the way you are."

His kindness made me feel worse, and the tears rolled down my cheeks. "Maybe now no one will want to hurt me looking like this."

"Is that what you think? That you did something to deserve that pig's hands on you?"

I nodded. "It must be my fault. Nearly every man I've ever been with has hurt me. That's not a coincidence."

Kane kissed me tenderly and whispered against my lips, "It's not your fault. Never forget that."

Wiping the tears from my cheeks, I couldn't help but think he was wrong. "Now I've hurt the only man who never did anything but protect me. I can't stand the idea that you'll suffer because of me."

"Shhh. The only suffering I'm feeling is seeing you like this. Let's get you out of these bloodstained clothes and cleaned up."

I watched him undress me, so careful as he gently tugged my white dress off my shoulders and down my body. A look of horror covered his face and I looked down to see some blood had seeped through the fabric from where he'd held me leaving a handprint of pale red on my skin. He stared at it and hanging his head, said quietly, "I'm sorry, angel. I'm no good for you."

"No! Please don't say that. You protected me."

"I didn't mean to get you involved in my problems. I'm sorry, Abbi."

"Your problems are my problems, Kane. Don't say protecting me is a problem."

"I couldn't think of anything but hurting him when I saw him put his hands on you. I wanted to kill him. I could have. I didn't want to stop hitting him, even when Cash and Stefan were pulling me off him. I'm not sorry for what I did. I'm just sorry it's touched you."

"It's a little blood. Some soap and water and I'll be just fine."

He kissed me like my lips held some release from all the ugliness of the past few hours, and for a few minutes I forgot about everything that could happen at any minute.

Taking my hand, he led me to the shower and cleaned every inch of me like I was something precious to him. His silence soothed me, unlike the first night when I so desperately wished for him to say more. Now I didn't need to hear him say the words. I felt them in his touch each time he caressed my body to clean the terrible events of the night from me.

When he finished, he smoothed my hair off my face with a towel and looked into my eyes. "Angel, no matter what, I love you."

I heard a knocking downstairs on the front door and for the first time since I'd met him, worry flashed in Kane's eyes. He covered me in a bath towel and wrapped one around his hips as I followed him into the bedroom.

"Don't answer that. Please."

"It can't be put off. Get dressed and come downstairs."

I hurried myself into one of his T-shirts and a pair of my shorts and took the stairs two at a time to find him standing in the living room with Cash. His eyes had that same worried look as Kane's. Taking a seat next to him on the couch, we listened to his half-brother update us on Jethro's condition and what Mason planned to do.

"Jethro's awake, but he's in bad shape. You really hurt him. Mason's not really in a talking mood, but from what I gathered, he's not going to be easily placated."

"What does that mean?" I asked as I squeezed Kane's hand tightly, afraid if I let go I'd lose him. "Because he survived, they won't do anything right? I mean, I know from when Aaron hit me once and I called the cops, they wouldn't do anything because he said he didn't do it, even though it happened in our house. So it'll be okay, right?"

Kane turned to look at me and shook his head. "No. His being awake is better than if I'd beaten him to death, but I'm not going to avoid charges."

I looked up at Cash hoping to hear him say something different, but he just nodded. "Kane's right. It's a sad truth that two men fighting gets more attention from the law than a man hitting a woman."

"But he was defending me. Doesn't that matter?"

Cash didn't answer. I saw by the look on Kane's face that it didn't. "No," he said quietly. "Not really."

"I'm going to talk to Mason again in the morning and hopefully I can convince him money can make this go away. He's a councilman, but the man loves money more than justice and the law. I just wanted to stop by to let you know and make sure you're okay, Abbi. I'm sorry this happened. I didn't know what kind of person Jethro was when I left him with you."

"I understand. I don't blame you, Cash."

Another knock on the door made my heart stop for a moment, and we all turned to see two cops standing on the porch. My emotions overwhelmed me as Kane stood from the couch. Reaching up to grab his hand again, I cried, "No, don't. Don't go."

"Don't worry. Just run upstairs and get me some clothes so I don't look like I belong on some episode of Cops, okay?"

I didn't want to leave that room just in case he let them in and they took him away before I could get back, so I ran as fast as I could up the stairs and grabbed a pair of black pants, a grey long sleeved shirt, and his boots he always wore and ran back to find the police standing in my living room. Everything got confused for me as they explained why they were there and that he'd have to go with them. Kane took his clothes and said something as he dressed, but nothing seemed to make any sense. All I knew was that his leaving scared me to death.

He left his boots unlaced, and stepping toward me, took my face in his hands. "Cash will make sure you're okay. I won't be gone for long. Don't worry, angel. I'll be okay."

The tears rolled down my cheeks as he spoke because I knew he was saying goodbye. "Don't leave. Please don't! You were only protecting me." I turned to look at the cops and tried to plead his case. "He was protecting me from being hurt. He doesn't deserve this. Don't take him away."

The police stood stone-faced as Kane turned my face back toward him. "Abbi, listen to me. I won't be gone for long. It will be okay. I promise it will. I love you, angel. Don't worry. Just promise me you'll be here when I get back."

"I'll be here," I sobbed. "I love you. I'm sorry."

He kissed me and whispered against my lips, "Don't worry. I'll be back soon."

Then he turned and silently held his hands out in front of him for the policeman to close the handcuffs around his wrists. I listened to one of the men recite those words I'd heard so many times on cop shows, but now each right he mentioned seemed so important. "…You have the right to an attorney. Anything you say can and will be held against you in a court of law."

He hung his head and nodded to Cash as they walked him out, "Take care of her until I get back."

"I'll have Jessup on it first thing, Kane," Cash said just before the screen door slammed closed and Kane was taken away.

My legs buckled underneath me, and I collapsed onto the couch, unable to stand I felt so sick. Closing my eyes, I tried to block out the image of the man I loved being taken away to jail because of me, but it wouldn't go away no matter how much I tried. Cash sat down next to me and gently put his arm around me, pulling me close as I cried uncontrollably.

"We won't let him stay away, Abbi. I promise. Stefan and I will make sure he comes home as soon as possible. For now, you can stay with Olivia and me so you aren't alone in this house."

I shook my head against his shoulder as I continued to sob. "No. This is the house he gave me. I won't leave until he comes back. I need to be here when he comes back."

Cash didn't argue with me, likely because he knew disagreeing with a hysterical woman was a useless idea. I promised I'd call him day or night if I needed anything, but all I needed was Kane back home with me again.

I took Angel to bed with me and cried myself to sleep thinking of the man I loved spending the night in jail. I couldn't just sit back and hope Cash could convince the councilman to help Kane. He'd gotten in trouble because of me. I had to do something.

✕

STRAIGHTENING OLIVIA'S SUNDRESS IN THE glass window outside Councilman Jennings' office, I took a deep breath and told myself I could do this. I needed to do whatever it took to help Kane. He'd protected me over and over. The least I could do was try to convince Jethro's brother to see what Kane had done was all for me and not because he was a bad man.

I knocked on the door and heard him yell for me to come in. Steadying myself, I pushed the door open a crack and stuck my head in. "Mr. Jennings, may I speak to you?"

"Please come in. I'm always available for my constituents."

I stepped into his office and instantly felt unnerved by the resemblance between Mason Jennings and his brother. The same slicked back hair, the same greasy look that screamed corrupt man.

"I'm not exactly here as a constituent. My name is Abigail Linde. I work at Club X as a dancer. Kane is my boyfriend."

In a far chillier voice than when he thought I was there as a simple voter, he said, "I see."

"I only ask for a few minutes of your time. I was the dancer in your brother's fantasy room last night."

He scanned my face and body and narrowed his eyes to slits. "You look very different now."

Tugging on the ends of my hair, I lowered my gaze. "I wear a costume and wig for work."

"What can I do for you, Abigail?"

He extended his hand for me to sit, and I gave him my nicest smile. "Please call me Abbi. How is Jethro feeling?"

"Better, thank you. I appreciate you asking."

"I know you probably think that Kane is a bad man for what happened, but he was just protecting me because he thought I was being hurt. He's a good person. Cash and Stefan are too. I know your brother got hurt, but if there was any way to make up for what happened without Kane having to go to jail, I really hope you'll consider it."

"I believe the case has already begun to move through the court system. I'm not sure what I could do, even if I wanted to. Kane's attack was vicious. I'm not sure anything can make up for that."

Tears began to well up in my eyes, but I needed to stay strong. "There has to be something I can do. He was just trying to protect me. Kane would never hurt someone without reason. I know your brother probably meant no harm either. It was all a horrible misunderstanding."

Mason Jennings stared at me with a look that I knew all too well. Like his brother, he wasn't above treating women like dirt, and I saw in his eyes that he'd already thought of something I'd be able to do for him to make this all go away.

"You seem like a determined young lady, Abbi. Kane is lucky to have such an advocate in his corner. You remind me of someone I once knew, in fact. I'll tell you what. My brother has a small bar he'd love to have you work at. No dancing. Just bartending, but if he had someone like you behind the bar for his patrons, I'm sure he could forget the unfortunate events of last night."

Bartend for Jethro, the man who thought grabbing at me had been perfectly fine? The man who had created all this mess? My stomach tightened at the thought of his hands on me every night, but maybe if he thought he'd get beaten again if he misbehaved he might not make the same mistake twice.

It didn't matter if he did as long as Kane stayed out of jail.

"I'd be happy to work at Jethro's bar, but I need your word that nothing will happen to Kane."

"You have my word, Abbi. I'll see to it. However, I don't see him agreeing to your working anywhere but Club X."

I wrote my phone number on a piece of paper and handed it to him. "Let me handle that. If anyone can convince him, it's me."

Mason stood and walked behind me as I made my way to the door, his hand pressed to my lower back and making me cringe. I stopped and smiled, hoping my disgust for him and his plan wasn't as obvious as it felt.

"You've been a pleasant surprise for me today, Abbi. Thank you. Good luck with your task. It's sure to not be an easy one."

I left his office to hurry home hoping that the lawyer Cash had mentioned the night before had been successful in getting Kane released. He'd only been away one night and already I felt alone and empty inside. I didn't want to feel this way ever again. If Cash could get him out of jail, I would do what Mason Jennings wanted to keep him out.

Kane deserved to have someone fight for him, no matter what it took.

Chapter Sixteen

Kane

After Cash and Jessup posted my bail, I could think of only one thing—getting back to Abbi. The sad look on her face had been too much for me as they led me out of the house, and I had to look away or I'd have done something stupid and made the situation worse. I couldn't do that. I wasn't sorry for what I'd done, but now that I had to pay for my crime, I saw that in my attempt to protect her I'd hurt her. If I had to spend years in jail, I'd continue hurting her. I hadn't meant that to happen, but now that it had, I needed to do anything I could to make things better.

I'd told Cash whatever it took and however much it cost, I had to stay out for Abbi. I had millions and it could all be Jethro's if that's what he wanted. Even if it took every cent I'd ever made at Club X, I didn't care.

As long as I was free and with her.

I bounded up the front stairs and stopped short as my hand touched the door handle. What if Abbi couldn't forgive me for what I'd done? She'd spent years with men who hurt her with their hands. How different was I from them? Either way, we'd all hurt her.

Slowly, I opened the door to see her standing in the living room with Angel in her arms, as if both of them had been there all night waiting for me. Her smile beamed her happiness, and she began to softly cry.

"I missed you so much. Cash told me you were out. Are you okay?"

She put the kitten down on the floor and wrapped her arms around me, burying her face in my chest. The feel of her body next to mine made everything I'd gone through fade away, and now all I knew was the happiness I always felt when she was in my arms.

"I'm fine. I thought about you alone here all night and hated that I'd fucked up so badly. Cash said you wouldn't go with him last night. Why?"

Abbi squeezed me tightly and shook her head. "This is our home. I couldn't leave. I belong here with you. I had to make sure I was here when you came back."

I smoothed my hand over her hair and pressed my cheek to the top of head. "I'm sorry, angel. I fucked everything up and now we have to deal with the consequences. I should have never put you in that room with him. It was stupid."

"Shhh. I don't want to think about what we'll have to do now. I just want to hold you and feel you next to me."

Tilting her head back, I kissed her lips after missing her like I'd never missed anyone before. "I love you, Abbi. I promise when this is all over I'll make it up to you, if you're still with me."

"I'm not going anywhere. There's no one else in this world who's shown me love like you have, Kane. You got in trouble because you wanted to protect me. How could I leave you after that?"

"I don't know what's going to happen now. I'm not going to lie. I'm probably going to do time, unless we can find another way out of this. I told Cash I'm willing to give Mason and his brother every last dime I have, so hopefully a few million can make this go away."

"I don't want you to worry about this, Kane. You were trying to help someone, so I believe it will all work out. Have faith."

Chuckling, I smiled at her mention of faith. I'd never had much belief in faith in anything—not people, not religion, nothing. But Abbi made me want to believe. Whatever I thought about faith, I believed her. From the moment I first saw her, I wanted to be the kind of man who deserved her. I wanted to protect and care for her and erase all the ugliness she'd seen.

But now with one stupid mistake, any future I hoped to have with her was in danger. If only I hadn't lost my temper and fallen back into what I'd always been.

A monster.

"I have faith in you, angel. Everything else in this world, no. But you make me believe."

"Then believe in me because I know we'll be okay."

As she pulled me into the kitchen to feed me after my night in jail, I couldn't help but admire how well she was handling everything that happened. I'd left her crying, and little over half a day later, she seemed able to be strong enough for both of us. She never ceased to surprise me with how tough she actually was. So gentle and kind, Abbi had a survivor streak in her I loved.

She cleared the table of all the dirty dishes and stood at the sink with her back to me. "I would do anything to make sure you're happy. You know that, Kane, don't you?"

Her shoulders hunched slightly as she spoke, and a spike of regret ran through me for what I'd done. I stood and walked over to her, wrapping my arms around her waist to pull her to me. "You make me happy just as you are. You don't have to do anything else."

Turning in my hold, she looked up at me and I saw something in her eyes. Fear. "I would, though. I would do anything to make sure you were happy."

I pressed my forehead to hers and confessed what I worried about as I sat in that jail cell all night. "Are you afraid of me now?"

She shook her head, but I knew the look of fear and I saw it in her eyes.

"Angel, I would give my life for yours. Do you know that?"

"I know. And I would give mine for yours, Kane."

I kissed her, loving the taste of her lips after a night away, and whispered against them, "Don't say that. I don't ever want you to feel like you have to give up anything for me."

Tears filled her eyes. "I couldn't think of anything last night but you stuck in jail because of me. Tell me to go away and I will. Then whatever it is that's inside me that makes men want to hurt me will be gone from your life."

Her words made my chest feel like someone was pressing down on it hard. "Don't say that, angel. You aren't the reason that fuck did what he did and I reacted the way I did."

She cradled my face in her hands and frowned. "You aren't like him, Kane. Don't mention the two of you in the same way."

Whether I was as bad as Jethro didn't matter. I knew what I was and I couldn't pretend any differently. "I told you the first night we made love you should leave, but now I can't bear to think of you not in my life. My demons are still inside me, though, Abbi. I can't change that."

"I'm not afraid of them. The only thing I'm afraid

of is not having you in my life. I can take anything else your demons want to do to me, but not that."

I took her by the hand and led her upstairs to our bedroom. Abbi sat on the bed quietly watching me undress to shower. I didn't want her touched by my night in jail any more than she had to be. We said nothing because there was nothing more to say.

I was who I was, and she'd accepted me.

The hot water streamed over me, but it couldn't take away the truth of what I'd done. I was home for now, but how long that would last I had no idea. Jessup had warned me that some jail time was likely because of my past record. The thought of my rage hurting Abbi for months or years made my heart ache.

Hanging my head, I sighed at the pain of missing her already.

"Kane, are you okay?"

I looked up to see Abbi standing on the other side of the glass shower door just like she had that first morning after I'd taken her back to my apartment. Choking back the mix of regret and sadness I felt just thinking about leaving her, I nodded.

"I'm fine."

She opened the door and stepped in. "You're torturing yourself over this, Kane. Don't."

I didn't know what to say to that. Only one other person had ever made me regret who I was, and I couldn't bear thinking of Abbi facing the same fate as her.

Her hands held my face, and she looked up at me with those blue eyes so sweet that she could have asked for anything in the world and I would have done anything to give it to her.

"I love you. I hate seeing you so torn up over this. You don't believe things are going to work out, but I know they will."

"I love you, angel. I want to believe. I do. But that's never been a strong part of my life."

Abbi stepped under the water and kissed me. "I believe, so I want you to believe too."

Pushing her hair back, I gazed down into that beautiful face that had enchanted me from the first night I met her and smiled in spite of my fear that someday soon I'd be locked up without her and the sweetness she brought to my life.

I kissed her as I silently begged for forgiveness, hoping whatever she believed in would let me stay with her.

"Do you remember that first night when you brought me back to your apartment at the club? I've wondered since then why you have DO NO HARM tattooed there right below your belly button."

I dried my hair with a towel and cracked my neck. Throwing the towel on top of the hamper, I sat down on the bed next to her and leaned back onto my elbows. She turned to face me and stared down at the tattoo.

"If it's too painful to talk about, that's okay. I was just curious."

Taking a deep breath in, I closed my eyes and thought about the night I'd gotten that tattooed on my body. "It was one of my first nights out of jail and I found out Holly had taken her own life. Her letters to me had gotten darker and darker as time went on, and then finally they'd stopped, but I was helpless to do anything from in there. The memory of what that man had done to her had tortured her until she couldn't take it anymore, and I wasn't there to be strong for her. She turned to drugs to erase the pain, and then finally one day, they took her away."

Abbi leaned over and kissed me softly on the cheek. "You don't have to go any further."

"Do you know that there wasn't a day when I was growing up that I didn't hear my mother tell me why I was named Kane? She used to tell me that I was meant to hurt. That hurting was who I was."

A look of sadness settled into her face, and Abbi quietly said, "That's not true. I don't think you're meant to hurt others."

"Maybe she meant I was supposed to hurt. I don't know. I never asked. Even as she lay dying in that hospital bed, the only thing that brought a smile to her face was telling me I was meant to hurt."

"I can't stand to see you like this, Kane. You've never been anything but caring and protective of me. How can anyone say you're meant to hurt? People are meant to love, not hurt one another."

"Maybe some of us can't do anything else but hurt—others and ourselves," I said as I thought about the reality of my life.

"I don't believe that. You're a good man. You got that tattoo because you don't want to hurt people. I don't know what these demons are inside you, but I believe you fight them with everything in you. If you didn't, you'd hurt me too, and you don't."

I pulled her on top of me and held her close, feeling her heartbeat against me. "What I did last night hurt you, and I'm sorry. I let my demons run loose, and that's what happens."

Abbi softly placed her finger up to my lips. "Shhh. No more about that. For now, I don't want to think about anything that happened. All I want to do is feel you inside me as you show me how much you love me."

My hands ached to touch her, to cup her beautiful breasts in my palms and squeeze those dark pink nipples between my thumbs and forefinger. I slid my hands down her soft back and gripped her ass hard in my hands.

"Stay with me, no matter what I do."

"I'm not going anywhere, Kane."

For the first time with her, I didn't hold back. She clung to my neck and with one sharp thrust I filled her. Her cunt was hot and wet, and I couldn't get enough of her. I'd have given anything to just get lost in her forever.

Her body met mine with each time I pushed into her as my demons whispered, "She's not frightened. Show her why she should be."

But I didn't want to hurt anymore. I wanted what Abbi gave me. I wanted to love.

Sliding out of her, I rolled her onto her back and slowly planted kisses down her body, loving the look of ecstasy in her eyes. With my thumbs, I spread her open and ran my tongue over her delicate skin to her clit, swollen and waiting for attention.

Abbi moaned softly above me and quietly begged for me to give her what she needed. "Oh, God…right there. Oh, that's it…"

I kept my eyes focused on her and sucked her clit gently into my mouth, flicking the tip of my tongue against her silky skin. She closed her eyes and bit her lower lip, and I watched as her expression softened as my mouth inched her toward release.

Lifting my head from between her legs, I ran a finger down her wet slit, adding another as I reached her entrance. Her hands urged me back to where I'd been, but instead I slid two fingers into her, curling them against the tender skin of her willing cunt.

"You're so wet," I whispered against her body and slowly pumped my fingers in and out of her, loving the sound of her moans. She was close, and I knew all it would take to send her over that delicious edge would be a few more deliberate drags of my tongue over her clit.

She pulled me by the back of my head to take her to that place, and a few seconds later her orgasm exploded inside her. Dragging her fingernails across my scalp, she closed her legs around my head and rode my mouth in that erotic way that never failed to thrill me.

When her thighs finally stopped quivering, I sat back on my heels and licked my lips to savor the taste of her as she grinned sweetly up at me. "You look beautiful lying there like that."

"Like some boneless creature totally satisfied by an incredibly hot man she loves?" she said with a giggle.

"Exactly, except that man loves her too."

I SHOWED UP TO THE weekly meeting with Cash and Stefan late, but as far as I was concerned, I had an excuse—spending time with Abbi before the shit hit the fan. It hadn't yet, which made me wonder what was going on in the D.A.'s office since I should have heard something by now. Every day I woke up expecting to hear something from Jessup, but he'd heard nothing and we'd taken the position that no news was good news.

"Nice to see you again, big brother," Stefan teased as I sat down next to him. "We were wondering if you'd ever show your face again or if you planned on spending the rest of your days playing house with Abbi."

"I would if I could, but then who would run our little funhouse upstairs?" I joked as I folded my hands behind my head.

"Any news from Jessup?" Cash asked with concern in his voice. "It's been over a week. Long enough he should have heard something."

I shook my head, as baffled as he was. "No. Nothing yet. I don't get it either. Have you talked to Mason?"

"No. I've called a few times, but his secretary always takes a message and he hasn't gotten back to me. I don't like that."

I sighed and blew the air out slowly. I didn't like Mason's behavior either. Stefan jabbed me in the arm. "Let's call him now. Enough fucking around with these two. If he's going to try and bury us, then let's hear it from him instead of playing these fucking cat and mouse games."

Turning to look at Stefan, I had to admit he'd really changed from the selfish younger brother who irritated me to no end to someone I knew had my back. It was a nice change.

Cash seemed less impressed with this new Stefan. "This is a delicate matter. We need to tread carefully."

"Talk about shit we're not doing. Cash, this guy thinks he has us by the balls. We need to show him and that brother of his that not only isn't Kane going to jail for a simple bar fight but that Jethro asshole should consider himself lucky Kane didn't fuck him up more for messing with Abbi."

"Thanks, Stefan," I said in near shock.

"We're brothers, Kane. When someone fucks with one of us or the women we love, they fuck with all of us. Right, Cash?"

We both turned to face him, and he sat with his mouth hung open in similar amazement at Stefan's brotherly behavior. "Okay, maybe you're right. I might have been playing this too cautious. It's up to you, though, Kane. You're the one who has to pay in the end if this is a mistake."

The real fear that stirring up the hornet's nest might cause me to have to leave Abbi sooner than I ever wanted to raced through me, but I couldn't just sit around and wait to find out my fate.

"Do it," I said, silently hoping that it wouldn't be just another mistake I'd made.

While I watched Cash dial Mason's number, Stefan said quietly, "Shay told me to say hi. She's worried about you with this. I told her not to worry. If anyone can handle this kind of thing, it's you. But when all this bullshit is over, she'd love it if you and Abbi would come over for dinner when she gets back and settled in."

"I have no idea how you got that woman, Stef, but she's done you a world of good. I can only hope Abbi can do that with me."

"I'll take that as a yes for dinner," he said with a laugh. "And don't worry about this."

"Mason, do you mind if I put you on speaker? Kane and Stefan are here and I'd like them to hear what you have to say." Cash put the conversation on speaker and put down the phone. "Okay, would you mind repeating what you just said?"

"Gentlemen, as I just told Cash, my brother is doing much better and has decided not to press charges. I've already set the wheels in motion so the D.A. won't be pursuing this. You did beat him up pretty well, Kane, so I don't think bumping up the monthly payments to twenty-five grand is out of line. If we're all in agreement with this, I say we put this ugly business behind us and continue with what has been a very successful business relationship on both sides, don't you agree?"

You could have heard a pin drop as we all sat there staring at the phone. Mason didn't sound like he was joking, but charges dropped and no time whatsoever for me? It sounded too good to be true.

Stefan looked at me with big eyes, and Cash

mouthed, "Take it." How could I say no? I'd make up the difference in Mason's monthly cost with my own money so my brothers wouldn't be hurt by my mistake.

"Okay, Mason. It's a deal."

The phone stayed silent for a moment, but then he answered, "Great! Cash, I'll call you later this week and we can iron out the money details. Have a good day, gentlemen."

Cash quickly picked up the phone to express his concern for Jethro's health, but in seconds he hung up and shook his head in disbelief. "I wish I could take credit for what happened there, but I don't think it was me. I have no idea how that came about, though."

"Always looking a gift horse in the mouth," Stefan said. "Who cares how it happened? All that matters is Kane is in the clear and we only have to pay five grand more a month."

"I'll pay that myself," I said, still not sure why Mason and his brother had decided not to do everything in their power to make sure I saw jail time. "You two shouldn't suffer for my mistake. I'm sorry about all this. I thought I'd changed, but when I saw that fuck's hands on Abbi, I lost it. I should have found another way to handle things, though. For that, I'm sorry."

Cash nodded, but Stefan refused to agree. "You didn't do anything wrong, Kane. If someone put their hands on Shay, I'd tear their fucking limbs off. I'm sure even Cash with his three-piece suits and business manners there wouldn't be all about talking to some guy who was manhandling Olivia. This place can be rough, and we're supposed to protect them."

Once again, my younger brother had stunned me with his new attitude. "Thanks, Stefan."

"I'm sure Abbi will be thrilled to hear the news. I don't see any reason we can't have the rest of our meeting tomorrow, so why don't you go tell her?" Cash offered. "Samson can run the top floors for another night. Go celebrate."

"I think I'll take you up on that."

"Good. Tell Abbi we said hi and we look forward to seeing her back here again too," Cash said with a smile. "And at the wedding."

In all the hassle of my beating Jethro and facing prison, I'd forgotten about Cash and Olivia's wedding. "I'm sorry this all happened so close to your big day, Cash. I didn't mean for any of this to end up causing so much trouble."

"Don't worry, Kane. Olivia and I are just happy you're not going to be hearing about our wedding through prison bars."

"Me too because if I have to get dressed up in a tux, so do you," Stefan chimed in. "So if you need to put the beatdown on someone else, wait until after the wedding, if possible. Olivia will never forgive us if Cash doesn't have all his groomsmen."

"Got it."

I turned to walk away and stopped, needing to say more than just thank you. "You guys have been really great through all this. I know we've all worked together here, but it wasn't always that way outside the club. I know that was mostly because of me, but when I needed you both, you were there. I won't forget that."

Cash and Stefan nodded. "You know what Stefan always says. We're brothers, Kane. Not by the same mother, but we all have our father's blood. That means something. You stood by me, and when I couldn't see the truth about Olivia, you could."

"And you were right there to give me advice when I was screwing things up royally with Shay. This is what brothers do. We bust balls, but when push comes to shove, we back each other up."

"Well, thanks. I won't forget this."

I thought back to all those years growing up when my mother worked every day to poison me against Cash and Stefan. All that time I could have had brothers instead of fake enemies. That was all in the past now. For the first time in my life, I felt like I finally had family and love around me.

I could get used to it.

Chapter Seventeen

Abbi

STANDING AT THE KITCHEN SINK, I felt Kane press up against my back and whisper, "I have good news."

I turned around with wet hands and looked up into his blue eyes to see all the worry from the past few days gone from them. "What? Tell me!"

He leaned around me to shut off the water and nuzzled my neck. "I have the night off from work and so do you. And Mason is making sure all the charges are dropped. I don't know what happened, but I'm guessing I have a guardian angel watching over me."

I threw my arms around his neck and pulled him close. "Oh, that's wonderful, Kane! I knew it would work out."

"You were right. I believed in what you said and it all turned out okay. He wants more money each month, but I'll pay that so Cash and Stefan don't have to suffer for what I did."

"Is it a lot?" I wondered, curious to know how

much he planned to make Kane suffer in that way.

Kane shook his head. "No. It wouldn't matter if he wanted every cent I have. I'd pay it if it meant getting to stay with you."

I held him close to me, loving his devotion and hoping he'd understand when he found out what I'd done. Like him, I'd give anything to have him free.

"I have to admit I'm a little surprised he didn't want anything else. A few grand more a month is a small price to pay for beating that brother of his. He didn't say he wanted anything more, though."

I looked up into his eyes and smiled. The stress and fear I'd seen in them for days was gone, replaced by that gentleness they always showed when he was around me. "Sounds like he's all about the money. Those kind of people are the easiest to deal with. They always have a price."

"Enough talk about them. I think I want to lay in bed all night with you, only getting up to get food and drink. How does that sound?"

How it sounded was perfect. The problem was I had to be at Jethro's bar by nine and with Kane home, there would be no way I'd be able to. As much as I hated lying, I needed to find a way to get out of the house so Gemma could take me to work at his bar.

"I heard from Gemma a little while ago. I need to go to her place tonight. She's feeling bad about how things are going with the new guy."

"I thought they were still in the honeymoon phase," he said with a smile.

"Guess not. I'd planned on staying with her until you got out of work."

He nuzzled my neck and whispered, "I'd rather you stay with me, but if she needs you, I can't say no. When do you need to leave?"

"She's not picking me up until eight, so we have some time."

Kane lifted his head and flashed me a sexy grin. "Good. I'm going to have to fit in a night's worth of lovemaking in just a few hours, though."

"I think I can handle that," I said with a giggle, loving how playful he was now that he'd gotten the good news that I'd helped make happen.

Lifting me into his arms, he kissed me and I wrapped my legs around his waist so he could carry me upstairs to the bedroom. We'd christened every room in the house already, so I joked as he laid me onto the bed, "I guess tonight's a bedroom night."

He kept his gaze on me as he slid out of his shirt. Licking his lips, he grinned. "You say that like it's boring."

"Not at all," I answered as I watched him slip off his pants and stand at the edge of the bed naked in front of me with his cock getting harder by the moment. "I don't think any man with a cock piercing can be called boring, Kane."

He flicked his tongue over his lower lip. "We'll get to that later. Right now, I had something else in mind."

Still fully clothed, I lay back and he slowly removed my shirt and shorts, kissing a path from my neck to my breasts. He slid his hands behind my back and removed my bra, tossing it to the side before he turned to take one excited nipple into his mouth. Flicking his tongue over the taut skin, he sent strings of need weaving through me straight to my core.

I ran my hands over his short black hair, holding him to me as he gently bit down on my tender skin. Even now, with his teeth marking me, Kane was gentle. I knew somewhere inside his demons could make that change at any moment, but that fact didn't frighten me.

Only the threat of losing him frightened me, but tonight I'd be at Jethro's bar to make sure that didn't happen. If Kane could protect me, I could do the same for him.

"Angel, everything all right?"

I looked down at him and nodded. "I'm all right."

"Did I do something to scare you? I didn't mean to hurt you, if I did."

"No, you didn't do anything wrong." I cradled his face in my hands. "It's perfect, like always."

Kane slid up my body to kiss my lips, softly and sweetly showing me he loved me as he whispered, "I would never hurt you intentionally, Abbi."

"You never hurt me, Kane. From the moment you came down to see me behind the bar that night, you've been kinder than any man I've ever met. The rest of the world may see the cold man, but I never do."

"I don't care about the rest of the world when I'm with you. All I care about is that you're happy. Tell me you're happy, angel, so while you're at Gemma's tonight I can be happy without you."

Never before had anyone been so able to make my heart ache with just words. I wanted to tell him the truth—that I had made that deal with Mason Jennings because I loved him and would do anything to keep him safe. I couldn't, though. He'd never let me go there to work for that man and then that awful councilman and his disgusting brother would make sure he went to jail.

I couldn't let that happen. For the first time in my life, I had a man who loved and protected me. That kind of man was worth any risk to keep.

"I love you, Kane. I would do anything to make you happy. I've never felt so loved and protected in my life, and that's all because of you."

"I swear I will never let anyone hurt you again. Never."

Kissing him, I ran my hands over his muscular back and whispered in his ear, "I know, and I won't let anyone hurt you either."

He made a contented sigh and slowly slid into me,

stretching my body to accommodate his cock. With every inch, I felt those metal studs drag along my tender skin, like the sweetest torture I never wanted to end. When we were completely joined, I wrapped my legs around his waist and tilted my hips to feel him against my most sensitive spot.

"You feel so fucking good, angel. Like your body was made for my cock."

Rearing back, he left me empty and desperate to feel him fill me again. Scratching my nails down his back, I pushed my hands against his firm ass and whimpered, "Come back to me. I want you so much."

Kane thrust his hips forward and buried himself inside me with a low groan. When he was like this—powerful and sensual—I wouldn't have been able to deny him anything. I adored him. His masculine smell. His throaty voice whispering sexy words as he fucked me. How his body brought me to heights of ecstasy no man had ever even come close to. Those beautiful blue eyes staring down into mine as his every movement aimed to please me.

His hands balled into fists in my hair, and he tugged hard, telling me he was close. Pumping into me, he groaned, "I can't hold back, angel."

"Don't hold back ever," I moaned as I wrapped my arms around his strong shoulders. "I want all of you, Kane."

He came with a rush, filling me until I was sure I

couldn't take any more of him. His mouth plundered mine, nearly taking my breath away as the first strings of my orgasm wound through my body. He made love to me until the very last tremor subsided and all that was left was the two of us in each other's arms.

"I love you, Abbi. You're my everything," he whispered against my cheek as he rolled off me and pulled me close.

Resting my head on his chest, I snuggled up against him and listened to his heart slowly return to its normal beat. "And you're mine. Whatever happens, I want you to always remember that."

Kane said nothing but squeezed me tighter against him. He didn't know what I planned to do for him later that night, but I just prayed he'd understand when he found out.

I KISSED KANE GOODBYE AND slammed Gemma's car door shut, wishing more than anything in the world I didn't have to leave the man I loved to go work at some place run by a pig. As she drove away, she looked over at me and said, "I still think this is a mistake, Abbi."

"Just drive. I have to do this."

"I just think this has the potential to be really bad. That man already grabbed at you. What are you going to do if he does it again?"

I'd thought about that question hundreds of times

since I'd agreed to this deal. The answer was simple. Nothing. I couldn't do a thing if he grabbed me again because if I didn't make Jethro happy, Kane would go to jail.

"I'll be fine. You know me. I'm much tougher than I look."

She gave me a sideways glance and a tiny smile. "By the way, I like this new look on you. Your hair looks cute."

I instinctively tugged on the bottom of my hair but remembered how much Kane loved my look, even this one. "I got rid of the wig after Kane got blood in it the other night."

"He really fucked that guy up, honey. If he finds out where you're going on your nights off, he's going to freak. I wouldn't want to be that guy when he finds out."

"Gemma, he can't find out. If he does and something happens, they'll make him go to jail. I can't let that happen."

"I have to wonder if there was another way, Abbi. I worry someone's going to get hurt."

I worried about that too, but I needed to do this. Kane deserved better than being punished because of who I was. Whatever made men want to hurt me, I had to take responsibility and protect the man I loved.

"Everything will be fine, Gemma. Just promise me that you won't say a thing to Kane, no matter what he does. I need you to promise me that."

She hesitated but finally said in a low voice, "I just don't want you to get hurt, honey."

"Please promise me you won't tell Kane. He can't find out because then he'll go after Jethro again. Don't worry, okay?"

Gemma and I rode along in silence for the rest of the drive to Jethro's bar in Bradenton, she likely worrying about what she saw as my latest huge mistake and me praying to God that my new boss would be too afraid to do anything to me in fear that Kane would kill him the next time.

She stopped in front of a rundown building with peeling white paint and a boarded up window. Not a good sign. Since he had a councilman for a brother who got all that money Kane and his brothers paid him every month, I expected something better than a dive bar. Suddenly, my decision to work for Jethro seemed like a very bad idea. Dive bars didn't get the kind of clientele places like Club X did, and they rarely had the kind of security Kane and his men provided either.

Gemma stared wide-eyed at the building and then turned to look at me in horror. "Abbi, you can't do this! Look at this place! No, no, no—"

I reached out and grabbed her arm to stop her from flailing. "I don't have a choice, so don't make this worse, okay? Just be back for two. And don't worry. I'll be fine."

"You have your phone, right? I want you to call me if anything happens. I'm not kidding, Abbi. If anything at all happens, you need to call me asap. I'll be right near my phone all night."

Leaning over, I held her to calm her nerves. "I'll be fine, sweetie. Remember? I'm tougher than I look."

Gemma hugged me tightly like she didn't want to let me go. "Please be careful, Abbi. I have a bad feeling about this."

"It'll be fine. Really. See you at two." I leaned back and saw the worry etched into her face. I was worried too, but I couldn't let her know or she'd never let me out of that car. "It's all good. Two o'clock, okay?"

Nodding, she knitted her brows, unable to pretend she was okay with any of this. "I'll be here. Just remember you get out of there if anything happens."

I lied and promised her I'd call her if I got into trouble, but I knew I couldn't do that. No matter what Jethro did, I had to deal with it. Kane's freedom depended on it.

THE INSIDE OF JETHRO'S BAR, The Greyhound, looked pretty much like the outside. Dimly lit, it had a feeling like somewhere you knew you weren't supposed to be. The old wooden bar that greeted customers as they walked through the front door looked like it had seen thousands of bar fights. Scratches, pock marks, and gouges marred the dark wood and made the bar look very much like a dive. The black paint on the walls did a poor job of hiding the years of neglect they'd seen, but at least it probably made the blood splatters harder to see.

I took a deep breath in and smelled the disgusting odor of stale nicotine, even though there wasn't an ashtray anywhere in sight. Looking above my head, I saw the source of the stink, ceiling tiles stained a golden brown from all the cigarette smoke they'd absorbed over time.

God, this place was gross, just like its owner.

Only a few men sat on ripped vinyl barstools watching some football game on the small TV at the end of the bar, old guys drinking cheap beer on tap from dirty glasses. I didn't see any women as I looked around, but as I studied my new workplace, I saw Mason come out of a back room.

Slightly less disgusting than his brother, he still fit in perfectly in The Greyhound. Unlike when I saw him sitting behind his desk in his councilman's office in a nice suit and tie, now he wore jeans and a black button down shirt that looked much cheaper. I suspected this was who he really was, no matter what act he put on for the voters.

He approached me and took my hand to shake it. "I'm so glad you decided to come tonight, Abigail. I wasn't sure you'd show up."

Surprised by the tightness of his handshake, I

hurriedly tore my hand from his hold and forced a smile. "I live up to my word, Mr. Jennings. I know you do too. Thank you for that."

"Please, no more Mr. Jennings. Call me Mason. We're going to be spending time together working here, so I think informality is called for."

"Oh, we are? Where's your brother?"

"Jethro is still on the mend, so until he's back up on his feet, I'm taking care of the bar."

A sense of relief washed over me. The news of no Jethro to deal with made me feel much better. Mason might look cheap, but as a public official, he'd know that attacking young women would endanger his political career.

"I'm glad to hear he's doing well. Just tell me what you need me to do and we can get started."

"I think for tonight just getting used to the bar will be good enough. It will get busier in a couple hours, so that should give you enough time to get your bearings."

Nodding, I smiled for real this time and turned to make my way to the bar, but Mason's hand caught my arm. "Oh, and Abigail, while what you're wearing is nice, you're going to have to wear something more revealing from now on."

Just the way he said those words, as if I was just a body to be leered at and nothing more, made my stomach drop. Mason stared at me, waiting for my answer, so I quickly said, "Sure. No problem."

I just hoped it wasn't a sign that everything I feared about working at The Greyhound was beginning to come true.

MASON LEFT ME ALONE FOR the rest of the night, and surprisingly, the patrons of Jethro's bar acted like perfect gentlemen. That they were all nearly three times my age might have been why, but whatever the reason was, they made my first night on the job painless and quite easy. A crowd did come in around ten, so I kept busy for a few hours, but I was always on the lookout for where Mason might be. I saw him speaking to a few men at one of the tables in a dark corner at one point, but when those men left, he returned to the back room.

The few patrons left by two o'clock quietly finished their drinks and pushed their glasses toward the inside of the bar before leaving. I cleaned up my area and wiped down the bar, thinking Mason would come out to say goodbye or something, but he never showed his face again. Even when I called his name, I got no response. As much as I dreaded going into the back room to find him, I couldn't just leave without telling him.

Opening the door, I poked my head in and saw him sitting at a table working on his laptop. I'd been so worried about what I'd find that I let out an audible sigh, and he turned to look at me with an expression that instantly made any relief I'd felt disappear.

"I'm sorry. I didn't meant to intrude. I just wanted to tell you that I cleaned up and it's after two, so I'm going to leave now."

His dark eyes scanned my body from head to toe and back up again before he spoke. "Very nice. I'll see you again on Sunday, right?"

"But state law doesn't let you serve alcohol on Sundays."

"We don't, but the bar is open on Sundays, Abigail, so I expect to see you here at nine sharp. Are we clear?"

I was anything but clear on what I'd be doing at a bar on a Sunday, but as I hesitated to give my answer, Mason stood and walked over to stand in front of me, glowering down at me. "That was our agreement, Abigail. You work here and I make sure Kane stays out of jail. I'd hate to see such a pretty girl heartbroken because her boyfriend had to spend time in prison for his violent tendencies."

This man frightened me, but what choice did I have? "No, no. I understand. I'll be here at nine Sunday. Since I'm not bartending, do I still need to wear different clothes?"

Mason gave me a sinister smile. "Yes, definitely. Let's try something more feminine next time."

"Oh, okay. I'll be here."

I ran out of The Greyhound, desperate to get away from Mason and that look on his face that told me he was who I should be afraid of, not Jethro.

Chapter Eighteen

Kane

I ROLLED OVER AND STRETCHED the sleep from my limbs, loving the feel of Abbi's warm skin touching mine. Of all the days of the week, I loved Sundays the most because we could stay in bed all day if we wanted to, and nobody and nothing interrupted us. Half-asleep, she curled up against my chest, nuzzling her face in the space between my shoulder and ear.

"What time is it?" she mumbled.

"Shhh. Go back to sleep," I whispered, touching my lips to the top of her head. Shimmying against me to find the perfect spot, she moaned softly as I slid my fingertips over the ends of her hair.

Even now that the evidence of that asshole ex's attack on her had faded and her hair had grown in, I still liked to feel the strands so soft against my fingertips. I knew she loved it too. That I had to fight the urge to rip the guy's fucking head off every time I thought about what he'd done didn't matter. All that mattered was when I played with her hair it made Abbi happy.

Only once before in my life had any person brought me such joy as she did. When she was near me, nothing could diminish my happiness. When she wasn't, she was all I thought of. I willingly admitted I was obsessed with her and making her the happiest woman on earth.

I'd lived alone for over a decade, and I'd planned on spending the rest of my life that way. Some people shouldn't be around others. They only end up hurting them. I believed that until Abbi showed up in front of me in Cash's office that night. I'd convinced myself that I'd never want to be close to anyone ever again, but all it took was one look from those gentle blue eyes and I was lost.

I didn't realize how lost until I saw her standing on that stage at The Carousel Club surrounded by all those men ogling her. I felt their eyes on her body and couldn't leave her standing up there for them. She was too gentle, too sweet. Suddenly, all those years alone evaporated and the need to protect her like I should have protected Holly became my only thought.

Abbi stirred in my arms and cooed next to my ear, "I could stay here forever, you know that?"

"Me too. There's nowhere else I'd rather be."

"Can we?" she asked.

"Can we what?"

She kissed my neck and squeezed me to her. "Stay

here forever."

I heard fear in her voice and eased her off me to look into her eyes. I saw the fear in them too. "What's wrong, angel?"

"Nothing. Why?"

"You're afraid of something. What is it?"

"I'm not afraid of anything, Kane. Why would I be? I'm here with you and you take care of me."

Abbi smiled, but there was something underneath her sweet look that troubled me. She was afraid of someone or something.

"Is it me? Are you afraid of me?" Just saying those words made me feel like my world was falling away from me.

Abbi looked up at me and shook her head. "No! Don't ever think that."

"I see the fear in your eyes, Abbi. I guess I wouldn't blame you after what I told you about my past and what you saw me do to Jethro. I would never hurt you, though. I hope you know that."

"No! I don't think that at all. Nobody has ever been as kind to me as you. Why would I be frightened of you?"

Lowering my head, I said, "Because I'm exactly what that judge said I was all those years ago. Violent. Dangerous. A monster."

Abbi lifted my face so I had no choice but to look at her. Now instead of fear I saw sadness in her eyes.

"You're not a monster, Kane. You hit Jethro to protect me. That judge was wrong."

I took her hands so small compared to mine and cradled them in my palms. "I knew it wasn't about protecting you after the first time my fist connected with his face. After that, it was about vengeance. That's the problem, Abbi. I say it's about protecting you, but it's about hurting people to make them pay for hurting you. There's a difference."

She said nothing but looked up at me, searching my face for some answer. I knew what question she wanted to ask.

"Did you do that to Aaron?" she asked, her eyes wide in anticipation of my answer.

I could have lied. She'd never know. I could have pretended someone else finally gave him what he deserved, but I didn't. I brought her hands to my lips and kissed them softly before murmuring the truth against her tender skin.

"Yes."

"Why? You could have gotten in trouble and then they'd take you away," she sobbed quietly.

Reaching out to touch her, I caught the ends of her hair between my fingertips. "That first night I came back to my rooms and saw you lying there in my bed with your hair all cut off. Then you told me he did that to you, and all I wanted to do was hurt him because he hurt you. I found him at his new apartment and did exactly what I did to Jethro. I knew it was wrong, but I'm not sorry."

Abbi stared at me but said nothing. I knew what she must be thinking. "You probably think I'm that monster now."

She pressed her lips to mine in a kiss that made my heart swell with joy. "Kane, I would never think you're a monster for that."

"I can't help that I want to hurt people who hurt you. This is who I am."

Abbi took a deep breath. "Aaron beat me over and over for months. One time I couldn't see out of my right eye for nearly a week. He tried to strangle me one time because I forgot to buy eggs. He pounded my head into the kitchen wall that time and I blacked out. I woke up alone covered in the raw bacon I was getting ready to cook when he went after me. I don't care what happens to him. I care about you being taken away, though."

I pulled her close to me and whispered, "I'm not going anywhere, angel."

"I can't live without you, Kane. If they took you away, I don't know what I'd do."

Stroking her hair, I tried to make her feel better. "Shhh. Nobody's taking me anywhere. Mason got the charges dropped. I'm staying right here with you."

We lay there with her face buried in my chest as I thought of how real the threat of me leaving had been.

For the first time in my life, I wanted to stay somewhere, but my demons had other thoughts. They wanted to make anyone who even touched the woman I loved feel the pain of my fists.

Abbi lifted her head and stared up at me. "I want you to promise me something."

Smoothing the stray hairs from her face, I nodded. "Anything."

"Promise me you won't ever leave. Promise me you won't do anything to make them take you away."

I knew what she was asking. She wanted me to say I wouldn't protect her if it meant I might go to jail. I couldn't make that promise.

"I can't. If someone hurts the woman I love, I'm going to do everything in my power to make sure they can't do it again, Abbi."

She pushed herself away from me and stood up from the bed. "Then you're going to make sure they take you away from me! You can't love me like you say you do and then risk having to leave."

I couldn't stand the pain in her voice. It was like it had my heart and was squeezing with every word. "I protect the woman I love. I have to. I didn't do that once and she suffered for it. I won't let that happen again."

"I'm not her, Kane. I need you with me, not in prison because you wanted to beat the fuck out of some guy because he touched me!"

"I can't change who I am, angel."

"So you don't care that you're going to leave me alone if you do that again?"

"I fucking care, Abbi. The thought of being without you makes me feel like someone's ripping my heart out. Don't think that I don't care. Don't ever think that."

Leaning on the bed, she took my hand in hers. "Then don't do it. Don't leave me here all alone."

"I can't fight the demons inside me when someone does something to hurt you. Don't ask me to. I can't."

"Baby, what kind of demons are these? How can you talk about them trying to control you when we make love and in the same way talk about them making you hurt people? Do you want to hurt me?"

"No. Never. I would never hurt you, Abbi. Never."

She climbed onto the bed and crawled over to sit next to me. "Then what are they?"

"I don't know. They've always been inside me. From the minute I met you, they made me want you, even though I worried I'd hurt you. They make me selfish sometimes. Other times they make me feel anger so completely I can't stop myself from hitting someone."

"They never want you to hit me?"

Shaking my head, I said quietly, "No. With you, it's something different. I can't explain it. From the first night I saw you, you were all I could think of. I tried, Abbi. I really did. I knew what would happen if I gave in and pursued anything with you. This is why I've stayed alone all these years. No woman wants a man who can't control himself."

Abbi took me in her arms and kissed me. "That's not true. I want him. I want the man who fights for me, who protects me. I want the man who's afraid to lose control with me even though I'm not afraid of that."

"I wish you would be afraid, angel, although it wouldn't make a difference now. You're inside me, part of me. I couldn't give you up now even if I had to. It would be like losing an arm or a leg."

"Kane, I love you. I love every part of you, including whatever demons you have inside you. I just want you to promise you won't do anything to get yourself in trouble over me. Why is that so hard for you?"

"Because I didn't do it for Holly and she paid the ultimate price. I'll never make that mistake again. If it means I go back to jail, as long as I know I stopped someone from hurting you, I can do whatever time they force me to do. She suffered because of me. I won't let that happen to you. I love you too much."

She tilted her head back and looked up at me with tears in her eyes. "Why me? Why did you have to pick me, someone who always seems to make people angry so they want to hurt me? If only you picked a Gemma or an Olivia, none of this would be happening. You'd be happy and never have to worry that someone's going to do something to make your demons come out."

"I didn't pick you, angel. You showed up one night and my heart never had a chance."

"If I never let Gemma talk me into that interview, you'd be safe and happy."

I kissed her forehead and shook my head. "No part of my life at Club X has ever been safe. Every night I run the risk of being led away in handcuffs. And I wasn't happy. I wasn't really living. It was more just existing."

"Will it always be like this? I know you don't like to think about the future, but it's what makes me happy."

"Then it makes me happy, angel. I don't know what's going to happen in the future. All I know is that I'm going to do everything in my power to make sure every morning you have a reason to give me one of your beautiful smiles and every night you have one of those smiles on your face as you drift off to sleep in my arms."

Abbi was quiet for a long time, but then she said sweetly, "You never talk about your happiness. Why? I want to know what to do to make you happier."

"Just having you by my side makes me the happiest man in the world. I have everything else I could want. Money, possessions, a successful business. Everything people think makes a person happy. But I'd willingly give up all of it as long as I know when I reach down to take your hand in mine it will always be there."

She weaved her fingers through mine and lifted my hand to her lips. "I will always be there to take your hand. Always, Kane."

"Then no matter what happens, we'll be good."

I believed that, but I knew something was scaring Abbi. I didn't know what it was, but when I found out, whoever was behind it better hope she didn't get hurt.

ABBI KISSED ME GOODBYE AT seven o'clock and promised to be home as soon as Gemma stopped crying, but I still saw fear in her eyes, no matter how many times she told me she was fine. I wanted to believe she'd told me the truth. My gut told me otherwise, though.

I settled in for a night at home with Angel, who seemed content to wrap herself around my right ankle as I sat on the couch to watch TV. Flipping through the channels proved to be a waste of time, and I closed my eyes intending to think about what to surprise Abbi with when she came home.

Instead, my mind drifted back in time.

"Tell me again how we're going to move to California and live on the beach. Can we really do it, Kane?" Holly asked as she squeezed my hand tightly in excitement.

I pulled her away from her front porch and toward the

street. "Shhh. We don't want anyone to find out or they'll try to stop us."

"I don't care what my parents say. Your mother's okay with you leaving, isn't she?"

"My mother doesn't care one way or another, but your father will come after me with a bat if he finds out, Holly."

She broke away from my hold and ran down the street giggling, her long brown hair flying behind her. "I don't care who finds out, Kane Jackson. We're going to be beach bums and live happily ever after in sunny California!"

I caught up with her as we hit the intersection and took her hand in mine. I loved when she was like this— light and sweet to my darkness and anger. Eight months had gone by since that first day I saw her at that ice cream shop, and every day I loved her more than the day before.

"Where are you running off to?" I asked with a smile.

"I want to take you to see something I found the other day. It's behind Center Street."

I followed her to an alleyway that led to where her surprise for me was and saw a Harley parked in front of someone's house. A black soft tail, it was a beautiful bike just like the one I'd always dreamed of having someday. Since my mother and I were poor, someday would be a long ways off, but I could dream.

She wrapped her arms around my waist and rested her head on my chest. "You'd look so good on that bike, Kane. We could ride out cross country on it."

"We could, but I think we're going to have to find another way."

She gazed up at me with longing in her soft brown eyes. "Someday we'll have one of those, won't we?"

"Someday, I promise."

I would have promised her I'd take the stars out of the sky for her. All she had to do was ask. Holly gave me something I'd never had before. Love. For that, I'd do anything to make her happy. When we finally left Tampa after she graduated, we'd get married and spend the rest of our lives together. After a life filled with hatred, I'd found the happiness I'd always dreamed of.

"Let's go down to the beach tonight. Melly said they're having a party near her house."

As much as I didn't want to spend the night drinking on the beach, I smiled and nodded my agreement. That's what I was supposed to do—make her happy—so that's what I did. Her happiness gave me mine.

My mind raced through memories of her like a painful movie made just for me. The birthday she got me my lip piercing. The warm summer night in my bedroom when I took her virginity and gave her mine. The feeling of her in my arms. The sound of her laughter. The smell of vanilla in her hair when she cuddled close to me and laid her head on my chest. The taste of her on my lips.

I knew how to control this walk down memory

lane. I'd done it for years. But tonight my demons had different ideas and the one memory I'd desperately tried to forget came raging back like it was just yesterday.

We turned and walked back into the alleyway and got halfway through when I saw four men coming toward us. Without saying a word, I pulled Holly close to me and reached down to hold her hand. She continued to talk about how great it would be if we had that bike when we left, dreaming out loud of the fun we'd have riding off with her arms around me into the sunset to our new life together.

The men passed us without a word, but I saw one nudge the man next to him in the side and every muscle in my body tensed. Quickly, I began walking toward the street just half a block away, pulling Holly's arm to help her catch up with my pace. If we could reach the corner, it wouldn't just be us against them. I might be able to take two of them, but four never and while I fought off the first two men, the other two could have their hands on Holly.

"Where you goin so quickly?" one yelled after us, but I kept walking, whispering to her, "Don't look back. Just keep walking."

"Kane, what's happening?" she asked in a terrified voice.

"Nothing. Just keep walking."

"Hey, come back here!"

I walked faster, but they caught up with us. Reaching into my pocket, I pulled out all the money I had. "Take it. It's all I have. Just let us go."

Holly's hand shook in terror against mine. I squeezed it gently to let her know I'd protect her no matter what they tried to do.

The one who looked the youngest with short hair and wide eyes grabbed the money from my hand, but the one closest to Holly spoke up and I knew it wasn't money they wanted.

"What's your name, sweetheart? You're a pretty thing."

"Please, let us go," she begged in a terrified voice. "We just want to leave."

He reached out to touch her long brown hair, but she cowered next to me, angering him. Before we could get away, they descended upon us, yanking Holly away from my side. I lunged toward the two men grabbing at her, but two sets of hands pulled me backwards and held me as her cries flooded my ears.

"Let me go! Don't fucking touch her!" I yelled as he held me down on the ground.

"We're gunna do more than just touch her, loverboy."

I screamed threats and thrashed against their hold as I listened to Holly cry and sob my name, but I was powerless to do anything. All I could do was watch as their hands tore at her clothing, ripping her shorts and T-shirt off her body. Then one held her down as the biggest one whipped out his hard dick and began stroking it. The man holding her ripped off her underwear and laughed as he let his friend know, "She's ready for ya! Go at it!"

Holly let out a blood curdling shriek, and as I watched the man lean over her body, I struggled to get free of the hands holding me before he hurt her. Two faces above me grinned and laughed as I watched that man thrust his hips forward. Holly's cries for me to help never stopped the entire time he raped her. I didn't know how long I fought against their hold, but at some point they began hitting me to stop me from fighting. It didn't matter. Nothing they did could drown out the horrible sound of them raping her.

By the time he'd finished with her, I could only see out of one eye and my mouth was full of blood. Everything seemed to spin around my head, and I felt a boot kick me in the stomach as they walked away laughing. I slowly pulled myself over to where Holly lay and saw a stream of blood slowly running down over the inside of her thigh.

"Holly?"

She lay there sobbing as I pulled her close to me, her body heaving against mine. The spinning around me grew darker, and then I felt myself slipping away.

I woke with a start, cold sweat running down my face and my hands clenched in rage like they always were when I thought about that night. Quickly, I scrambled to find the time and saw by my watch that I'd only been asleep for a little while.

9:14. I didn't know why, but something inside me told me I needed to speak to Abbi right at that moment. Grabbing my phone, I called her but her phone just rang until the voicemail kicked in. I tried three more times and got nothing. My mind racing with fear I knew was unreasonable, I dialed Gemma's number and hers just rang too.

They could be watching a movie. Or they could be doing each other's makeup or whatever else women did when they hung out to get over some guy. I had no idea what they could be doing, but that they weren't answering their phones bothered me.

I tried Abbi's phone again and got the same result. Gemma's rang three times and I was about to give up when I heard her say tentatively, "Hello?"

"Gemma, it's Kane. I need to talk to Abbi. Put her on the phone."

"She's busy right now, but I'll have her call you as soon as she's done."

"Now, Gemma. I want to talk to her now."

"She can't, Kane, but I promise she'll call you as soon as she can."

Suddenly, my chest felt empty and my mind whirled with a thousand reasons why Abbi couldn't talk to me. I knew Gemma. She was lying for her friend.

"I'm coming over then."

Before she could give me some excuse, I hung up and grabbed my keys. Gemma's house wasn't too far, so I'd be there in a few minutes and find out what the fuck was going on.

By the time I pulled up, I knew something was wrong. I could feel it in my gut. My palms were already so damp from gripping the steering wheel so tightly that when I tried to grip Gemma's front doorknob, my fingers slid right off.

Frustrated, I pounded on the door. "Abbi! What's going on?" I yelled.

Gemma flung the door open and stared up at me with fear. "Kane, come in."

"Where's Abbi? I want to see her."

"She's not here. Sit down and I'll explain."

I looked around Gemma's living room and saw no evidence that Abbi had been there that night. "What the fuck is going on here? Why did she lie to me and say she was coming here?"

"She's got herself into something I don't think she knows how to get out of. She couldn't tell you because she didn't want to risk you getting in trouble. I need you to be calm, okay?"

"I need you to tell me what's going on right the fuck now or this level of calm I've got going on is going to vanish fucking quickly, Gemma."

"Please sit down and take a breath. I can't talk to you when you're like this."

I did as she asked and tried to keep it together, even though I was this close to exploding. "All right. I'm sitting. Now tell me what's going on and where Abbi is."

"She's at a bar called The Greyhound. She's bartending there."

"Why?"

She had no reason to bartend anywhere. She made enough money to live on at my club, and I took care of everything else. Why would she need to bartend at some bar named The Greyhound?

"She made a deal so you'd stay out of jail. The Greyhound is that guy's bar, the one you beat up. Whenever she has a night off from the club, they expect her to bartend there. She had her first shift the other night and she said everything was fine. The guy wasn't even there. Only his brother was, the councilman? It's a dive bar, but she doesn't think it'll be bad and if it keeps you out of jail, she's willing to do it."

My heartbeat pounded in my ears as I listened to Gemma explain how the woman I loved was sneaking off to bartend at some dive bar to keep me safe. Everything inside me said to go to her and take her out of that place.

"So this is why Mason was so willing to get the charges dropped. How could you let her go there, Gemma? Jesus Christ, that guy grabbed her when she was dancing. What made you think he wouldn't do that again?"

I looked at Gemma in disgust as she tried to excuse

her behavior.

"I couldn't stop her, Kane. She would have found a way there with or without my help. I wanted to make sure I knew where the place was so I could help if she got into trouble. She's doing this because she loves you and is terrified of losing you. I couldn't say no."

Then it dawned on me. It was Sunday. State law didn't allow alcohol served in bars and clubs on Sunday. "Why is she there tonight? Bars aren't allowed to be open on Sunday."

Gemma's eyes flashed her fear. "I don't know. I didn't realize bars couldn't serve on Sundays. We have to get there in case something bad is happening, Kane!"

"You've already done enough. I'll go by myself."

I turned to leave, but Gemma grabbed my arm and wouldn't let me go. "Please, Kane! I need to know she's okay."

I didn't have time to argue with her. Shrugging, I yanked my arm from her grip and barked, "Fine. Let's go."

All that ran through my head as I stormed out to my car was God help Mason and Jethro if Abbi was hurt. This time, there'd be no one who could stop me.

Chapter Nineteen

Abbi

I PUSHED OPEN THE FRONT door of The Greyhound to find the bar dark and not a soul inside. The door had been unlocked and Mason had been very clear about how he expected me to be here tonight, so I held out my cell phone in front of me to light my way through the building, wondering why he'd demand I show up if the bar wasn't even open.

My phone showed five missed calls, and as I swiped the screen, I saw Kane had called me four times and Gemma had called me right after him. Something was wrong. I quickly dialed her number and continued to walk toward the bar with my one hand out in front of me to feel my way.

She answered her phone on the first ring, and instantly I heard the panic in her voice. "Abbi, are you okay?"

"I'm fine. There doesn't seem to be anyone here. It's a Sunday and Mason said I had to work, but I can't find him or anyone else. The bar was dark when I walked in. Why did you call?"

There was silence for a long moment and then I heard Kane's voice come through loud and clear, the hurt in it shooting straight to my heart. "Angel, you don't have to do this. Get out of there now. We'll be there in a few minutes. I want you to stay on the phone with me and keep talking. Do you understand?"

"Oh, Kane, you can't come here. I have to do this or Mason and Jethro will make sure you go to jail for what you did. Don't be mad at me. Please. I couldn't sit back and do nothing. I had to make sure you were safe."

"I love you for that, baby, but there's no good reason why they'd want you there tonight. The bar can't open, so whatever you're doing there isn't bartending. Get out now and wait in the parking lot, and if they come after you, run as fast as you can and stay on the road. I'm driving there right now. Abbi, do as I say."

I felt the bar beneath my fingertips and stopped walking. "I'm okay, Kane. I have to do this. You protected me, so I have to protect you."

"Angel, get out of there now! Did you hear me? Leave now. We're almost there."

Something touched my sleeve, and I turned to see Mason looking at me with a stare that instantly made a shiver run down my spine. I stood stunned that he'd suddenly appeared, my brain unable to form words. I heard Kane telling me over and over to get out of there, but Mason took my phone and ended the call.

"Time to get to work, Abigail."

"Kane found out and he's coming here. I told him I was okay, but he's still coming," I explained in a shaky voice. "I know when he sees everything's on the up and up, he'll be fine. Just give him a chance."

Mason smiled that vicious smile I saw when I was leaving last time and shook his head. "I've got something else in mind. Time to go."

He pulled me toward the back room as I struggled to get free of his hold. Nearly frozen in fear, I tried to think of some way to escape, but it was so dark and I couldn't see anything in front of me.

"Mason, let me go! You're hurting me! What are you doing?"

My arm burned where his fingers dug into my skin, but he refused to answer me. Instead, he walked faster toward the back room, but why? We quickly reached it, but no one waited for us and we passed through and out a door that led to a parking lot behind the building.

Mason yanked hard on my arm to pull me toward a car, and I cried out from the pain. "Let me go! Where are you taking me?"

"Get in and shut your mouth or this will hurt for much longer," he snapped.

"No!"

The back of his hand skidded across my cheek, and

for a moment my skin felt like it was on fire. My vision blurred, and he took advantage of my confusion to stuff me into the backseat of the car. As I tried to shake off the pain jutting up into my temple, he tied my hands together with a cord and covered my mouth with duct tape.

"One more sound out of you and that shot you just took will be nothing compared to what I do to you. Keep quiet!"

He jumped in the driver's seat and started the car, flooring it out of the parking lot. I rolled around on the leather seat and worked to pull myself up to look out the window, praying that I'd see Kane's car and somehow make him know Mason was taking me away somewhere. No streetlights lit up the road from the bar, so hopefully it would be easy to see a car coming at us, but Mason was driving so fast I was afraid I'd miss him.

Suddenly, I saw a pair of lights coming at us and began to flail my arms in the hope that whoever was driving would see me and come after us. As the car got closer, I recognized it as Kane's and banged on the window, knowing that he couldn't hear me but desperate to have any chance to get his attention.

Driving even faster than Mason, Kane passed us without ever looking at the car. Devastated, I slumped against the seat and screamed his name. All it did was anger Mason, and as he raced down the road, he reached his arm around to punch me across the face.

Everything blurred and then it went dark as I fell down onto the floor.

I opened my eyes and the pain in my cheek came raging back, making me wince in agony. My mouth hurt, I guessed from when he tore the duct tape off, but my hands were still bound together. Bright lights shined above me, and I couldn't see anything past them. I had no idea where I was or even if there were any people around me.

Mason's voice next to my head told me at least he was there, and I turned to look at him. "Where am I?"

"Where I want you. I told you not to talk, Abigail. You should have listened. You ask too many questions."

Just like every other man who'd hit me, Mason had his excuses ready. I hung my head and closed my eyes as the memory of Kane passing us on the road and never seeing me flooded back into my mind.

Whatever was about to happen to me, he wouldn't be able to protect me.

Tears began to roll down my swollen cheeks. I'd done this to myself, as usual. God, I was so stupid! Like with every man who ever beat me, I thought everything would work out and I could handle things and Mason would let me work at The Greyhound in exchange for Kane's freedom.

I had to wonder if I didn't deserve the pain for being so naïve.

"I want you to feel what my brother felt because of you, a common whore. You think you should be able to look like you do and dance for men and they shouldn't be able to touch you without getting a beating from your boyfriend there? What makes you so special?"

"Kane was only trying to protect me," I said quietly, sure he'd knock my teeth down my throat if I said much more.

"That boyfriend of yours should have remembered what he was. Ex-cons don't get to protect their sluts."

I looked away from Mason's angry gaze so I didn't defend myself. I wasn't a whore or a slut. I never sold my body for any money or gift. But he grabbed my face and jerked it back to make me look at him, and I saw the disgust in his eyes.

"Why do you hate me so much?"

"You make me sick. That club you work at makes me sick. Women should be chaste and innocent. You look like you're innocent, but it's all an act. Beneath the big blue eyes and blond hair is a cheap whore. You're the worst kind of female. You make men think they're getting one thing, but it's all a façade."

I knew I shouldn't, but I pressed him for more details, hoping that if I kept him talking he might not do whatever he planned to do to me. "But you're a member of Club X. If you hate us so much, why did you join?"

"You ask too many fucking questions, Abigail."

He glowered down at me and cocked his arm back to hit me. Squeezing my eyes tight, I braced for the pain of his thick knuckles smashing into my face but nothing happened. I waited for what seemed like forever, listening to him breathe just above me, but he didn't move. Finally, I slowly opened my eyes to see him staring at me like he was studying something about my face.

"You remind me of someone, Abigail. Do you want to know who that someone is?"

His voice sounded distant, frightening me more than his fist ever could. Nodding, I whispered, "Yes?"

Mason smoothed the hair from my face and ran the tip of his forefinger from my temple to my chin. His eyes had a crazy look in them. "You remind me of my wife."

As the words came out of his mouth, I wondered why he'd want to beat me if I reminded him of someone he loved, but then he continued and I began to understand why I was there.

"My wife was beautiful, like you Abigail, and innocent. So pure that I could look into her eyes and know I was the luckiest man in the world. I bet Kane thinks that when he looks into those big blue eyes of yours, doesn't he? The eyes are supposed to be the windows to the soul. At least that's what they say. Did you know that?"

"Yes."

"But that's not true. The eyes aren't the windows to the soul. They lie," he hissed. "My wife's eyes lied. She wasn't pure and innocent like she made me believe. She was tainted and corrupted. Like you are. I see in your eyes the foulness in your soul. You're foul, Abigail. It's clear as day right there in those eyes of yours."

As he spoke, his face twisted in a horrifying expression full of hatred and disgust. I moved my head to look away, but he forced me to turn back toward him.

"Don't you fucking look away, you whore! Don't you look away from me like you're better than I am! I'm a goddamned councilman! People respect me. They believe me. People don't respect you. You're garbage. You're a dancer who tempts men with your body and the promise of innocence long thrown away!"

I couldn't stop myself from crying at his words. I'd heard every one of them before from every man who'd told me he'd loved me and then used his fists to show me just how much I meant to him. Mason was going to beat me like Kane did to his brother, but he wasn't going to stop until he'd gotten his vengeance for not only Jethro but whatever his wife had done to hurt him so much.

With his thumb, he wiped my tears away, and I dragged my gaze up to see sadness in his eyes. "Please don't do this, Mason. Please. I'm begging you. I'll do whatever you want, but please don't kill me."

He began to pace back and forth, looking up to the ceiling as he walked. "I gave my wife her birthday present the night she left me. A beautiful diamond necklace I'd had specially made to show her how much I loved her. I gave it to her and three hours and fifteen minutes later she told me she was leaving me for someone she'd met online. We'd been married for ten years and she left me for some guy with a house in Jacksonville and a boat."

I wasn't even sure Mason was talking to me anymore. He didn't seem to notice I was even in the room with him as he recounted his wife's cheating and then leaving him. Silently, I prayed to God to help Kane find me before Mason remembered why he'd brought me there and killed me.

"I gave her everything, and she left me for a fucking carpenter!" he bellowed into the room, still looking up at the ceiling.

Closing my eyes, I prayed to God to rescue me from this nightmare. *God, please save me. Please help Kane find me here and save me.*

"I bet you wouldn't do that to me, would you, Abigail?" Mason asked.

My eyes flew open to see him standing in front of me. Trembling in fear, I said quietly, "No. I would never do that to anyone."

"See? I knew that," he said as he nodded his head,

his demeanor back to the kind way he'd been when I'd met with him in his office. "I can see that in you. You're not like her, Abigail."

"Why do you call me Abigail?" I asked without thinking, immediately regretting my question. Asking questions was what always got me in trouble. I waited for his face to grow dark with anger and for him to pull his fist back to hit me, but he just smiled like I'd said something that made him happy.

"Her name was Abigail. Do you know the moment you entered my office that day you reminded me of her. My Abigail. Sweet and innocent, you wanted to protect the man you loved, but I see you for who you really are. You're just like her."

In a flash, his expression morphed into one full of rage. I shook my head over and over as I tried to convince him I wasn't like the woman who'd broken his heart. "No! No! I'm not like her. I would never do that to you. I would never hurt someone like that!"

Out of the corner of my eye, I saw something move, but instantly my attention was on Mason's fist crashing into my face. His knuckles smashed right into my eye, sending my head flying back into the wall behind me. Pain shot through my skull from all sides, and in seconds another punch landed just lower on my cheek, sending my head rolling on my shoulders.

I struggled to keep my eyes open. He cocked his arm back and then from the left side of the room someone launched at Mason and slammed him to the ground. Through my blurry vision I saw the man begin to beat him, repeatedly smashing his head on the floor. As I tried to make out who the man was, I felt hands untie the cord on my wrists.

Turning my head, I saw Gemma standing beside me. "Honey, we need to get out of here. Follow me."

Suddenly, the scene in front of me made sense. I looked again and saw Kane pummeling Mason's face, his fists smashing his nose as blood sprayed everywhere. My hands freed, I tried to stand, but my legs buckled. Gemma grabbed me from behind to pull me out of harm's way, but I fought her, not wanting to leave without Kane.

"No! I won't leave him here!" I screamed when she wrapped her arms around me and tried to move me toward the door.

"Abbi, we need to get out of here. Kane can handle himself. At least let me get you to the car."

"No, I don't want to go," I sobbed as Mason gained the upper hand on top of Kane and began to land punches to his face.

Gemma shook her head. "No. I won't leave you here! Come on. He'll be okay."

Much stronger, she forced me out of the room, even as I screamed for Kane. By the time we reached the car, I was crying uncontrollably, sure he was hurt and needing me while I was outside saving my own skin.

"Abbi, let me look at your face." She touched my cheek with her sleeve, making me recoil back in pain. "Oh honey, I'm sorry. I didn't meant to hurt you. He hit you bad. You're all bloody, sweetie. I need to clean you off."

I sagged against Kane's Mustang and watched for him to come out. "Gemma, I need to go back in there. I can't let him get hurt. You have to let me go."

She shook her head violently. "No way. He made me promise I'd get you out of there as soon as I could. You have to trust him. He can handle himself."

The tears flowed down my face and I tried to push my way past her, but it was no use. She was just too strong for me. Defeated and sure something terrible was happening inside the house, I buried my face in my hands and sobbed. If Kane got hurt because of me, I would never forgive myself.

Gemma hugged me and rubbed my back to soothe me, but nothing would make me happy until I saw Kane come out of that house safe and sound. Burying my face in her shoulder, I cried, "What if something happens to him? We can't leave him in there. We have to do something."

"Don't worry, honey. Everything's going to be fine. I know it will."

I pulled away from her and looked into her eyes to see she was as worried as I was. "How can you say that?

No matter what happens, it won't be fine. Kane is going to get in trouble again, and there's nothing that can be done to stop that. And that's if he doesn't get himself killed in there. Mason is crazy, Gemma. He thought I was his ex-wife who left him and he wanted to punish me for that."

"I thought he did this because of what Kane did to his brother."

"I thought so too. He said he wanted me to feel the pain Jethro felt when Kane beat him, but then he started talking about how I reminded him of his wife whose name was Abigail too. He's crazy! Kane can't fight that."

"It's going to be okay, Abbi. I don't know how, but it will be. All we have to do is wait for Kane like he made me promise and it will all be okay."

I closed my eyes to pray to God again. He'd saved me. Now I needed him to save the man I loved. *Please don't let him get hurt. Please. I love him. Please, God.*

Just then, I heard a noise that sounded like a gunshot go off somewhere inside the house. Had someone else come to help Mason and shot Kane? My blood ran cold at the idea of him on the floor bleeding to death alone. I pushed past Gemma, who stood trying to figure out where the gunshot had come from, and ran back toward the house.

I needed to see Kane, no matter what happened.

My legs buckled under me at the sound of a second

gunshot and then everything went black as I fell to the ground, my mind filled with one terrible thought.

Kane was dead.

Chapter Twenty

Abbi

K*ANE'S LIPS PRESSED GENTLY AGAINST my forehead, and he whispered, "Everything will be okay, angel. I'm here. You're safe now, Abbi."*

He lifted me into his arms and carried me, but I didn't know where we were going. He yelled something about a car—the words seemed to get lost in my head, rattling around and crashing into one another as I tried to understand what was happening.

I felt hands touch my face and looked up to see Gemma crying as she stroked my forehead. I opened my mouth to tell her it was okay and she shouldn't cry, but the words didn't come out, instead trapped with all of Kane's words in my mind.

I had the sensation of going fast one minute and then being still the next. I thought I was in Kane's Mustang, but I couldn't be sure. From somewhere far away, I heard voices and turned to see a woman and a man looking down at me. I recognized Cash, but I didn't know the woman. She reminded me of my mother, her dark eyes staring down at me with sadness.

Slowly, the words around me became clearer. Someone was dead. Who? I frantically searched the faces around me for Kane's, but I couldn't find him. He'd just told me everything would be okay. Had I dreamed that? Or was I dreaming this?

Struggling to speak, I croaked out the only word I knew to say. "Kane?"

I watched the looks on the faces around me for any sign he'd been hurt. They didn't seem to react to his name. Did that mean he was okay?

Gemma kissed my cheek. "Kane's right here, honey."

And then he appeared, smiling down at me with one of those genuine smiles that went all the way to his eyes. Everything would be okay if he was happy. He cradled my face in his hands and brushed the pads of his thumbs over the tender skin of my cheeks. I winced and saw the happiness leave his eyes as he moved his hands away.

"No," I pleaded as I raised my hands to cover his. "Don't move them. I don't care if it hurts. As long as you're holding me, I'm okay."

"I have to go now, Abbi. It's too risky for me to stay here with you. Gemma and Alexandria will make sure you're safe and taken care of for a while."

Terror raced through me as the memory of Kane being taken away in handcuffs flooded my mind. "No! Don't go, Kane. Please don't go."

He kissed me softly on the lips and then placed a kiss

on the tip of my nose, finally looking down into my eyes with a look so full of pain my heart felt like it was being broken in two. "I have to, angel. Just for a little while. As soon as everything's cleared up, I'll come get you. Until then, don't forget how much I love you."

Tears filled my eyes. "How long will you be gone?"

"I don't know, but as soon as I can get back to you, I'll be here. I promise."

"Promise me you'll come back? You won't forget me because of all the trouble I've been?"

"Oh, baby, you've never been trouble. As soon as I can, I'll come get you and we can go back to living in that little house of ours. You, me, and Angel."

Somebody warned him that he needed to leave and he kissed me one last time. Pulling away, he tried to smile, to put on a good face for me, but I saw the sadness in those dark blue eyes.

"I love you, Kane."

"I love you, my angel."

He stood and hurried away, leaving me feeling lost and alone. I closed my eyes, wishing I could shut out the rest of the world until he came back to me.

The sound of purring next to my ear woke me up, and I slowly opened my eyes to see Angel sitting on my chest and nuzzling my neck. Her adorable little face made me smile, and as soon as I did I felt the all too familiar pain of a beating shoot up through my cheek.

Rubbing my nose on hers, I felt the cold wetness on my skin.

"Good morning, Angel."

She licked my cheek and bounded off the bed to scamper away through the doorway out to the hall. Fully awake, I looked around at the room I was in and realized I wasn't at home. Where was I?

"Kane? Kane!"

I heard footsteps coming quickly down the hall and then saw Gemma standing in front of me. But I wasn't in her apartment either. Where was I?

"Where's Kane?"

"Good morning, honey. How are you feeling?"

"I'd be feeling a whole lot better if you'd answer my question. Where's Kane? Why isn't he here? Where am I?"

Gemma sat down on the bed next to me and took my hand in hers. I knew by her expression that what she was about to say wouldn't be good. "I'm glad you're awake. You've been asleep for a while, honey."

"Please tell me what's going on."

"Okay. You're at Cassian and Stefan's mother's house on Anna Maria Island. We brought you here after what happened with Mason. Kane's not here, though. He's in Tampa."

"Why? Why isn't he here with me? Gemma, what aren't you telling me?"

"Honey, he can't be here right now. But when he

can, he'll come for you. Don't worry."

I sat up in bed and swung my legs off the side. "If he can't be here with me, I'm going to him. Get me my clothes, please."

"No, you can't go to him now, Abbi. It's not safe. Olivia!"

"What do you mean it's not safe and why is Olivia here too?" I asked as I looked around the room for any of my clothes.

Olivia appeared in the doorway full of smiles like she was happy to see me. Since we'd never really spoken, I couldn't imagine why.

"Hey, you. I'm glad to see you're up. Are you hungry?"

"I want to know where Kane is. Gemma doesn't seem to want to tell me, so I need you to right now."

"Okay, I'll tell you, but I need you to get back into bed. You're still pretty banged up and the doctor said you might have a concussion, so you need to rest."

I didn't want to get back into bed, but if that's what I was going to take to get some answers, I'd do it. To be honest, my head was beginning to feel like the room was spinning. "Fine. Just tell me where Kane is and what's going on."

As Gemma made sure the sheets and blanket were neatly tucked in against me, Olivia sat in a chair on the other side of the bed and began to explain everything. I lay there staring at the pale pink walls all around me trying to absorb the story she told.

"Kane is still in Tampa, Abbi. He's back living in his rooms at the club. He's been there since the night we brought you here."

"How long ago was that?" I asked as I watched the white ceiling fan above me slowly turn.

"Four days ago. You've been in and out for that time, but Alexandria's doctor says you're going to be okay."

I turned to look at Olivia, confused. "Who is Alexandria?"

"Cash's mother. It's her beach house we're at on Anna Maria Island. We brought you here because we needed to hide you away while the police investigate Mason's death."

"Mason's murder?"

Gemma tucked my hair behind my ear and said quietly, "He had a gun. He'd intended to kill you, and when he and Kane fought, the gun accidentally went off."

A memory of gunshots at the house Mason took me to flashed through my mind. But I'd heard more than one shot. Then a spike of fear raced through me.

"Did Kane get shot too?"

"No," Gemma said with a smile, not knowing her answer created more questions than comfort in me.

"The police are treating Kane as the number one suspect in what they're calling a murder," Olivia said quietly.

All those horrible feelings of losing him I'd experienced that night when he was arrested and led away came back with a vengeance, and I began to cry, wishing I never woke up to hear all this. Kane was going to jail because he wanted to save me, and there was nothing I could do about it this time.

"Abbi, it's going to be okay. Don't cry."

I looked at Gemma and shook my head, not believing what she was saying. "How could it be okay? Kane killed someone to save me and now he's going to go to jail. Nothing will ever be okay again!"

Olivia leaned over and squeezed my hand in sympathy. "Don't worry just yet. Cash and Stefan vouched for him and said he was with them all night, so he's got an alibi."

"So why is he still in Tampa and I'm here?"

"Well, it's not that simple. After the problem with Jethro, Kane is naturally the one they'd look at since Mason was beaten before he was shot. Even more, your injuries would make them think Kane did it to avenge what Mason did to you. That's why we need to hide you out here for a while."

"Don't worry, honey," Gemma said in her usual sweet way. "Kane's going to take care of everything."

Olivia walked toward the door. "Are you hungry? I can get you something to eat."

"Yeah. Sure. Maybe some toast or something," I

said, not really hungry but not wanting to talk anymore.

She left and Gemma sat with me, silent for a long time before she said, "Abbi, he's going to be fine and as soon as the cops stop investigating him, he'll come here for you."

"He killed someone, Gemma. They're not going to just let that go. Mason was a councilman. A politician's death isn't something they're just going to spend a few days on and forget."

"Kane was careful, honey. He's got this covered. Don't worry."

"He killed someone, Gemma! Murder!" I began to sob, unable to handle the truth. Because of me, Kane was now a murderer for the second time and certain to be sent to prison. I'd turned the man I loved into a murderer for me.

"That man was going to kill you, Abbi Linde," she scolded me. "Do you understand me? He had a gun and he wanted to kill you." She got up from the bed and grabbed a mirror from the dresser. Holding it in front of my face, she said, "Take a good look at what he did. That's four days out and you still look like someone took a fucking bat to your face. He kidnapped you, beat you, and planned to kill you. And you want to blame Kane for doing what any man should do for the woman he loves?"

I sat stunned at her words. Looking at my

reflection, all I saw was what I'd always been. A victim.

"I can't help it. He killed someone, Gemma. After all those times boyfriends beat me and how many times I wished someone would make them feel what I felt, now that it's happened all I feel is sick. How can I ever look at him the same again?"

"I told you this when I first suggested you come to work at Club X. Kane is a good man. He's crazy in love with you, probably going out of his mind missing you, and you'd be insane to think of him as anything else but that. Would you rather be dead and Mason be alive?"

It wasn't that easy. Mason's death made Kane something I wasn't sure I could handle. I loved him with all my heart, but what if I never could look at him the same again knowing what he'd done because of me?

"I'm tired, Gemma. I'm going to lay down a little while," I said, needing to avoid this conversation.

She reached into her jeans pocket and pulled out an envelope. "Okay, honey, but I want to leave this with you."

I took it from her hand and looked at it. "What's this?"

"A letter from Kane. Olivia brought it yesterday."

Gemma left me and I opened the envelope to find a single sheet of paper. In his own hand, he'd written me things he'd never said to me before.

My angel,

I'm sorry I'm not there with you when you need me most. I told you I'd never leave you alone, but I swear I had no choice. Every night I lay on the floor next to my twin bed in my rooms at the club and think of the time I spent there with you. You're the first thought I have every morning and the last thought I have every night. In between, it feels like someone's carved into my chest and taken my heart out, leaving an emptiness there only you can fill.

There's a darkness in me, angel—my demons demand I protect you—and I don't regret letting them rule me that night. For you, I'd give up everything, including my freedom, if I could know you were safe. I promise I'll make this up to you if it takes the rest of my life. Please don't give up on us, angel.

Never doubt I love you more than anyone or anything in this world.

Kane

His letter made my heart ache and I missed him so much at that moment, I couldn't think about those doubts I'd had just minutes before. I feared they'd return sometime, though, and I'd have to deal with them or lose him. There was no other way.

✕

DAY AFTER DAY, I WAITED to hear that Kane had been cleared of the charges, but each time Olivia came to see me, all she could report was the investigation was continuing and at least he hadn't been charged. The days became weeks and even though I wanted to write back to him to say I loved him and missed him more than I thought I could ever miss another person, I couldn't just in case the police searched his rooms. Any connection to me could endanger him, so all those words I wanted to say to him remained unspoken and hidden in my heart.

I missed our little house where we'd made a home together, even if I began to like Alexandria's house on Anna Maria Island with its warm breezes that blew through the French doors of my bedroom and porch right outside where I sat at night and wished Kane was there beside me as I watched the sun set. I told myself that this was only temporary and tomorrow Kane would come and take me and Angel home with him.

But tomorrow always came without him. My face healed over time until there was no evidence of what Mason had done to me, but still I couldn't go back home.

Three weeks went by without another word from him, and each day became harder to deal with. Gemma and Olivia tried to keep my spirits up, reminding me to keep in mind that at least he hadn't been arrested, but I didn't want at leasts or anything else that was supposed to make me feel better.

I only wanted him.

By the beginning of May, four weeks had passed and getting out of bed seemed like a useless attempt at pretending I was happy. Even worse, I came down with a bug and couldn't keep a thing in my stomach. My misery was complete. I was alone without the man I loved and not even sure I'd ever see him again, away from my home, and sick.

One morning as I knelt over the toilet, disappointed that even though I'd felt better the night before whatever this was had come back with a vengeance again, I realized in all the time I'd been there at that house I'd never had my period. Standing at the bathroom mirror, I counted back to the last time I had and the last time Kane and I made love and the answer became obvious.

I didn't have the flu. I was pregnant.

Behind me, Gemma knocked on the door. "Not feeling any better this morning? I thought you'd shaken it last night."

I rinsed my mouth and walked out past her to sit on the bed. My legs felt like they were made of rubber and would give out at any moment. My hands began to shake as I thought about how I would break this news to him.

"Olivia's bringing up some toast in a minute. Maybe you should get under the covers. You're shaking, honey."

I hung my head and sighed. How was I going to have a baby when its father might go to prison any day?

What a mess my life was.

Gemma sat down next to me and rubbed my back. "Why so sad? It'll be gone in a few days."

"No, it won't. This isn't the flu, Gem. I'm pregnant."

I heard her gasp and then she hugged me tightly as she made a squealing noise in my ear. "Oh Abbi! That's wonderful! Wait until Kane hears. He'll be over the moon!"

Turning to look at her, I couldn't fathom what the hell she was so happy about. "Do you never see anything but the positive side of life? I'm pregnant, living here away from Kane, who may be hauled off to jail at any time. Could there be a worse time to bring a baby into our lives?"

Gemma kissed me and jumped up off the bed. Spreading her arms wide, she smiled and said, "I've been waiting for a sign for weeks. This is it. Finally, some good news out of all of this. A baby is the best news ever too. When are you going to tell him?"

"I have no idea. I haven't heard from him in a month. At this rate, I'll have the baby before we see each other again. And I can't write to him anyway, at least not until the police stop looking at him."

"You can tell Olivia and she can tell him," she suggested.

"No. I want him to find out from me, not secondhand, so don't say a thing to her, okay?"

"Of course." Gemma looked like she was thinking of a solution and then pointed at me excitedly. "I got it! You could ask her to give him a message from you that only he would understand."

"Like what?"

"I don't know. Think of something only he would know so you can tell him. Imagine how happy he's going to be when he finds out. After weeks of all the police stuff and being away from you, he'll be thrilled to find out the good news."

"No. Then he'll risk coming here to see me and all that time away from each other will be for nothing. No. I won't tell him until he comes back to me on his own."

"You sure?"

"Yes, and promise me you won't say a thing. I'd never forgive myself if everything was ruined because of this."

With a frown, she nodded. "I promise."

I knew Gemma would have a hard time keeping this a secret, but thankfully, I didn't think she ever saw Kane either so there'd be no chance she'd be able to tell him. I just had to hope she wouldn't break her promise and tell Olivia.

CHAPTER TWENTY-ONE

KANE

I SAT IN CASH'S OFFICE with him and Stefan as he made his daily call to the lawyer to find out the latest news on the investigation into Mason's death. Six weeks had gone by since that night, and although I didn't regret what I'd done, I did regret that it meant I had to be away from Abbi for so long. Listening to Olivia's reports about her nearly broke my heart. She may have been fooling Olivia and Gemma into believing she was okay, but my gut told me otherwise.

I knew my angel. She was going through everything I was, and I wasn't there for her, the strength I'd promised her when she needed it most.

Cash hung up the phone and began talking, but my mind was miles away with Abbi. Stefan nudged me out of my daydreaming, and I looked up to see them both grinning like they'd heard a funny joke and I'd missed it.

"Sorry. My mind was somewhere else."

"No problem. I've got good news. Jessup says it

looks like they're onto a different line of investigation. Seems none of us panned out, even though we'd been paying him every month and you looked like an obvious suspect because of what happened with Jethro."

"That's great! But we were all suspects?" Stefan asked.

"Yes. Since we were paying him protection every month, we'd have a good reason to want him dead," Cash answered. "That it overlooks the reality that if he's dead we have no one to help us didn't seem to occur to the police."

"So I'm in the clear?"

"Looks like it."

The idea of finally being able to go back to my life slowly sunk into my brain. I could return to Abbi now and our life together. A sense of relief washed over me. Six weeks of worrying every day that I'd be taken away to jail finally over.

"I want to thank both of you for all that you've done during this. I couldn't have done this alone."

Cash smiled and nodded his head. "This is what family does, Kane. You're our brother. We protect each other."

"Yeah, you're blood," Stefan continued. "When one of us is in trouble, he can always count on his brothers."

"Thanks. But what's going to happen to the club?

We've been closed ever since Mason's man in the police department didn't get his payment three weeks ago. What are we going to do?"

Deep down, I knew the answer to my question. I just didn't want to admit it. Without someone like Shank or Mason, Club X couldn't stay open. Too much of my area would get us shut down the minute some eager cop found out we weren't protected.

"Unfortunately, until we figure out what to do, whether we can find another Mason or not, I think we have to stay closed. The nature of our business means we need someone like that," Cash said.

"I'm sorry for that. I never meant to do this to you two and to the club," I said quietly. I hadn't meant to ruin their livelihoods with my demons.

"Things were changing anyway, so maybe it's just the way it's meant to be," Stefan said as he chucked me in the shoulder. "Shay's going to be back soon, and we were going to wait to tell everyone, but she's taken a job at a school in Texas. I was going to be leaving you guys, believe it or not."

Cash and I sat there in stunned silence. I looked over at him, and like me, the look of amazement on his face told the whole story. Neither one of us just a year earlier would have imagined Stefan settled down with a good woman, a soon-to-be college professor no less, and moving away from Tampa.

"Will you be getting married?" Cash asked like the

big brother he was.

Stefan grinned and shrugged. "We don't know yet. We're just having fun and loving every minute together. I keep telling you guys. I'm a changed man."

"I guess you are," I said, still shocked from his news.

"And your wedding is right around the corner," Stefan said to Cash. "Just a few more weeks. I guess this vacation from the club is good."

"Yep, and then a long honeymoon in Italy for three weeks. I haven't had that much time off since we began this. I'd say I'd get bored not working, but something tells me that's not going to happen."

"While you're gone, Stefan and I can keep the nightclub section open at least," I suggested.

"I'm game," Stefan chimed in. "I mean, my section was always the one that brought in the people."

"Yeah, right," I joked. "I think we know what section brought in the money, Stef."

Before he could take my bait, Cash shook his head. "I don't think so. We've had a good run here, but Club X means the upper floors. If we do open up again in the future, it's got to be with Kane's section too."

The three of us sat there silently as the reality of the situation became clear. Club X would be no more, at least for the time being.

"So this is it?" Stefan asked with more than a hint of sadness in his voice.

Cash looked at me and then back at Stefan. "I think so. We've made a lot of money here, gentlemen. More than even I ever thought we could. Our father would be proud. It was a good run, but things are changing. I'm getting married. Stefan, you're leaving. What are your plans, Kane?"

"Just bringing Abbi home. I lived so long alone that having someone in my life is a big change."

"Olivia says she's doing fine out there at the house, other than a touch of the flu, right?"

"Yeah. Right after we're done here, I can finally see her again now that I'm no longer a suspect. I'm going to bring her back to the house and hope I can make up for lost time."

"So it's agreed Club X will stay closed?" Cash asked looking at Stefan and then me for our answers.

Quietly, we both answered and agreed. The business we'd built into the multi-million dollar a year hottest nightspot in Tampa would stay closed. The three of us sat silently as the reality of that decision began to settle in.

For six days a week for most of my twenties I'd worked with these two men. It had been awkward in the beginning. I'd never met them before our father died and dictated in his will that if any of us wanted any money from his estate we'd have to work together. At first, it felt like a punishment none of us thought we deserved, but after a while we grew to like each other.

Cash, the brother nearly my age I wished I'd known all those years growing up, and Stefan, the younger pain in the ass brother I suddenly couldn't imagine not having around to joke and bust ass with. I'd always been the outsider, but now as I sat there with them after all they'd done for me in the past two months, I didn't feel like that outsider anymore.

I just felt like their brother. For someone who'd never really had a family in his life, it was a feeling I'd miss.

A knocking on the office door roused us all from our thoughts, and Olivia walked in with her usual sweet smile. "Am I interrupting? It sounded as quiet as a church in here."

She walked over to Cash's side. Wrapping his arm around her waist, he looked up and said, "We've decided to keep the club closed for the time being."

"Oh," she said with a pout.

"It's okay, Olivia," Stefan said. "We've all got things going on. You two are getting married. Kane and Abbi have to make up for all this time apart. And Shay and I are going to be moving when she comes back."

"Moving? To where?" She looked down at Cash and poked his shoulder. "Why didn't your brother tell me any of this?"

"He didn't know. I just told them today. Shay got a job in Texas for next semester."

"Listen to you talking like that," she teased him.

"Please tell her I said congratulations. You're not planning on moving too, are you Kane?" she asked. "You can't move now."

"Abbi and I aren't going anywhere," I said with a smile, silently remembering a time when the dream of leaving with the woman I loved was all that I could think of. Now, all I wanted to do was take Abbi back to our little house with the squeaky screen door and little backyard and live there in peace.

"All right, it's decided. Until further notice, Club X is closed and we're moving on. I'll take care of talking to the staff."

Cash's announcement brought Olivia's frown back, but it was for the best. I would have liked to talk to my people, but Cash was better at that anyway. As Stefan and Cash talked about the legalities of our decision, I headed up to my area for one last look around the place I'd spent so many nights.

I climbed the stairs up to the fifth floor and walked around where I stood every night, by habit immediately turning to look at the monitors, but now they all sat there dark in front of me. I walked the halls of each floor, looking in on the rooms I'd watched over for years and feeling a sense of some kind of accomplishment. We hadn't invented the wheel or saved the world, but our members had found a place to enjoy themselves.

It wasn't world peace, but it was some kind of

happiness.

On the fourth floor, I walked back to my old rooms where I'd lived from the day we opened Club X. Three small rooms never meant to be a home, they'd served as a place for me to hide out from the world and all the pain that came with it. Then one night, Abbi walked into them and I didn't want to hide anymore.

Gathering up my clothes, I looked down at the blanket on the floor and remembered the night I came back to find her still wearing my shirt and asleep in my bed. So small and innocent, she didn't know it as she lay there all curled up but even then she'd found a way into my heart.

I cleaned out the last of the food in the refrigerator and threw it in the garbage, the final task to end my life there. I'd returned when Abbi went to Anna Maria Island because I couldn't live in that house without her, but now if she'd have me, we'd go back to our home and begin a new life.

I wasn't a fool. I knew no woman should want a man who'd done what I'd done, even if I could claim the best of intentions. Abbi had spent years with violent men. Would she see me as one of them now? If she did, I couldn't blame her. I just had to show her I wasn't like them.

Even now, my demons told me I had good reason for killing Mason. They always had good reasons for the bad I did. But now, I needed to work harder than ever to control the demons inside me. They may not ever push me to hurt Abbi, but I couldn't continue to expect her to want to spend her life with me if I couldn't control them.

In a choice between them and her, the decision was simple. Whatever I had to do to keep Abbi, that's what I'd do.

I headed down to my car, ready to see her and show her I could be the man she needed and the man she wanted. Olivia caught me as I walked out the back door and looked like she had a secret she couldn't wait to share.

"Hey, I wanted to talk to you, but you disappeared."

"Just a small trip through the past. I've spent a lot of time in this club."

Olivia's smile grew bigger. "Well, it's probably best that you won't be doing this anymore. It's not really the kind of job you should have now."

"You're probably right. After being arrested and the main suspect in a murder all in the past couple months, I probably need a break."

"That's not what I meant, actually. Gemma told me what Abbi thought was the flu was actually something else. Sickness women get in the morning."

I stared down at Olivia, who stood there practically beaming, and tried to figure out her riddle. My thinking about what she'd said took too long for her, and she blurted out, "Morning sickness! Jeez, you men are so slow with this stuff."

"Morning sickness? You mean—"

Olivia bounced on her toes, finally able to say the words she'd been holding in since she arrived at the club. "Abbi's pregnant! Gemma says she's worried you won't be happy because of everything that's happened."

Abbi pregnant? I felt myself fall back against the wall, stunned at what Olivia had just told me. Abbi the mother of my child. Me a father. For a moment, all I could think was at least I had enough money because that's all we had going for us, but then the truth pushed all the doubts out of my mind. We'd been through a lot together, but that didn't mean we couldn't do this.

We were having a baby.

"Are you okay, Kane? You look like you can barely stand up."

I nodded, still getting a handle on the fact that I was going to be a father. "Yeah, I'm…I'm fine."

"I'm so happy for you two. You're finally able to go to her, so what are you doing wasting your time with me and an armful of food and clothes?"

Olivia's words confused me, but looking down, I saw what she meant. "I was cleaning out my rooms. I better go. Should I bring her anything?" I asked, suddenly feeling like I didn't know how to act.

"Get some flowers. Women love flowers. Other than that, all she wants to see is you. Now go!"

I quickly headed out to my car and threw everything in my arms out in the trash dumpster before racing over to the florist near the club for a dozen roses. I had one hour before I had to be ready to be a father, and I knew I better use that drive to figure out how to be the man Abbi needed now.

ALEXANDRIA'S HOUSE ON ANNA MARIA Island was typical her—opulent in a way that didn't seem off putting. Far wealthier than either of her sons or me, she wore her money like it belonged on her. Cash took after her in that way, unlike Stefan, who forever seemed to want to look like some frat boy, even after his life change because of Shay.

I walked up the stairs to the front door with my heart in my throat. Six long weeks was enough time for a woman to decide she didn't want a man in her life who couldn't control his demons. Six long weeks of not hearing a word from me, except for that one letter Jessup told me I could sneak to her. Six long weeks of every night alone. Six long weeks of worrying about me again.

What woman would want that?

"Hello, Kane."

Alexandria opened the door for me to come in, speaking to me for one of the few times since we'd met all those years ago. I entered the house, instantly feeling like intruder as I always did when it came to Cash and Stefan's mother.

"Hi, Alexandria."

She silently led me down the hall to the foot of the stairs and turned to look at me as I stood there with the bouquet of roses in my hand. "Abbi's feeling better. I'm sure she'll be happy to see you after all this time."

"Thank you for helping me with this. I know we've never been close and you likely agreed to let Abbi stay here because Cash asked, but thank you all the same."

Alexandria looked up at me, staring into my eyes for so long that I wanted to look away, but finally she said, "I noticed when I saw you at Cassian and Olivia's engagement party how much you look like your father."

I'd only seen my father a handful of times in my life. How much I looked like him never entered my mind. I only knew I looked like Cash.

"You look more like him now because all that hatred and anger isn't in your eyes anymore."

"That's all Abbi."

Alexandria smiled. "I had a feeling. She's a very sweet girl. Your father would like her."

"I didn't know him, so I wouldn't know what he'd like," I said quietly, trying to hide the resentment I still carried for Cassian March III.

"I know. That was one of the many mistakes he made, Kane, but I think it's about time I told you. You weren't one of those mistakes."

We stood there not saying a thing, me because I didn't know what to say to the woman I'd believed always hated my very existence, and her because I had a feeling now that she could accept me I was more like a stranger to her than ever before.

Alexandria gave me a smile and walked back toward the kitchen, and for a moment I thought about the father I'd never known and all those years growing up hearing the terrible things my mother had said about Cassian March and his wife. After all this time, I could finally say I knew she'd been wrong.

I made my way up the stairs to Abbi's room at the far end of the house. My hand clutching the roses' stems cramped from how tightly I gripped them. Her room was empty, but I saw the kitten sitting on the bed all curled up into a little ball. My eyes scanned the porch for any sign of Abbi, but she wasn't there either.

Angel's purring made me look over toward her, and I saw underneath her lay a sheet of paper folded in half. Scooping her up, I dropped the flowers on the bed and held her to my chest, nuzzling her fur.

"What are you and Abbi hiding there?"

As she kneaded my shoulder, I opened up the note and read what Abbi had written.

Dear Kane,

By the time you get this letter, I'll be gone so I want to make sure this makes sense. It's been a long wait for us to be together, and in that time I've missed you so much. I know you deserved to hear me tell you all of this in person, but it's better this way.

I've brought you nothing but trouble since I came into your life. Gemma told me you've never been arrested or even in a fight in all the time she's known you, but now in the span of just a few months you've done all these terrible things and I don't think it's your demons.

I think it's me.

I don't know what it is about me that brings trouble, but I love you too much to see you suffer anymore because of me. You deserve so much more than what I can give you.

I never meant for any of this to happen to you. All I ever wanted was someone to love who wouldn't hurt me, and you've been that and so much more. But now I'm hurting you, and I can't do that to you anymore. I love you too much.

Please don't come after me. It's best this way. You deserve to have that life you and Holly dreamed of, and you can't if I'm around. I love you.

Abbi

My hands began to shake as I read Abbi's letter again, still not believing the words she'd written. No. This couldn't be goodbye. We'd been through all that shit and misery just to come through it and not be together?

No. I couldn't let that happen.

I sat down on her bed and tried to figure out what to do. She was gone and I had no idea where she could be. Pregnant, alone…what if she got hurt? What if that asshole ex-boyfriend found her again? Where could she be? I had to find her.

My mind raced. She couldn't have gotten too far on foot. Was she even on foot? Where was Gemma? Gemma must have taken her somewhere. Fucking Gemma! Did Alexandria know? Was that why she stopped me downstairs?

I hurriedly placed Angel on the bed and ran to the porch to see if Abbi was still close by. Fuck! I looked out and only saw water. My gut felt like someone was ripping me apart. Where was she? I had to find her.

"Abbi!" I yelled so loud my lungs hurt. "Abbi! Where are you?"

I yelled until I couldn't anymore. I turned back into her room and Alexandria stood in the doorway. I saw it in her eyes. She knew something and wasn't telling me.

"Where is she?"

"I don't know what you mean."

Holding Abbi's letter up, I shook my head as I felt the anger rise in me. This woman was keeping me from the woman I loved. I didn't care why. I just knew she was in my way.

"Fine. I don't have time to fuck around with you. But if I find out you had any part in why she left—if you turned her against me—I'll find a way to make you pay. I don't give a damn whose mother you are."

I stuffed Abbi's letter into my pocket and went for the door, but Alexandria stopped me and placed her hand on my forearm. "Stop. Let her be for a little while. She's not in danger."

"You know where she is? Tell me. Now."

"She's just confused, Kane. She thinks she's the reason you do the things you do."

This woman stood between me and my happiness, and every second I wasted with her was another second I didn't get to spend with Abbi. "Alexandria, I'm going to give you about three seconds to tell me where she is."

"Kane, she's afraid and doesn't know what to do. Let her have a little time."

"She's had six weeks to realize she doesn't love me anymore. Time isn't something that works in my favor."

"She thinks she's ruined your life."

"Why? Because you sat here for over a month and filled her head with how much she should hate me?"

Alexandria frowned and shook her head. "I meant

what I said downstairs. I'm sorry you didn't get to know your father, Kane. You deserved more than just money from him. If you had known him, maybe you wouldn't be like you are."

"This has nothing to do with who my father was," I said as a lump formed in my throat. I couldn't handle this on top of losing Abbi. "I can't spend the rest of my life apologizing for being born and being the child no one wanted. I don't want my son or daughter to feel that way. I have to find Abbi, and you can either step aside so I can get past you or stand in my way and deal with my demons, which at the moment can think of nothing else but finding the woman I love. Your choice."

She stared up at me for a long moment with a look in her eyes that told me she was deciding what to do, but then without another word she stepped aside and let me by. I gave her one last chance to tell me where Abbi was. One last chance to be something other than the person who'd always hated me.

Stopping in front of her, I asked, "Will you please tell me where she is, if you know?"

"I can't. I promised her I wouldn't."

"Why? Do you hate me that much that you want to see my one chance for happiness gone?"

"I don't hate you, Kane. If anything, I've grown to think of you as another one of my sons because of the way Cassian and Stefan feel about you. I grew very fond of Abbi since she's been here, and I know she loves you. Just give her some time."

"Some time to do what, Alexandria? Realize she can't live with the man I am and doesn't want me in my child's life?"

"Time to find the strength to be the person she needs to be to be with you."

"What does that mean? I just want my Abbi, the person I fell in love with. Why is that a problem?"

Alexandria said nothing, and I knew I wasn't going to get anything useful from her. She hated me, no matter what she said, and somehow had poisoned Abbi against me.

"I never asked to be born. I'm sorry my father wasn't the kind of man who cared about the women he claimed to love. I'm not like him, though, and when I find Abbi she'll see that."

Racing down the stairs, I got to my car and called Abbi, but her phone went directly to voicemail. With her phone off, I couldn't even try to track her. I didn't know if she'd ever get my message, but I texted her anyway, desperate for her to know I needed her.

Abbi, don't do this. Don't leave me. I need you. I swear I'll promise you anything if you'll just tell me where you are so I can bring you home to our little house.

I couldn't just wait and hope she'd see my message, so I called John Kearney, the private investigator we used at the club. If anyone could help me find her, if was him.

"Kane, I heard you guys were closing up shop, so I'm surprised to hear from you."

"I need you to find someone for me. I'm in a hurry."

"Find someone? Who?"

"Her name is Abigail Linde. Goes by the name Abbi. She's petite, blond with shorter hair but she might be wearing a wig. She's also pregnant. I need to find her as soon as possible. She might be headed north from Anna Maria Island to her mother's house in Panama City."

"She owe you money or something? You sound like you're a man on a mission here, Kane."

I slid behind the wheel and took one last look at the house. "Nothing like that. I just need to find her now. Don't worry about the cost. Price is no object. Spend whatever you have to but find her. I'll throw in an extra twenty grand if you can find her within the week. Deal?"

John's breath caught and he said, "I can't turn that down, so deal. I'll find your girl. What do you want me to do when I do find her, though?"

"Let me know and I'll come to you. She's not to be hurt. Do you understand me, John?"

"I don't hurt people, Kane. I just find them. I leave the hurting up to the people who want them found."

His comment made me wince, but I brushed it off.

I needed to keep focused. "Call me as soon as you know something."

"You got it. Stay by your phone."

I threw my cell on the passenger seat and drove out of there back to my rooms at the club. I couldn't go back to our house. It just wasn't the same without Abbi there to share it with me.

WITH THE CLUB CLOSED, I had the entire building to myself, alone with nothing but my thoughts. During the day, I sat in my office and waited to hear from John about where she was hiding, and at night I lay on the floor next to my bed where I held Abbi in my arms that first night. Every minute my mind stayed preoccupied with the real fear that I'd never see the woman I loved again or ever see my child.

That when everything else was stripped away—the money, the club, everything—who I was wasn't who she wanted. That the man I was made her run away.

Three night later, I lay on the floor of my bedroom in the dark when John called with the news I'd been waiting for. "What did you find out?"

"Kane, was this job some kind of trick or something? You testing me?"

Sitting up, I tried to figure out what he meant. "I told you I needed you to find Abbi Linde. Did you find her?"

"Yeah, but I don't get why you couldn't. She's right

there on Anna Maria Island at Cash and Stefan's mother's beach house. From what I can figure, she never left there. Why did you send me looking for her if she was right there the whole time?"

Abbi had never left the house. She'd hidden from me and stood by as Alexandria made me believe she wasn't there. Stunned, I mumbled, "Thanks" and dropped the phone to the floor.

I knew I could go there at that moment and find her, but what good would that do? She didn't want to be with me now.

Chapter Twenty-Two
Abbi

I STOOD ON THE PORCH with my heart in my throat as I watched Kane drive away. I'd hidden myself in the next room and listened to everything he'd said to Alexandria as the tears rolled down my cheeks. I knew he loved me, but he deserved better than the life he'd have if he stayed with me.

Alexandria placed her hand on my shoulder. "Did you hear what he said?"

Nodding, I choked back the tears. "Yeah. Everything. Why didn't you just let me go when I wanted to?"

"I couldn't let you do that to him. If you did what you planned to, he'd never get over it. You two would never have a chance. I didn't want to see you do that to him or you."

I turned around and saw that same sympathetic look she always wore around me. How she could when she knew what I'd wanted to do confused me. "He doesn't need me or a baby in his life. He deserves to finally be happy, and it's obvious that can't happen with me. I just bring misery to him."

"You underestimate yourself. And him."

"I still don't know if I should keep this baby. Nothing's changed."

"Abbi, he's never known love like you gave him."

"And now because of me he's killed someone. It was bad enough that he'd hurt others for me, but that…I can't be the reason someone does that."

The pain in her expression bothered me. If she felt that way about what I said, what would Kane feel?

"I'm going to let you have some time alone to think about this."

"Do you hate him like he said?" I asked, needing to know why she would help someone if she didn't care at all about him.

She smiled and shook her head. "No. Not anymore. I told him the truth. I care about him like I do my own sons."

"Why?"

Alexandria thought about my question and frowned. "Maybe I think he deserves it. Neither of his parents seemed to care enough about him, so perhaps I should."

"Is it because he reminds you of Cash since they look so alike?"

"No. He actually looks more like his father than even Cassian does. Maybe that's why I don't want to see him lose this chance to be happy. I always did have a soft spot where his father was concerned."

"Was your husband like him—I mean with the demons like Kane has?" I asked, wanting to know more about his background he'd never really wanted to talk about with me.

"The demons in Kane come from his mother," Alexandria said sharply as she walked away.

There alone on the porch I looked off in the distance, wanting to see Kane's car. Had I made a mistake? No, I couldn't let him stay with me just because of the baby. He deserved the happiness he gave me, and I couldn't give that to him.

It was better this way.

THE FIRST LETTER CAME FOUR days later. Alexandria brought it to me as I lay in bed crying with Angel. I knew the minute she held out the envelope that he'd found out where I was. But why hadn't he come to get me?

She left me alone and with trembling hands, I opened the letter and read the words as the tears rolled down my cheeks.

Angel,

I can't go on without you. Whatever I need to do to convince you I love you, I'll do it.

Kane

I wanted to believe I wouldn't ruin his life, but I couldn't help thinking I was what brought out those demons in him. Naturally protective, he'd only find more battles to fight with me. I couldn't do that to him. He deserved to be happy.

That night I cried myself to sleep with Angel cuddled next to me, and the next morning when I awoke there was another letter on my nightstand. I knew he'd been there. Maybe he'd even come to my room while I slept. That he knew where I was and wasn't coming to get me made me think I was right, no matter what his letter said.

I held the second envelope in my hand, wondering if I should read it at all. What good would any of this do when being with me would only hurt him? I thought of how happy he'd looked that day he showed me our little house, and as my heart broke at how much I missed him and our life, I read his letter.

Angel,

I'm lost without you. Don't leave me to live this life alone.

Kane

I wanted to write back and tell him I was lost without him. I wanted to tell him how I spent every minute of my days missing how it felt when he held me in his arms and protected me from the world and every night I lay in my bed alone wishing he was next to me.

His third letter was waiting for me when I awoke the next day, and I didn't know how I would go on if he kept breaking my heart. With every word he wrote me, I was beginning to think I'd made a mistake hiding from him.

Abbi,

I can't go on like this. I know about the baby, but maybe it's better he or she never knows what I am. I'm sorry.

Kane

Oh, God! How could I spend the rest of my life without him? I turned on my phone to call him and saw dozens of texts, all from him. I read each and every one of them and sobbed as I realized how much he was hurting. I could only hope that it wasn't too late.

I sat there in bed listening to his phone ring once, twice, three times. Had I waited too long and he'd realized what I'd feared all along? I held my breath as my heart slammed in my chest at the thought that I'd lost him, but finally he answered.

"I miss you, Kane."

Like hearing my voice was all he needed to be happy, he said quietly, "Abbi…"

I wanted to be next to him, to have his arms around me. "I'm sorry for everything. I didn't mean to hurt you. I just didn't want to ruin your life."

"Angel, you could never ruin my life. You are my life."

My words caught in my throat as I sobbed. "I want to go home to our little house with the squeaky screen door, Kane. Come take me home."

"Abbi, I'm no good. You don't need someone like me."

"Don't say that! I do! Our baby needs you. I can't do this without you."

"What child wants a father like me? Like the kind of man I am?"

The tears streamed down my face as the real fear that I was losing him settled into my heart. "Kane, don't leave me here all alone without you. I want to come home. Please take me back to our little house."

The phone stayed silent for so long I wasn't even sure he was still there, but then he said the words that made me happier than I thought I could ever be again.

"Okay, angel. I'll take you home."

ALEXANDRIA HELD MY HAND AS I stood on the front porch waiting for Kane. She hadn't said anything when I told her it was time for me to go home, but I had a sense that my decision had made her happy. At the sight of Kane's black Mustang coming down the road toward the house, I squeezed her hand tightly and held Angel to me, suddenly worried about seeing the man I loved again.

"It's okay, Abbi. He loves you. There's no reason to be scared."

I turned to look at her and saw the same sympathy in her dark brown eyes that I'd seen since the night I arrived here. It had been a source of comfort in all the time I stayed at this house, and now it calmed me when I needed it most.

"What if nothing has changed and everything I fear comes true?"

She cradled my cheek and smiled. "Do you love him?"

"I do. I'm only happy when I know he's happy. That's love, isn't it?"

"It is. So if you love him and you've accepted who he is, there's nothing to fear. Once you truly accept who the man you love is, you can handle anything that comes your way."

"I don't want to mess this up. Kane's the best thing to come into my life in a long, long time."

Alexandria smiled and pulled me close to hug me. "Just be yourself. He loves you, so take one day at a time and stand with him against his demons."

I could do that.

Straightening my clothes, I watched as the car stopped but Kane wasn't driving. Stefan got out of the car and walked toward us wearing an expression that told me something was very wrong.

"Why isn't Kane here? What happened?" I asked frantically.

Alexandria took my hand in hers to calm me, but even she was frightened. "Stefan, why you here?"

"Abbi, I need you to come with me. I'll tell you everything, but we need to go."

I read the fear in his eyes and panicked. "What's happened? Is he alright?"

Stefan forced a smile and nodded. "He'll be fine. We'll make sure everything's taken care of, but for now, I need you to come with me."

Turning, I looked at Alexandria, my eyes pleading with her to make Stefan answer my questions. She understood instantly, and said, "Stefan, you need to tell her what happened now. She deserves to know."

He took a deep breath and held out an envelope. "Here. This is for you."

As Alexandria demanded to know what was going on, I walked away with what I knew was a letter from Kane. My hands trembling, I opened the envelope and began to read his words, my heart breaking with each one.

Dear Abbi,

I wanted to come get you and take you home to our little house, but you and our child are better off without me. That first night we were together I told you I'd hurt you because I hurt everyone. All my life I've known I was born to hurt. I can't change, no matter how much I wish I could.

I'm no good, and you and our child deserve better. I thought life had given me you to show me I wasn't supposed to be alone, but I messed everything up and that will never change. I'm a murderer. A killer who can't even say he feels bad about the men he's killed.

I love you. I never meant to hurt you. It's just who I am. I'm sorry.

Kane

"Abbi? What is it?" Alexandria asked as I stood stunned by Kane's goodbye.

"He's not coming." I let the letter drop from my hand and covered my face as I sobbed the truth.

"He's not coming for me."

"Stefan, what's going on?"

"I don't know. All I know is that Cash found that letter under his door at the condo and told me to come get Abbi and get her back to the house as soon as possible."

"Where's Kane?"

"We don't know. His rooms at the club are locked up. I banged on the door, but got no answer."

"I want to go there," I said as I scooped Angel up into my arms. "He's there and he's hiding away from the world. I need to go to him, Stefan."

"The club is closed, Abbi. The place is just an empty building now."

"He's there. I know it. I need to go there."

I kissed Alexandria goodbye and as I rode off to find the man I loved, I silently promised Kane I'd be the one person in his life who'd prove to him love didn't have to hurt.

EPILOGUE

KANE

I SAT STARING AT THE white cinder block walls of my rooms as the alcohol finally began to take effect after nearly a bottle of whiskey and prayed for some release from my mind's racing about Abbi and the baby we were having. A tiny voice in my head screamed for me to go to her, but I knew better.

She didn't need someone like me. I only brought pain, and she didn't deserve that. And no child deserved a man like me for a father.

Not that I had any real frame of reference for what a good father was. Cassian March III wasn't exactly the kind of role model a man wanted. A selfish bastard, his claim to fame seemed to be his skill in getting women to fall for his game. I never wanted to be like him.

All I wanted at that moment was to black out so at least I wouldn't have to feel the pain of not having Abbi by my side or think about all the shit my mind wanted to use to fuck with me tonight. I didn't need to beat myself up again over the mess my parents had been and why I was like I was. Closing my eyes, I especially tried not to think of my father, but the few memories I had of us together had different ideas about how I should spend my time drunk off my ass.

He stood by a black Mercedes dressed in a grey three piece suit that likely cost more than what my mother made in a month at the diner. Tall with black hair and blue eyes just like me, he'd likely have a hard time convincing anyone he and I weren't father and son.

"Kane," he said in a deep voice as he waved me toward him.

I didn't know what to call him. Father sounded wrong, as did dad. Dads tossed baseballs around with their sons in the backyard on sunny Saturday afternoons and taught them how to ride a bike and how to swim. Dads sat at the head of the table for dinnertime and stopped in as you were falling asleep to check up on you.

Cassian March III had never done any of those things with me. He'd never done anything with me in the seventeen years I'd been alive.

I stopped about three feet from him and stood silently, unsure why I was even there with him. We were strangers, brought together by my conviction and my mother's impending death. Neither was a good reason to start any kind of relationship since neither would lead to anything. For the next four years, I'd be locked up and the woman he'd once loved enough to have a child with would be dead.

Maybe he was hoping for me to say thank you for paying for my lawyer. I had to admit the guy was good. Four years for premeditated murder. I wondered what he'd gotten Cassian March out of if he could do that for me.

"Kane, I'm glad you came, son."

I felt my eyes grow big at that word. Son. I was that, not that he'd ever noticed much.

"What did you want to see me for?"

My terse answer surprised him, and like mine always did, his eyes grew big for a moment before he regained his composure. "I'm sorry to hear about your mother. I hope she's not suffering."

"They have her on strong drugs, so she's not much of anything anymore."

His blue eyes so much like mine stared at me, and for a second, I was struck by how much he reminded me of myself. Did my eyes ever look that cold?

"Well, I'm sorry. We may not have been on good terms for a long time, but…"

His sentence faded off, and I couldn't stop myself from asking, "But what? You loved her? If that was the case, I think you would have wanted to see me before this, or is it that you loved her but didn't want anything to do with me?"

"Is that what she told you?"

I shook my head in disgust. I didn't come here to do the whole true confessions I loved you from afar bullshit with him. "She never told me anything other than the night she told you she was pregnant with me, you left her and she knew she should name me Kane because I caused pain from the very beginning."

He couldn't hide the horrified look that came over his face at hearing the truth, but I saw those cold blue eyes soften as he said, "I didn't leave her because of you. It's hard to explain, but it was never because of you. When you were born, I offered to take you, give you my name, and bring you up with my son. She refused. She said you were hers. Even if I wanted to go back to her, I couldn't, but I'm not going to lie to you. I didn't want to."

"Nice. At least I don't have to wonder anymore if her hatred of you is deserved. Thanks for answering that question."

He took a deep breath in and let it out slowly. "I didn't want to go back to her, but I wanted you to have the kind of life I could give you. That should count for something."

Hanging my head, I said quietly, "Yeah. You got her pregnant and then didn't feel like doing the whole family thing with her. I get it. Is this what you wanted to meet with me for? To tell me I was wanted but she wasn't?"

"You have two brothers I'd love for you to meet, Cassian and Stefan. You and Cassian are about the same age. Stefan's a couple years younger. I guess I just wanted you to know that you aren't alone."

"I'm sure your wife would love that. Bring the bastard

child to dinner and see how that goes. Sounds like a great time, but as you know, I'm going to be a little busy for the next few years."

He winced at the mention of my upcoming incarceration, and a frown settled into his features. "I know. My lawyer did the best he could, Kane. I know four years sounds like a lifetime now, but it could have been worse."

"I know. I'm lucky they only gave this monster four years."

Shaking his head, he frowned even deeper. "That judge was way out of line. You aren't a monster. You just did something because of what that man did to your girlfriend. But that doesn't make you a monster."

I leveled my gaze on the man considered my father. "This is who I am. That judge called me a monster, but he wasn't wrong. My demons make sure of that."

"You sound like your mother. You don't have to be like her. I'm in there somewhere too."

Chuckling at his attempt to act like a supportive father figure, I said, "All I got of you is on the outside, Cassian."

We stood there next to his expensive car in that parking lot as the distance he'd always kept between us shrunk just a bit. It was barely noticeable, but it shrunk all the same. Maybe it was because in just a few days I'd be sent away and my mother would be dead, but I didn't want to hate him, even though that's all I'd ever been taught to do.

With a look of pride in his eyes, he said, "Well, I'd like to think you have some of me on the inside too, although I do have to admit there's no denying you're my son."

I shrugged, unsure of what to say since all I'd ever felt was his denial of everything about me.

He reached out and touched my forearm as if he cared that I had nothing to say to that. "I know your mother has never had a nice thing to say about me, but would it be so bad to be like me in some way?"

"I probably wouldn't mind having your money." I realized how that sounded as soon as the words were out of my mouth. Not meaning to insult him, I quickly said, "I didn't mean it like that. I just meant I wouldn't mind being rich like you."

Cassian grinned as I fumbled over my explanation. "I understand. Someday when I'm gone you and your brothers will get a lot of my money. But I hope you're more like me on the inside than you think. You don't have to be angry at the world, Kane. I know it's been hard, but there's a lot of good in this world."

I thought about Holly and her love, the only real good I'd ever experienced in my life. For the next four years, I'd have to live without that good. How I'd get through without it—without her love to keep me from becoming nothing but that anger I held inside—I didn't know. Already I felt myself hardening over as I felt my freedom slowly slipping away.

"Maybe you're right. I just haven't seen a lot of that

good."

"I know it's going to get a lot a worse for you, but when you get out I hope you and I can have a fresh start."

"Yeah, that might be nice," I said knowing any promises he made might not ever come true when I was finally out four long years from then. "I better go. I only have a couple more days of freedom. I want to spend as much of that time with Holly and my mother."

"I understand. If you need anything, I'm here, Kane."

He held out his hand and gave me the kind of handshake I'd always imagined my father would give me when I made him proud. Not that I'd done anything to deserve that. But maybe after I got out I might have the chance to do something.

Fucking whiskey making me reminisce about things that did no good. My father was gone by the time I got out of prison, dead from a heart attack before he'd even turned fifty and just four months before my release. Fate had fucked me again by dangling the chance to finally get to know him in front of my eyes only to take it away.

I left those four years behind to find both my parents and the only person I'd ever truly loved dead and gone. Whatever my father had seen of himself in me I never really knew, but he believed it was inside me and to prove it, he decreed in his will for Cassian, Stefan, or me to get any of his money, we had to work together and make something in this world a success.

More a punishment than anything else at first, we'd fulfilled his wish and I'd found two brothers. But I'd never found that something good inside me my father had seen.

Now I was going to be a father but nothing had changed in me. Two men dead at my hands and my demons happy to make excuses for my actions. I wasn't the kind of man a child needed as a father. For all his faults, Cassian March III hadn't been a murderer like me. I had money and anything I wanted to buy like he had, and if that was all I could offer, at least I could give my son or daughter a better life than I had growing up.

But those things didn't make up for the horrible things I'd done and the demons inside me who would never let me go.

Abbi and our child deserved more than who I was.

"KANE, PLEASE OPEN THE DOOR. I know you're in there," Abbi pleaded as she banged on my door.

I stumbled off the couch and opened the door to find her standing there looking up at me with her gentle eyes full of sadness and Stefan standing behind her.

"Abbi, go. I told you not to come for me. Go back to that little house that's yours now. I'll make sure you and our child will never want for anything. But go away from me before you get hurt."

She reached out to touch me, but I backed away. I watched the tears well in her eyes and hated myself, but this was for the best.

"Why are you doing this? You said you'd come for me. Why did you send Stefan instead?" she asked as the tears began to roll down her face.

Shooting him an angry look, I said, "I didn't send Stefan. I told Cash to make sure you got home, not to bring you here. You need to go."

"I don't want to go. I love you. I'm carrying your child. Don't you love me anymore? Is it because of what I wrote in that letter? I was just being stupid. I wasn't sure a child was something I could handle, but I know I can now. I can do this, but I can't do it without you."

I pushed the door to close it and said, "I'm not what you need. I can give you all my money, but you don't want me around when the baby comes. Go."

Abbi pushed all her weight against the door to stop it from closing and in my drunken state, I didn't fight her. I just didn't have it in me.

The two of them came in, and she stood there in front of me sobbing, "I'm not going anywhere. I belong with you, and if that means in these little rooms, then so be it. As long as we're together, that's all that matters."

"Stefan, get her out of here. Take her to the house like I asked Cash to do."

His expression told me he thought I was being the world's biggest dick, but he said nothing. All the better. I didn't want to explain myself to him too. Instead, he tapped Abbi on the shoulder and said quietly, "I'll be downstairs if you need me to give you a ride to the house."

As he closed the door behind him, she turned to look at me with those blue eyes that never failed to weaken my resolve. "I'm sorry I ever wrote that letter. I was wrong. Please, just listen to me. I love you, Kane, and I know you love me too."

I hung my head and tried to think of the words to say to convince her she didn't want me in her life. "Angel, sometimes love isn't enough. You have a chance now to go wherever you want. I'll make sure you're taken care of along with baby. Start a new life like you'd planned before you met me. Just go and don't look back."

She took my hand and pressed her damp cheek to it. "I told you before I don't want to leave you. Your demons don't frighten me. The only thing that scares me is not having you by my side."

"I thought my love for you would be enough to change who I am, but I'm still that monster that judge said I was all those years ago. I can't promise what happened with Mason and Jethro won't happen with someone else, and no child should be around that. You shouldn't be around that."

"What if don't want to go? Don't I get a say in this?"

I moved my hand from her soft cheek and walked away toward my place on the couch where all I wanted to do was drink enough to forget how much it hurt to tell her to go away. She followed me, unwilling to accept the truth. I said nothing but lifted the bottle of whiskey to my lips for a gulp I hoped would take some of this pain away.

"Kane, what happened between when you sent me those letters telling me you missed me and today? What changed?"

"Nothing. That's the problem. Nothing changed. I'm still the same person I was when I killed that man who raped Holly. The same man who killed Mason because of what he did to you. Why can't you see that no child should have a father like me?"

"All a child needs is love. You love me and I love you. It doesn't matter who you were in the past. Our son or daughter won't care what you did. All they'll know is that you're the kindest man and you take care of me."

I wanted to believe everything she was saying, but I knew the truth of who I was. She wasn't going to listen to that, though, so with a lump in my throat, I said the hardest words I'd ever spoken in my life. "Abbi, I want you to go."

She clung to my arm and cried, "No! Don't do this, Kane! Don't send me away. I need you!"

I stared into her eyes and struggled to do the right thing, no matter how much it was breaking my heart. "You need to go. Have Stefan take you back to the house. I'll make sure you have everything you need."

"I need you! Why are you doing this?"

Standing, I walked to the door and held it open for her. "I'm doing what I said I would. I can't take the chance that you or the baby could be hurt by me. I'd rather you hate me than me hurt you anymore."

She followed me to where I stood and took my hands in hers, pleading with her eyes for me not to make her go. "I love you, Kane. Please don't do this to us. I can handle whatever your demons do. Just don't push me away."

I looked down into that beautiful face so sad from everything I was doing and couldn't help but want to kiss her. Pressing my lips to hers, I wished so much that I wasn't what I was and that all her dreams of a wonderful life with me could come true, but I knew better.

"This is the way it has to be, angel. I'm doing this because I love you."

"You're doing this because you don't want to hurt me, but you're breaking my heart! Don't you think that's hurting me?" she screamed as she beat her fists against my chest.

I wanted to take her in my arms and make all the bad we'd been through go away, but I couldn't because I'd caused it. Whatever hurt she was feeling at that moment would pass. In the end, she was better off without me.

Backing away from her, I said quietly, "I'm sorry, angel. I never meant to hurt you."

"Well, you did. I don't care about your money or houses or anything else. Why can't you see that?"

I couldn't stand there and watch her cry anymore or I'd give in to my own pain and never let her leave. Hating myself more than ever before in my life, I closed the door and listened as she sobbed that she loved me and would never give up on us.

When she finally left to go downstairs to Stefan, I walked to my bedroom and lay down on the blanket I'd spread out on the floor and let the loneliness I'd felt for years come back and take me over. Some people are meant to be alone because all they do is hurt others. I was meant to hurt, no matter how much I wished that wasn't true.

Abbi was better off without me, and someday she'd realize that. If only it didn't hurt so much to let her go. I couldn't think about what this did to me, though.

You were meant to hurt, Kane.

I knew who I was and what my place in the world was. I had no choice.

I had to hurt her to save her.

LOOK FOR SATISFACTION (CLUB X #4), AVAILABLE NOW!

AND DON'T MISS K.M.'S THE SILK SERIES
A STORY OF LOVE AND OBSESSION

SILK

I want her. I crave her. She's my addiction.

The world knows me as Ian Anwell, New York Times bestselling author, but Kristina makes me want more.
Much more.

I need him. I love him. He's my obsession.
Everyone thinks they know Kristina Richards, but I'm more than what they see on the screen.
So much more.

I'm his muse, and this is our story.

READ ON FOR AN EXCERPT OF SILK VOLUME ONE!

SILK VOLUME ONE

EXCERPT

I SIGN MY NAME AND a few words about her being my biggest fan, but all I can think of is how her knee feels nudging against my thigh as she sits next to me with her legs folded underneath her. When I hand her the book, she smiles so sweetly at my inscription.

"Thank you. It's perfect."

More perfection from the world's most imperfect soul. If she only knew.

Kristina shifts her weight and begins to fidget with her hands. "I guess you know all about that whole thing with John Stinson and think I'm just the biggest fool, don't you?"

I truly have no idea what she's referring to, but I can see by the pain in her gorgeous eyes that it's something she's embarrassed by. With a smile, I say, "I don't know what you mean."

"You don't?"

Shaking my head, I explain I rarely watch anything that would tell me about Hollywood gossip. "So you see, I really don't know what you mean."

"Oh. I thought maybe that was why you didn't make a move when we got back here."

She presses her lips together as she waits for my

answer, but I'm not in the mood to explain why I haven't tried to kiss her yet. Better to just do it. Sometimes words get in the way.

The fantasy that's been playing on a constant loop in my brain is about to come true. Taking her chin between my thumb and forefinger, I gently pull her face toward me and kiss that delicious mouth I first noticed days ago, dying to know what her perfectly formed lips will feel like as I press mine to them.

My cock is rock hard already, and I haven't even touched her yet. Normally, it takes at least some decent foreplay to get me going, but that's probably because of the poison flowing through me. Now my bulge is practically busting out of my pants before we even kiss.

Just before her mouth meets mine, she moans ever so slightly a tiny whimper, and then we kiss. Her lips are soft and full, and all I can think of as her tongue slides tentatively into my mouth is how much I want to feel those lips and tongue on my cock.

Her hands caress my cheeks as our kiss intensifies, and then she's on my lap straddling my hips, her black skirt up around her waist. My hands instinctively move to cup that beautiful ass I'd admired as we left the bar, and a jolt of excitement courses through me when I feel skin instead of the cotton of panties. Fuck, she's wearing only a garter belt under her skirt!

That gorgeous, full ass feels incredible in my hands. My fingers knead her silky skin as she grinds against the front of my pants, and I lift my hips off the couch to push my cock against her.

Our kiss deepens and our tongues dance together. Kristina moans into my mouth, and I squeeze her cheeks hard, loving how eager she is. She tugs on my hair, her desire ratcheting up against mine and I slip a finger down toward her drenched pussy.

I want her. I want to live the fantasy that's played repeatedly since that first moment I filled my eyes with her beautiful face.

Kristina's fingers slide down over my neck to my shirt, and she begins to unbutton it, whispering against my lips, "I want you, Ian. That's why when my manager told me you wanted to meet me, I made the meeting for as soon as possible. Tell me you want me. Tell me what you want me to do."

I push her hands away and groan, "Take your sweater off."

She obeys my command and slips it off, revealing a pink lace bra. I want to see the gorgeous tits under it, so I quickly unhook it and throw it off to the side as I fill my eyes with the sight of her breasts. Full and firm, they look real, which thrills me even more than I imagined. I cup them in my hands and take one full, deep pink nipple in my mouth, sucking gently at first.

Looking up, I see her watching me, biting her lower lip and whimpering, "Yes...harder..."

Her wish is my command, and I suck her pebbled

skin harder into my mouth. I close my eyes and listen to her moans as I bite down gently on her excited nipple. Fuck, she's responsive! I hadn't expected that.

Kristina rolls her hips and begins to rub up against me in earnest. I love the idea that my mouth on her is going to get her off even before I whip my cock out. I feel her juices dampen the front of my pants and look up to see her face show the ecstasy building inside her. Releasing her nipple, I move my head to the other one and take it into my mouth, sucking hard as she pulls my hair.

Her hand slides between us and she fingers her wet pussy, but it gets in my way, so I pull her hand away. Disappointed, she frowns and admits quietly, "That's the only way I can get off."

I say nothing but shake my head, determined now to make her come from anything but her fingers touching her clit. Holding her hands behind her back, I slide my cock out of my pants and stroke it from base to head. I position it at her entrance and look up at her.

"Not with me."

SILK VOLUME ONE AVAILABLE NOW

LOOK FOR K.M. SCOTT'S CORRUPTED LOVE SERIES, A STORY OF FORBIDDEN LOVE AND WHAT TWO PEOPLE WILL DO TO BE TOGETHER!

IF I DREAM (CORRUPTED LOVE #1)

If I dream, will you dare?

All I wanted was my freedom. It's all I'd dreamed of from the first time I stood in the ring. Until I entered Robert Erickson's world. Until Serena. Cruelty and ugliness surrounded me, but she was beautiful and good. I wanted to protect her from her father's world, even though I knew being with her could mean the end of me.

I wanted for nothing as the daughter of one of the richest men in the world. But all my father's money couldn't buy what I truly craved. Until Ryder. I wanted all he was, all he brought out in me. All he made me desire.

Our love was forbidden by the one person who had the power to harm us. We dreamed of more than living in that world, though. We dreamed of having it all, but did we dare?

About the Author

K.M. Scott writes contemporary romance stories of sexy, intense, and unforgettable love. A New York Times and USA Today bestselling author, she's been in love with romance since reading her first romance novel in junior high (she was a very curious girl!). Under her Gabrielle Bisset name, she writes erotic paranormal and historical romance. She lives in Pennsylvania with a herd of animals and when she's not writing can be found reading or feeding her TV addiction.

Be sure to visit K.M.'s Facebook page at facebook.com/kmscottauthor for all the latest on her books, along with giveaways and other goodies! And to hear all the news on K.M. Scott books first, sign up for her newsletter today and be sure to visit her website at www.kmscottbooks.com.

BOOKS BY K.M. SCOTT:

The Corrupted Love Series
If I Dream (Corrupted Love #1)

The Heart of Stone Series
Crash Into Me (Heart of Stone #1)
Fall Into Me (Heart of Stone #2)
Give In To Me (Heart of Stone #3)
Heart of Stone Volume One Box Set
Ever After (Heart of Stone #4)
A Heart of Stone Christmas (Heart of Stone #5)
Unforgettable (Heart of Stone #6)
Unbreakable (Heart of Stone #7)
Heart of Stone Volume Two Box Set

The Club X Series
Temptation (Club X #1)
Surrender (Club X #2)
Possession (Club X #3)
Satisfaction (Club X #4)
Acceptance (Club X #5)
The Complete Club X Series Box Set

The SILK Series
SILK (Volume One)
SILK (Volume Two)
SILK (Volume Three)
SILK (Volume Four)
The SILK Box Set

K.M.'S BOOKS ARE IN AUDIOBOOK TOO!

Books by Gabrielle Bisset:

The Sons of Navarus Series
Vampire Dreams Revamped (A Sons of Navarus Prequel)
Blood Avenged (Sons of Navarus #1)
Blood Betrayed (Sons of Navarus #2)
Longing (A Sons of Navarus Short Story)
Blood Spirit (Sons of Navarus #3)
The Deepest Cut (A Sons of Navarus Short Story)
Blood Prophecy (Sons of Navarus #4)
Blood Craving (Sons of Navarus #5)
Blood Eclipse (Sons of Navarus #6)
The Sons of Navarus Box Set #1
The Sons of Navarus Box Set #2

The Destined Ones Duology
Stolen Destiny (Destined Ones Duology #1)
Destiny Redeemed (Destined Ones Duology #2)

The Victorian Erotic Romances
Love's Master
Masquerade
The Victorian Erotic Romance Trilogy